CHERISHED BY THE RANCHER

JEN PETERS

BLUE LILY BOOKS

To my mother, who had me on a horse before I could walk

CHERISHED BY THE RANCHER

"Thank you, Mr. Black. You won't regret it," Maddy Johnston said, relieved to have a job again. A cattle ranch was not where she'd expected to end up, not as a die-hard city gal, but it would be a perfect refuge for now.

The old cowboy smiled. "I'm sure I won't. You've got the experience to clean up the mess our last accountant left, and Black Rock Ranch could use a new face. A younger, prettier one, too!"

Maddy blushed.

"Now, let me practice that name you want us to use. Rich-o-leen-ee," Mr. Black pronounced carefully.

"O," she corrected. "Ricciolin-o, close enough."

"How'd you come to pick that one?"

Maddy smiled. "My grandmother. Nonna is very special to me, but not many people know her maiden name."

"Ricciolino, Ricciolino," he said, grinning proudly. "I can do that. And if it will keep you safe, it will be worth any tongue-tangling I might do. You sure I can't tell the boys?"

She gave a sharp shake of her head. "Somebody might let something slip. I just can't chance it."

"All right then, Missy. Let's get you settled."

Outside, he whistled to a couple of cowboys near a complicated set of fences. "My sons," he said.

The two men approached, both muscled and tanned and wearing cowboy hats that seemed part of them. The blond met her with a wide grin and cheerful eyes. The dark-haired one...that perfectly chiseled jaw and intent expression told Maddy he was more reserved.

"Adam, Caleb, this is Maddy Ricciolino. She's going to be our new accountant."

"Nice to meet you," the dark-haired one said. "Adam Black." He tipped his worn hat to her.

The blond stretched out a work-roughened hand. "Hi, I'm Caleb. Welcome to the ranch."

"Thanks," Maddy said. "I'll learn as fast as I can."

"I guess you'll meet my daughter and my other son later," Mr. Black said. "One's at school and the other is probably elbow deep in tractor grease." He chuckled. "Let's introduce you to your cabin now, and you can move in whenever you're ready."

Maddy nodded to Caleb and Adam and followed their father down another driveway, away from the house and barns and admin building. Not quite half a mile later, the lane curved and opened up.

"Some of our ranch hands live here," Mr. Black said, sweeping his arm out to a cluster of compact houses. "That one on the far right should do you and your daughter just fine."

Maddy was speechless. She'd been grateful that housing was included with the job, but she'd expected a cabin—the old, run-down type. These were snug homes with front porches and a common grassy area in the center of the horseshoe drive. "Wow," was all she could say.

She repeated the word when Mr. Black showed her the inside. A living area, eat-in kitchen, a bath between two bedrooms, and a door to the back where the view went on forever. Pasture, cattle, mountains…it was like paradise.

She ran her hand down a doorway, along a countertop, and closed her eyes. She felt the hominess here, but safety as well. This cabin, this ranch, would be a refuge for her and Mia.

She blinked back tears. "I can't say thank you enough. This is…incredible."

"Aw, just our normal stuff," Mr. Black said. "People need a good home to do good work. Even cowboys. Now, you go get your little girl, and I'll see you in the office on Monday."

Two DAYS back in Denver to gather what Maddy could fit in her Toyota and for six-year-old Mia to play with cousins one more time. Two days to say her goodbyes and convince her mother that she couldn't give out her address.

Two days to bake with Nonna and soak up her wisdom. To watch her twin nephews wrestle, to do make-up with her niece. To have a last, tearful heart-to-heart with her sister.

"Don't cry, Mama," Mia said as they drove their packed little car away.

Maddy swiped the tears away. "You got it. No more tears. We won't get to come back for a long time, but we're going to have a great adventure. Right?"

"Right! And we can see everyone next week."

Oh, to have a child's view of time. It would be much more than a week before they could return.

• • •

Now, exhausted from the whirlwind days, Maddy had slept through the Sunday church service Mr. Black had told her about. She yawned and stretched and, for once, decided the Lord wouldn't mind.

Maddy listened to Mia's cartoon coming in faintly from the living room, then pulled clothes on and went out. "Hey, kidaroo. I see you've had breakfast." Mia was surrounded by spilled cheerios, grape stems, and a paperback copy of *Dinosaurs Before Dark*.

"Yup! And I didn't put my bowl on the coffee table to make a ring, see?"

No, instead it was balanced precariously on a stack of towels Maddy hadn't found a spot for yet. She sighed. "I do see. Now, I'll help you clean up, and then we'll get dressed and go for a walk around the ranch. Maybe we can find a nice cowboy to show us around."

In just a moment, they stood on the front porch of their new home, inhaling the warm air. A soft mountain breeze stirred Maddy's curls, and she wondered how she ever managed to breathe in Denver. All air should be required to smell this fresh.

The other small cabins were quiet, all the ranch hands out working already. Ranch hands. She almost snorted. Who would have imagined Maddy Johnston, who lived for shopping and cooking and close family, would ever end up on a ranch in the back of Colorado's beyond?

Grand Junction, only a tenth the size of Denver, was more than an hour away. The closest thing to civilization was tiny Beaver Falls, still twenty-minutes down a winding, hilly road. She'd go through shopping withdrawal, but it would be worth it—it had to be.

They walked toward the ranch homestead, Mia skipping

and singing a nonsense song. Caleb Black welcomed them with a jovial, "Howdy there!"

They walked out to the group of confusing fences, and he explained how the chute system worked, sending the cattle in different directions depending on what was wanted.

"What's that," Mia asked, pointing to a sort of wide hole in one area.

Caleb tipped his hat back. "Oh, we fill that every week and throw all the cowboys in there for a bath," he said. "Anyone new to the ranch has to do it, too."

Mia squealed. "Noooo!" Then she looked at him more closely. "You do not," she exclaimed, hands on her hips. "Mama and I take showers in our cabin."

Maddy grinned as Caleb crouched down to Mia's height. "You don't say." He sniffed. "Well, you smell right pretty, so I guess I believe you."

Mia sniffed back. "*You* don't smell very pretty. I think we should fill it and throw you in."

Caleb roared with laughter and stood up. "Got me there, little one. Want to come see the horses?" He reached his arms out for her.

Mia backed up quickly and clung to Maddy's leg. Maddy couldn't help stiffening herself.

Puzzled, Caleb asked, "Can she have a piggyback ride?"

Of course. Not every man reached out with anger in his hands. Maddy knelt next to Mia. "Would you like that, sweetheart? It's okay."

Mia looked at her with big eyes, but nodded.

"Hold my shoulders tight," Caleb said, swinging her up. "I can take it, as long as you don't strangle me. Then I'd collapse, and you'd land in a tumble."

Mia giggled, a sound Maddy hadn't expected to hear

around a strange man, and tightened her grip. "Giddy-up," she said.

Caleb neighed, Mia giggled again, and Maddy relaxed as she watched them trot through the big barn.

She'd been holding a lot of tension in. The worry of staying out of her ex-husband's way, the trauma of leaving their home, the uncertainty of what to do and how far to run —it had all taken its toll. Now, safe in this hidden valley with its protective mountains, Maddy began to let go.

"This is my home turf," Caleb said when they reached a set of horse barns and a large outdoor arena. "Dad, Adam and Micah run the ranch, and probably Seth too, whenever he leaves the Army, but the horses are mine to manage."

He took them around one barn to a field in back. Maddy counted twelve mares with foals frolicking around them.

"Baby horses, Mama!" Mia cried, wiggling down from Caleb's back. "Can I pet one?"

Caleb shrugged. "Maybe tonight when we bring them in."

"Do you have baby cows, too?" Mia pointed to a pasture with large cattle.

"Mia, too many questions is not polite," Maddy reminded her.

"She's all right," Caleb said, leading them back past the barn. "But no, those are the bulls. The daddies. They spend a few months with the mommies and then come live over here for the rest of the year."

Maddy bent to Mia's level. "Remember the TV shows with bulls? They're mean and cranky, and you need to stay away from them." She thought of the horses in the pasture and the stallions. "Actually, don't bother any of the animals. Okay?"

"Oh. Okay." Mia looked at the livestock warily.

6

"And that's about it," Caleb said. "You obviously know the admin building and the cabins for the ranch hands—"

"Are we ranch hands, Mama?"

Before Maddy could speak, Caleb laughed. "Do you have two hands, Mia?" he said. "Are you on a ranch?"

Mia nodded.

"Then you're a ranch hand!"

Maddy grinned. Caleb reminded her so much of her brother Alex—knowledgeable without acting superior, gently teasing, and getting along well with children. She suddenly missed her family terribly. How long would it be before she could see them again?

It happened in the few seconds she'd been thinking about Alex.

She looked over to Mia. The child was no longer at the fence watching the colts. Where was she? Maddy spun, her breath catching, searching frantically for her daughter.

Then she glimpsed Mia's bright pink jacket, clear out in the bull pasture.

"Mia!" she screamed. "No!"

ADAM LET Mister amble through the winter-dried grass at his own pace. He'd ridden farther than he'd expected, but he had truly needed the break. The peace of the mountains and the soaring of the eagles filled him with a sense of grandeur and God, and helped him get a handle on his workload.

Bringing Black Rock Ranch into the twenty-first century was more than enough for any one person, and now he kept finding things that his father had left undone. It added unexpected tasks to his own chores, and his frustration level became unbearable if he didn't get away once in a while.

A good gallop on his horse and extra time in God's backyard had done him a world of good today. Only reluctantly did he turn Mister back to the ranch and the work that awaited him, even on Sunday.

They crossed the river at the lowest spot Adam could find —the spring flow was strong with snow melt. Mister nosed the water and threw up a splash before he drank. Adam watched the current rush twigs downstream, some of them getting caught in eddies near the rocks. He hoped the level would continue high long enough to irrigate this summer.

He nudged Mister on through the home pastures, thinking about the tasks awaiting him this week. He had renewed the BLM lease back in February, but he wanted to talk to the Watkins Ranch about leasing some acreage from them. They weren't running cattle anymore, so he figured it was a good possibility. The yearling heifers were growing well and should be ready for breeding next month. He needed to arrange a day or two for the vet to do the bull evaluations, make final decisions on solar wells, arrangements for water-witching and well-drilling and—

There was a kid in one of the bull pastures! Adam kicked Mister into a gallop.

Thirty bulls and one small child were a recipe for disaster. Knocked down, shoved against the fence, trampled… Where had the kid come from? And where were its totally irresponsible parents?

Adam leaned low, urging Mister faster. They jumped a small creek and then were racing past the horse barns. By the time he pulled Mister to a sliding stop and leapt off, the girl was out of the pasture and being scolded by her mother.

While Caleb just stood there.

"What the devil is going on?" Adam shouted at his too-easy-going brother. "Do you realize what could have happened?"

From the corner of his eye, he saw the little girl's lower lip quiver. "I'm sorry, I'm sorry, I'm sorry," she whispered, keeping her eyes buried in her mother's pant leg.

Adam's heart half-stopped at the girl's reaction, but his panic at the danger still rode high. He whipped his eyes to Maddy. The new accountant was unaccustomed to ranch life, but still... "You let her go in—"

She backed up two steps, her shoulders hunched and one arm tight around her daughter. "I know!" she squeaked. "We told her not to go near the animals, but—"

Great. Now he was frightening women. Still charged with energy, Adam flipped his attention back to his brother. "And what were you doing, Caleb? Got your head in the clouds again?"

"It was a mistake, Adam, okay? The bulls stayed on the other side of the pasture and nobody's hurt. Just calm down for a minute."

"Calm down? You want *me* to calm down?" Adam realized his voice was rising. He stopped to take a breath.

"It won't happen again," Maddy said, eyes now bright with defiance. "Mia and I won't be coming anywhere near here again." She kept an arm around the girl's shoulders.

He stared at her. "You need to make sure of it—kids are almost as unpredictable as bulls." He paused. "I didn't even know you had a child."

Caleb huffed. "You might be good at managing this ranch, brother, but you're lousy with people. Don't you think they're scared enough already? And I'll bet you don't even know Maddy's last name, let alone why she was willing to take a job out here."

"I know enough," Adam spat, temper rising again. "And I do know her last name—it's Richoletta."

That was enough of that—he had better things to do than argue with his brother. He stalked toward the stables, Mister trailing after him.

"Riccio-*lino*," Caleb called after him.

ADAM SPENT LONGER than necessary grooming Mister before turning him out.

He hadn't lost control like that in a long time. Then again, he hadn't been faced with a child in danger before. Never dreamed he would be. The adrenaline had pounded through him, and even now he shoved away images of what could have happened.

The long strokes with the brush were soothing and the work, along with a few snuffles from the gelding, helped slow Adam's rushing pulse.

But Caleb had been right—no one had gotten hurt. He shouldn't have been so caustic with his brother or Maddy, should have controlled himself more. He remembered the fear still in her eyes, even with her daughter back in her arms. And the girl's crumpled little face when he'd started shouting. He'd never meant to scare her. And when Maddy's own fear had settled, her brown eyes had flashed fire at his tirade.

There was something intriguing about the woman. She seemed to be a bit of a contradiction, and it wasn't just her crazy corkscrew curls that didn't belong on a real person's head. During those few moments, she'd gone from cowering to feisty.

Adam leaned his head against Mister's neck and inhaled the familiar horsey smell. "Lord, give me strength," he murmured. Then he chuckled. He'd been taught young that if you asked God for something, He was likely to give you a situation to teach you. He shouldn't have said that out loud, or Maddy could become his opportunity to learn strength.

Nah. He fully believed God had a sense of humor, but sending Maddy to teach him a lesson seemed a little too trivial. Adam would just do his own work, let her do hers, and hope she kept her little girl out of harm's way.

"What do you think, Mister?"

The horse flicked an ear at him. Adam reached into his pocket for a piece of carrot. Mister lipped it from his palm and crunched contentedly.

2

Turmoil rocked Maddy's stomach like a herd of stampeding cattle as she stormed off, pulling Mia behind her. Her daughter could have been *killed*. What had she been thinking, to take her eyes off a six-year-old in a strange place?

"Why in the world were you in the field with the bulls? Didn't I just tell you to stay away from them?" Maddy wanted to continue her scold, but Mia was half-crushed by Adam's yelling already. She didn't have to complete the job just to vent her own frustration.

"There was a bunny in the pasture," Mia explained, jogging to keep up. "It was way far away from the daddy bulls."

Maddy jerked to a stop. "Mia, just being in the pasture was dangerous. It didn't matter how far away they were." She forced back the image of a rampaging bull trampling her precious girl, but it kept returning in full color. "Promise me you'll never, ever go in any pasture again."

"Not even with you?" Mia's eyes filled with tears. "I can't pet the baby horses?"

"After all this? Not for..." What was an appropriate grounding? "For the next two days. You can't go anywhere near any animals. After that, only if you're with me."

Back in the cabin, a much-subdued Mia quietly picked out a book and retreated to her bed to read. Maddy leaned against the kitchen counter and rested her forehead against the cupboard above.

She was still shaking with nerves over Mia's close call, but that wasn't the only reason. Adam Black had been furious, and Maddy had responded with fire of her own. She was amazed she had actually stood up to someone's anger. When Brock had lashed out, she'd had to melt into the wall. Stay still, stay quiet, don't set him off any further.

She must be feeling safer than she expected at Black Rock Ranch, or she wouldn't have talked back to Adam. He hadn't raised a hand to her, hadn't even come close, but still...it was obvious he had a temper, and she didn't want to stick around to see it build. She could pack them up in one evening and go look for another job.

Maddy moved to the living room and slowly sank into an armchair as reality set in. This job at the ranch was a huge blessing, considering that she didn't have to use her real name in day-to-day living or to sign a rental agreement for an apartment. Where else would she find someone who would go along with her subterfuge and provide housing as well?

And who was she to turn away from a blessing that had so obviously come from the Lord? She needed to work through what she could on her own instead of running away from relatively minor issues. She was as safe as possible right now; she had a comfortable home, a place for Mia to play outdoors, and a job that would challenge her.

She'd just have to get on with that job and do her best to avoid Adam.

MADDY WOKE to the alarm clock Monday. She shut it off, turned over and stroked her sleeping daughter's hair. Mia hadn't wanted to be by herself in a new place, but Maddy didn't mind.

Technically, she should be getting Mia settled into school today, but there was only so much adjusting a child could do at once. She figured Mia could spend this week relaxing into ranch life instead. They'd tackle registration on Thursday or Friday, and the daily school bus rides could wait until next week.

At six years old, with a mostly obedient nature, Mia should be happy to color or read in her office while Maddy worked.

Speaking of work...

"Come on, little one, time to get up."

Mia smiled sleepily. "Hi, Mama," she murmured. Then she opened her eyes and wrapped her arms around Maddy's neck.

They ate croissants and Nutella for breakfast—not quite the *cornetto* that Nonna made, but close enough. It was one of Mia's favorites, and although it went straight to Maddy's hips, she didn't care—the flavors and the memories that went with it were worth it. Besides, she could always do an extra twenty minutes of exercise.

She rolled her eyes to herself as she dressed. Twenty minutes of daily exercise wasn't going to change her body shape. She normally ranged anywhere from curvy to plump, but right now was on the slender-curvy side—all the stress had worried ten pounds right off her.

She wouldn't trade her shape for the world, though. Her Italian heritage was part of her, and if it gave her more flesh than northern Europeans, it also provided her olive skin and luscious curls. Glorious tiny spirals that fell well below her shoulders. Her hair made people turn their heads for a second look, and she'd rather be known for that than have to live on salad just to fit a size eight.

Maddy swiped a coat of gloss over her full lips, then dabbed some on Mia's mouth, too. "Do you have enough coloring stuff? Your mystery?" Mia was only in kindergarten, but she was already reading books.

The young girl nodded, holding up her T-Rex book bag. She was seriously into dinosaurs, as well as princesses and ponies.

"Good job. Now remember, you're Mia Ricciolino, not Mia Johnston, right?"

"Right. I'll remember, Mama." Mia zipped her lips and turned an imaginary key.

THE RANCH ADMIN building boasted a wide open space with a desk against one wall and a few scattered chairs, all empty at this time of day. Beyond that were two offices, a large one for Mr. Black and Adam, and a smaller one for the accountant. Once Maddy had settled Mia in a corner of her office, she turned to her new workspace in dismay. Haphazard papers covered the desk surface, an old vase of dried-up flowers sat on one corner, and dust coated the computer. And two sets of taxes were due.

She took a deep breath, wiped her hands on her jeans, and sat down to see what order she could bring out of the mess.

An hour later, Maddy had one stack of invoices and statements to be entered, a smaller pile of correspondence, and too many leftover papers. Not quite the order she craved.

She wiped off the computer keyboard and the monitor, then turned it on and opened the accounting system. She ought to make some headway if she just entered one invoice at a time.

The problem was that she couldn't really tell what the invoices were for. Gasoline was easy, but what were ivermectin and tags, for goodness' sake?

She looked over at Mia, engrossed in coloring a dilophosaur's crest pink. Maddy started to rethink her decision about school, but surely a few days off wouldn't hurt. "You doing okay, sweetie?"

Mia nodded without looking up.

Whatever. Maddy stood, two invoices in hand. "I have to go ask some questions. I'll be right back. Stay in here, okay?"

"Okay, Mama."

Maddy trotted down the steps of the admin building, out into the wide, paved area that spread to the equipment shed, the loading chutes and another barn.

She poked her head into the equipment shed, although *shed* didn't seem the proper term for this huge building. She heard some clanging in back and walked in that direction.

Two men, both of them with grease covering their hands and a smear or two on their faces, held wrenches and pry bars and were trying to get something to move. She backed quietly away. These invoices seemed to do with livestock anyway, not machinery.

Back in the yard, she spied a figure coming from Caleb's stables. Finally!

It turned out to be Adam, who undoubtedly judged her as useless and irresponsible. There was nothing for it, though, so she took a deep breath and walked toward him.

"Can you help me with some information about these invoices?" She thrust the papers out to him. There, that wasn't so bad.

He scanned them with a frown. "Looks pretty straightforward to me. Ivermectin and tags." He held them back out to her.

Maddy crossed her arms. "Yes, I can see that. But just what are they? Feed supplements? Veterinary expenses? I can't categorize what I don't know."

Adam's sigh was so put-upon that she wished he would just give the snarky comment he was obviously holding back. "Ivermectin is for worming livestock—veterinary," he said. "Tags are ear tags for the cattle, so that's ranch supplies." He canted his head. "Did Dad know you were such a greenhorn when he hired you?"

"Of course. It didn't bother him. And I learn fast."

Adam shook his head and muttered something, then held the papers out to her. "Anything else?"

She snatched them. "No, that's all, thank you. I won't trouble you again." She turned and managed several steps before he called after her.

"Better to ask questions than not!"

Maybe, but Maddy would go elsewhere for her answers.

A man lifted a greasy hand in greeting as she passed the equipment shed—it must be Micah, but she couldn't remember if he was the middle or youngest brother.

She watched him for a few minutes. "You really like fixing things, don't you?"

He just smiled and shrugged.

Micah really was a man of few words. The three brothers were all so different, but all so good looking, especially when they smiled. It didn't matter much to her—she'd dated some since her divorce, but now wasn't the time to be thinking about romance—but she wished her sister could come out. Maybe some interesting sparks would fly.

She shook her head at her foolishness. She couldn't even tell her sister where she was; there was no way she could have her visit. They'd been such a close-knit family back in Denver, and it was killing her to have to make do with just phone calls. From a burner phone, no less!

But it was what it was, and she'd just have to deal with it. As long as she had Mia with her...

Unfortunately, as soon as she opened her office door, she had to close her eyes and count to ten. Her daughter's artwork now adorned not only the coloring pages but both walls in the corner.

"Oh, Mia. Couldn't you be good for five minutes?"

"But Mama, it said to draw a *big* picture of the dinosaur. And an apatosaurus is very, very big—I *had* to use the walls!"

Maddy closed her eyes. This precocious six-year-old would be the death of her yet. Reading at second or third grade level, questioning everything, but not having the maturity to make good decisions. She opened her eyes and squatted down to meet Mia eye to eye.

"Sweetheart, I'm glad you're reading the directions, and I'm glad you're trying to follow them. But you need to use some common sense, too. Does Mr. Black want his walls to become drawing paper? Or would he want them to stay white, like a business?"

Mia sighed. "White, I guess. But if I scrub it off, will you get me some BIG drawing paper?"

"I will. I'll even help you scrub. But we need to do that when I'm done with work today. So can you stick to the coloring pages or read your new book while I do my work?"

Mia colored sixteen dinosaurs in the time it took Maddy to work through a set of invoices and statements and prepare a list of questions. She didn't need to go running for one answer at a time.

It would be easier if she knew anything about ranching, but she knew a whole lot more about Italian cooking than she did about beef on the hoof.

Then again, the whole reason she was out at the ranch was that it was a place where Brock would never think to look for her. His obsession with her hadn't stopped after he'd violated the restraining order and gone to jail. When he got out, he'd threatened her when he could and stalked her when he couldn't.

Maddy had been surprised he had done nothing more than verbally run off her almost-boyfriend, but he really wasn't the type to physically go after anyone else—he saved that for people he considered his.

Namely, her.

She'd had no choice but to leave Denver.

The senior Mr. Black hadn't cared that she didn't know ranch work, just that she had enough accounting experience. Especially after their last accountant had quit more than a month ago, and he hadn't been able to find anyone who wanted to work so far out. She had reluctantly given him her real name for the official paperwork, but convinced him to introduce her as Maddy Ricciolino, her grandmother's maiden name, instead. If Brock ever came looking for Maddy Johnston, he wouldn't find her.

As for the handsome, younger Mr. Blacks, they were her boss's sons and that was all.

3

A dam stared after the infuriating woman. Why in the world had Dad hired her? It would take months for her to learn what she needed. He deliberately ignored the whisper that he'd just had a perfect chance to apologize for the day before and hadn't taken it.

He watched her stalk away, that incredible mass of curly brown hair swinging with each stride. He wondered if she curled it every morning. The lengths some women went to for fashion...

He shook his head to clear it. He didn't need to spend time thinking about a feisty accountant, no matter how luscious her hair or her curves. She wasn't his type—did he even have a type?—and he didn't have room for those kind of thoughts, anyway. Lately his dad seemed to be doing less, or accomplishing less, so keeping the ranch running well took all Adam's energy these days.

Adam poked his head into the equipment shed. "Find the leak?" he asked his brother.

"Yup." Micah wiped his hands on an old red rag. "The

plug wasn't seated properly—shouldn't have any problems now."

"Have you welded the hooks on the new bucket yet?"

Micah gave him a look. "Not yet. I will."

With hooks to carry other loads, the replacement bucket would put another tractor back to full use, and Adam liked things running at full capacity. "Any idea when?"

"It's on my list, Adam. Leaking oil comes first, though."

"I know, I know. Just trying to keep things current in my mind."

Micah nodded curtly before turning back to Jesse. "Let's clean her up before we put her away."

Adam watched as they began cleaning the remaining oil off various parts, as well as the grass and debris that had built up. They didn't need him around—that was obvious.

He couldn't help himself sometimes. He knew the more he could keep situations and events under control, the fewer chances there were that something could go wrong. Having something go wrong was never good.

Outside, he ran his eyes over the cows that were close. He stopped one of the ranch hands as he walked past. "How many calves are we going to have today, Wes?"

The cowboy shrugged. "We've got three in the calving shed now, maybe two more by tonight. Jesse and Luis are taking the night shift."

Adam nodded. Wes was a good ranch hand, had a way with animals that some of the others didn't. "Give a shout if you need help." He'd check in periodically anyway, and probably do one of the night checks as well.

He caught motion from the corner of his eye—the farrier had arrived at the stable yard. He let Wes go his way and headed for Caleb's domain.

Fifteen minutes later, Adam was filled with the sounds

and smells of one of his favorite parts of ranching. He watched the farrier work, trimming and rasping, then shaping steel horseshoes to fit individual hooves, tapping little nails into the hoof wall, then moving on to the next.

He heard the barn door slide open and looked up to see his father come in. Samuel Black was a tall man still, although his back seemed a bit more bent and his shoulders a bit bonier than in years past. Adam fought the idea that his dad was getting on in years, that it wouldn't be too long before Adam would need to take over completely. Dad had always said that he'd work until he dropped—preferably somewhere out on the range, but definitely not in any forlorn nursing home.

Now he wondered if his father might need to retire before that time came.

"Hey there, John," his father greeted the farrier. "Adam, I wanted to ask you…" His voice trailed off. He looked at the horse being shod, the barn rafters, and finally back at Adam. "Dang it, I don't remember why I came out here."

"Must have gone through a doorway," Adam said, smiling. That had been their standard joke ever since one of Adam's younger brothers read a quasi-scientific comment about doorways causing forgetfulness. "That's all right—you'll remember in a bit."

"Right," Dad said sarcastically. "As soon as I get back to the equipment shed. Stupid senior-itis."

Adam chuckled. "I ought to check on the guys working on that cross-fencing. Want to come?"

Dad's face brightened, enjoyment replacing frustration. "Sure. Horses or the four-wheelers?"

Adam shrugged. He had loads to do, but it wouldn't hurt to spend a little extra time with his father. "It's a nice day— let's go horseback."

They saddled Mister and Cobbler, Dad's black-and-white paint gelding, who both stood quietly for the ritual. Swinging a leg over his well-worn saddle put a smile on Adam's face—two days in a row on a horse. He'd been using the Gator and the four-wheeler way too much.

They left the homestead and followed the fence line out a mile, the mountains above their little valley sharp against the sky.

Dad suddenly shaded his eyes and peered into the distance. "What're they doing?"

Adam looked over to where ranch hands were working on the fencing. "We talked about this, Dad. We're replacing the top and bottom strands of barbed wire with smooth, and we're putting vinyl flags on it. Too many deer and elk are getting hurt on it."

Dad grumbled. "So they can get in and eat our pasture, huh?"

Letting out a long sigh, Adam said, "So they can move where they need to, Dad. Aren't you tired of finding a cut-up deer hanging on a fence?"

Dad grunted.

"Besides, hurt animals only draw predators. You wouldn't want more bear or mountain lion down here, would you?"

"Hmmph."

Adam loved his father, but the old man was so frustrating sometimes. They were butting heads on several things besides fencing—the solar wells being another. He hoped they worked as well as they were supposed to, or Dad would never let it go.

Needing to lighten the mood, he nudged Mister into a jog. "Come on, let's see how they're doing."

Five minutes later, Adam leaned on his saddle horn while he spoke with the ranch hands. It wasn't terribly hard work, but most of them were grateful for the pause, taking a moment to take a long swig of water. "That is water, isn't it?" he asked.

One of the cowboys nodded. "Want some?"

Adam shook his head. "Ty?"

Ty shrugged, tucking a flask back in his hip pocket.

"I've warned you, Ty. No liquor while you're working."

Dad reached a hand in Adam's direction. "Later, son," he said firmly.

Adam fumed, but kept silent. He wasn't going to lessen his father's authority in front of the hands. Mister took a step sideways.

He looked at the markers now sitting on the top wire—nice and visible for any kind of animal. "Looks good. You guys need anything?"

Another ranch hand spoke up. "If it's not too much hassle, I could use another pair of gloves. Kind of ripped these to pieces."

"Been here a year and still learning about barbed wire, huh?" Dad joked. "I'll send someone out with them." He nodded and turned Cobbler back towards the homestead.

Adam caught up with his father. "They're doing a pretty good job," he said.

"I know," Dad said. "And I'll talk to Steven about his drinking this evening. Not something you need to deal with until you're the big boss."

"Steven? You mean Ty."

Dad waved his hand. "Of course, Ty. Want to stretch these horses' legs a bit?" He pushed Cobbler into an easy lope.

Adam and Mister followed suit, the wind rushing past Adam's face and threatening to blow his hat off. He clamped it down with one hand, grinned, and pushed Mister into a full-blown gallop. He wasn't too old to have a little fun.

. . .

WHEN THE HORSES were cooled off and brushed down, Dad turned them out in the pasture while Adam walked back to the admin office. His mind filled with fencing plans and the solar-powered wells. If they could get water into areas without river access—

He came to a quick halt in the main room. Maddy stood in the hallway, one hand on Mia's shoulder and the other over her mouth as she looked into her office. Thumps and muttering came from inside. Maddy backed up as Caleb stepped carefully out, plaster dust in his hair. "It looks pretty bad," he said.

Adam strode forward. "What's bad? What happened?"

Maddy stepped back quickly, pulling Mia with her. Did she do that to make room for him or because she was afraid of him? He cleared the regrets from his head and peered inside.

Her office looked like a tornado had come through. Chunks of drywall covered her desk, the floor, and everything in between. Maddy's chair was bent awkwardly, and a torn box lay on its side. The ceiling was mostly a dark, jagged hole, except for where he could see the edge of another box. Was it teetering?

Adam whipped his head around. "Were you in there? Are you hurt?"

Maddy shrugged. "Mia and I were cleaning," she paused and looked at some streaks of color in the corner, "so I wasn't at my desk."

He looked her over. Her face was three shades paler than normal, and her hair and clothes held bits of debris amongst the chalky dust. He felt her eyes on him as he turned to her daughter and hunkered down.

25

Mia leaned away from him immediately, clutching her mother's hand.

"I'm sorry I yelled the other day, Mia," Adam said softly. "Are you okay now? The ceiling didn't hit you?"

She shook her head solemnly.

"I'll bet you were brave," he said.

Mia shook her head again. "I cried. And Mommy did too."

Adam nodded. "But even though it was scary, you're not crying now. To me, that's brave. Do you want me to see if I can get it cleaned up?"

She nodded. "But I don't want to go in there again."

"We'll see what we can do about that." He stood and found Maddy with a soft smile on her face, and Caleb with his eyebrows raised to the ceiling. Whatever.

"Right, then." Adam knew his voice was authoritative again, but so be it. That was how he rolled. "Caleb, go round up a couple hands and supervise the cleanup. Someone not on calving duty. And Maddy, if you and Mia want to head home for the night, I'll see about finding you a new space for tomorrow."

MADDY WALKED Mia back to the cabin, dumbfounded over it all. The ceiling had caved in, but not until they had moved to the other corner. Caleb had stopped by just in time to help them out. And Adam had actually been nice. Rather bossy, but nice.

God was being very good to them.

By the time she had Mia cleaned up and into fresh clothes, her daughter was recounting how it had sounded, how it was dusty to breathe, how she had to step on a wobbly piece to get to the door. If the youngster could chatter about the adventure, she'd be just fine.

And Maddy? The scariest moment had been when the second box had landed with a crash, toppling her chair over. Now she was filled with what-could-have-happened imaginings and what-should-she-do-now questions. She supposed she could work through the tax returns in the main room there. She'd have to ignore the cowboys who came and went, and keep confidential information locked in the file cabinet.

When they returned the next day, Adam motioned her back to the large office he shared with his father.

Their huge partner's desk sat to one side instead of the center of the room, and they had rearranged chairs to make room for a computer desk by the other wall. She had a printer table, her file cabinet, and a small table for a work surface.

Which held a vase of daffodils.

Her heart melted. "Adam, this is wonderful. And I love the flowers."

He lifted one shoulder and let it drop. "I'll take credit for the desk and the old computer—I hope it runs what it needs to—but the flowers are my dad's doing. He thought you needed something to make you smile."

And smile she did. One thoughtful, older gentleman and one handsome man who might turn out to be a nice guy, plus a place to work—it all gave her a lot to smile about. Being under the eye of two bosses might be stressful, though.

With Mia settled on a floor pillow with her book, Maddy ignored the weight of Adam's gaze and opened up the old computer. She groaned as it booted up. Windows Vista! She wasn't sure it would even run the current software.

"What's wrong?" Adam asked.

Maddy could only shake her head. "I'm not sure how much I can do on this. I'll let you know."

Adam didn't answer directly, but the next thing Maddy heard was him on the phone. "Hey, Brad. Any chance you can speed up the work on the computer we sent down? This old one isn't going to work out... Uh huh... Well, do what you can."

Wow. This was one cowboy who didn't mess around. "Thanks," Maddy said when he hung up.

"I'm sorry. Cattle and horses I can handle. Computers, not so much." He tapped his pen against his desk and frowned.

"That's all right," she said, smiling. "Everything's backed up to the cloud, and I can do the tax worksheets online. That deadline is more important than the pile of invoices."

Adam nodded and turned back to the article he was reading.

By the end of the day, though, Maddy knew it wasn't going to work. Not that she couldn't concentrate while Adam was on the phone or talking to his father—headphones would work if she needed them. But her curious daughter was another story.

"What are the trophies for, Mama?"

"Where did Mr. Black go, Mama?"

"What's a bull exam?"

"Who is Mr. Adam scolding?"

No matter how much Maddy urged Mia to read or color, the questions kept coming with every small happening in the office. At three o'clock, the end of Maddy's workday, she took her daughter in her arms. "Sweetie, we're going to go down to the school tomorrow." She turned to Adam. "Do you mind if I only work a half day?"

Adam gave a rather bemused smile. "Take what you need."

Maddy drove Mia to school herself Wednesday—riding the bus could start the next day. Mia's chatter didn't distract her from her nerves, though. What if the principal wouldn't agree? What if they insisted on using Mia's real last name? Even if the school wouldn't release her to Brock's custody, Maddy couldn't trust that a secretary wouldn't slip and confirm that she was a student there.

Brock was a master at manipulation. He could be understanding, polite, sincere, all to get you to do what he wanted. She could just hear him: "Does Mia Johnston have enough lunch money today?" And of course someone would look it up and tell him.

His abuse should have kept him locked up for a long time, but he'd been able to talk his way out of everything except the blatant violation of the restraining order. And ever since he'd been locked up for those months, all he could think about was getting back at her. If taking Mia would make Maddy give in, she was sure he'd do it.

Thankfully, the principal agreed to put "Mia Ricciolino" on all their records except a confidential file. With a lightened heart and a major worry off her shoulders, Maddy walked Mia to her new class before treating herself to a mint chocolate ice cream at Two Scoops. So what if it added to her curves? Then it was back to the ranch, humming all the way up.

Country roads, take me home... The Black Rock Ranch was feeling more and more like home.

4

When Adam finished checking the soil samples and returned to his office Tuesday, the admin building was quiet. Dad was at the house, and Maddy must still be in town.

He settled in at his desk and tried working out a lease offer to use the Watkins' land, but kept getting distracted by memories of yesterday. Young Mia's questions about anything and everything. Maddy's problems with the wretched old computer. Heck, *he'd* had problems with it when it was new!

And then trying to concentrate with Maddy sitting only a few feet away.

Why? He'd only met her a few days ago. And sure, she was pretty, but there was something else about her. He just couldn't put his finger on it.

He gave a shake of his head. He didn't have time for this —there was too much paperwork to do before he could get back outside.

Adam tried again to concentrate on the proposed lease. He dozed a bit, then jerked upright, barely catching himself from tipping over. Stupid chair. He really ought to get a new one.

"Do you do that often?" came Maddy's amused voice.

"What?" he growled. "Fall asleep or tip over?"

"Either. Both."

"It's calving season. I do both on a regular basis."

Maddy's brow furrowed, creating two small lines between her eyebrows. "No one can work 24/7."

Was she being critical or caring?

"The hands do most of it, but I like to know what's going on." So he was a bit of a control freak. But he couldn't head off problems if he wasn't there to catch them early on. Being out with the cows in the middle of the night might leave him worn out, but he wasn't going to give it up.

"Mia's all set up for school?" he asked as Maddy settled in at her desk.

"Yup. And when I explained, they even—" Her words broke off, and she stared at the computer screen as the Windows logo slowly appeared.

"They even what?"

She just shook her head. "Nothing. Mia's teacher seems nice."

Adam watched her, but she said nothing else. Her private life was her own, though, so he turned back to his papers. He wondered if he would have followed in his father's footsteps so eagerly if he'd known how much desk work it entailed.

He flipped his pencil in the air and gave up half an hour later. Between watching Maddy and trying to work with a bleary mind, he wasn't getting anything done. "If Dad comes in, tell him I'm out riding."

. . .

"Hey, Mister, want to get out of here for a bit?" Adam crooned as he offered the bay gelding his piece of carrot. He rubbed behind Mister's ear, then rested his forehead against the horse's neck. There wasn't much that time with a horse couldn't make better.

He saddled Mister, and they headed out. Past all the expectant cows, past the ones with new calves at their sides, even past the yearling heifers. He ought to stop and check them, but other than a quick glance for anything amiss, he just wanted to ride.

He closed the last gate, then reined Mister to the right fork of the trail, past Black Rock and up toward the high lake where a pair of bald eagles were raising their chicks. He couldn't wait until they fledged and he could watch them soar with their parents. There was something about the freedom and fluidity of watching eagles fly that thrilled his soul.

Adam breathed deeply, letting his cares wash away. Despite his enjoyment of Sunday church services, *this* was where he came to feel close to God. He just wished the Lord would send him some help once in a while.

If ranching only had to do with animals and pasture, he'd be in heaven. But there were people, too. People who came with issues.

He wondered if Ty was going to be a continuing problem, and if so, what he should do about it. Drinking at his cabin was Ty's right, but if he was drinking on the job... The animals they handled and the equipment they used could both be dangerous. Dad really should be the one pulling Ty aside for a serious conversation, but Dad seemed to be letting the hard stuff slide.

His father was pushing seventy, even if he didn't want to admit it. Sometimes Dad sort of zoned out. He had checked the fence line the day before, and Adam wondered if he ought to run past it himself on the way back.

He lifted his face to the sky. "You could help me out a little, God. I wouldn't mind. Really."

And then Maddy's face was in his mind. Totally unexpected. Was she his help? He rolled his eyes at the idea. She might be a good accountant, but she didn't know the first thing about ranching. *What's a tag?* she'd asked.

He laughed at a different thought. On Sunday, Pastor Rich had suggested that it was trials that made people strong and developed their character. Maybe Maddy was here to be a trial, to develop his character. She could certainly frustrate him, no matter how quietly she sat at her desk.

No, time would tell whether she was a trial or blessing, if either.

He ducked under a branch and thought of what else Pastor Rich had said: *Leaning on the Lord through trials deepened a person's relationship with Him, and the Lord could then use that depth and strength for His purposes. Usually to help someone else.*

Adam snorted. Their biggest trial had about broken them instead. Adam had been sixteen when the phone call came saying that Mom had been in an accident. She was dead by the time they got to the hospital, killed by a drunk driver.

It hadn't made them stronger people. They were just like they had been, now with a massive hole in their lives.

Aunt Sarah had come to take care of them, especially with Lacey so little back then, but even when she left, Adam didn't think Dad had ever considered remarrying. He didn't talk about Mom, either, and the brothers had all taken their cue from him—she was a treasured memory but not an open conversation. Which was fine.

Since then, Adam worked hard to make sure there were

33

no unexpected difficulties, especially the type that Pastor Rich claimed would make someone stronger in his faith. Maybe the thing he should take away from the pastor's words was to lean on the Lord more through his current trials, instead of trying to do it all himself.

The lake sparkled ahead, blue against the snow lining the banks. He'd have just a few minutes to enjoy it before he needed to head back, but it had been worth it.

Dismounting, he kept a loose hold on Mister's reins and found a large enough rock to sit on. His thoughts meandered from Pastor Rich back to his mother, to Maddy, to what his mother would think of Maddy. She'd probably like her, and especially envy her curls—Mom's hair had been curtain-straight.

Mister shied suddenly, and the reins jerked against Adam's hand, pulling him backwards. He scooted to his feet, following the motion of his horse. "Whoa, boy, easy there."

But Mister kept backing up, eyes wide, nostrils flared.

"Come on, nothing's going to hurt you." Adam looked to see what could have spooked him. Was there a predator around? But as he moved to keep up with Mister, one boot twisted on a piece of a branch.

Gasping as pain shot up his leg, he pulled harder on the reins. "Stop it, silly, you're fine." His voice wasn't as calm as it should have been, but he couldn't help it. He limped after his horse, finally getting him to stand still.

Mister blew harsh breaths, and his eyes were still a bit wild, but he stood long enough for Adam to mount. With difficulty. Standing on a twisted or sprained ankle while he got the other foot in the stirrup had him gritting his teeth and keeping a close hold on the swear words that wanted to come out.

He grunted as he settled in the saddle, keeping a tight rein on Mister. "Thanks for nothing, bud." His ankle throbbed. It would be swollen tight by the time they got back to the homestead, and he would *not* be happy if they had to cut his boot off.

Adam turned Mister back to the trail and lifted his face to the skies. Branches and treetops cut down his view of the blue expanse above, but he spoke anyway. "Is this what you mean by trials building character, God? Just what am I supposed to learn from a sprained ankle?"

MADDY WORKED by herself for another hour, the office seeming too quiet with Adam out. Mr. Black eventually came in and lowered himself slowly into his chair. "It's no fun getting old," he said.

Maddy smiled at the weather-worn rancher. "No, I imagine not. The only problem with that statement is that you're not old."

"That's what you think. I turned sixty-seven last month, Missy. I know, I know," he said, eyes twinkling, "I only look like I'm sixty-six. But raising four boys when you started late wears you out even more than a hard ranching life. And then adding a little girl…"

"Mr. Black, I —"

He held up a hand and cut her off. "Please, I've told you before, no 'Mr. Black.' It's Samuel."

Maddy tipped her head. He seemed to engender the respect that called for Mr. Black, but if that was what he truly wanted…

"Samuel it is, then. But you are *not* old. You're strong and working hard, and you will be for a lot of years."

"Yeah, well, let's just say that I'm glad Adam is taking on a bit more." He paused, looking at his ranch-roughened hands. "These old things have done a lot of the work around here, but they're not as strong as they used to be."

Maddy didn't know what to say. She hadn't realized he was past regular retirement age, but did ranchers ever really retire? What she did know was that he wouldn't appreciate any more platitudes from her. And she could use a break from income and expenses.

"Tell me about your family," she said. "I mean, I know Adam is the oldest, and Caleb takes care of the horses, but I don't know much about them. And I haven't met your daughter at all."

The older man waved a hand. "Lacey's been chomping at the bit to come see you. She finally got some big school project done, so I imagine she'll find you soon." He looked pensive, then glanced at her and chuckled. "So you want to know about the boys, huh, Missy? I can't say as I blame you—they're downright good looking, all of them. Take after their mother, you know."

He looked suddenly out the window, keeping his gaze there while he blinked a few times. Maddy waited, not wanting to intrude, but couldn't help wondering how his wife had died.

Samuel finally turned back to Maddy with a half-smile. "Well now, I'd say Caleb does more than just take care of the horses. He's about the best trainer I know. And he's got a knack for breeding the right mare to the right stallion. Our three stallions are known across the west now for the things their get are doing."

"Get?"

"Their progeny. Colts and fillies. Children." He waved his hand at her.

"Caleb seems pretty happy," Maddy said, wanting the

attention off her lack of knowledge.

"Oh, happy-go-lucky, that one," Samuel Black said. "Always has been. He always looking for the silver lining, and he could charm a sparrow from a tree. Got girls eager for him to come dancing in town.

"Now Micah, he's just the opposite. Quiet, hardly hear a peep from him. But he watches and sees, and he's thinking a lot behind those eyes. When he does talk, you oughta listen."

"And does he have a lot of girls, too?" Maddy asked. Quiet, brooding cowboys could be quite attractive to some women, even if they weren't her type.

Samuel grimaced. It was a moment before he spoke again. "No, Micah's gone through a pretty rough time. His wife left and won't hardly let him see his son. My grandson."

Maddy gasped. "Doesn't he have visitation rights?"

"Huh. Don't do much good if she won't follow them. And he won't push so hard that she lands in jail."

"How old is your grandson? How long since you've seen him?" She couldn't imagine not being able to be with her own child.

"Jacob is two-and-a-half now, I think, and I ain't seen him since they left a year ago." He looked away again, then down at his boots.

"Hey, boss, you in here?" came a voice from the hall. A short, swarthy man appeared at the doorway. "I've got some of Lacey's fudge for you. She wanted to come herself, but Adam didn't want her bothering your new accountant." He limped slightly as he brought the plate of goodies in.

"Thanks, Bart," Samuel said, reaching for a piece of light-colored fudge. He turned to Maddy. "Bart's been on this ranch almost as long as I have, and I was born here."

"Ma'am." Bart tipped his hat to her.

"Nice to meet you, Bart," Maddy said. She looked over

the peanut-butter fudge.

"Actually," Samuel said with a grin, "most everyone calls him Uncle Dirt."

Maddy jerked her head up. "Uncle Dirt?"

Bart—Uncle Dirt—put the plate on the big desk and tipped his cowboy hat to her. "'Cuz I'm older'n dirt, not 'cuz I never bathe."

Samuel laughed. "That too, Bart!" He turned to Maddy. "Lacey heard someone call him that when she was little and carried it on for the rest of us. Now everyone calls him that."

Uncle Dirt chuckled. "And now it's time for me to brighten your day…by leaving!"

Maddy took her own bite of the slightly grainy sweetness and smiled, both at Uncle Dirt's humor and at memories of her own early attempts at fudge. "He's…an interesting character."

"That he is," Samuel said, taking another piece and stretching his legs out. "We go back a long, long ways. Well now, the boys. You probably heard that Seth is in the Army, off in Iraq. We're pretty proud of him."

Maddy waited, but Samuel got lost in his own thoughts again. It couldn't be easy having a son fighting in the middle East.

When the tension finally eased from Samuel's shoulders, Maddy shifted the subject. "What about Adam? I mean, we were all in here yesterday, but is he more like Micah or Caleb?"

Samuel snorted. "Oh, he's the lead bull in the pasture. Loud, in charge, knows what he wants and gets it."

Maddy cringed inwardly, remembering Adam's reaction to her and Mia. And then his decisiveness taking care of the office situation, demanding and getting results. "A bull in a pasture" described Adam Black to a tee.

"Have you always been a rancher?" she asked.

"Long as I can remember, and my father before me. Black Rock, up the hills from the bull pastures, was named after my grandfather. Besides being mostly black granite." He grinned. "So when the boys take over, this land will have owned by," he counted on his fingers, "four generations of Blacks."

"Wow," Maddy said. With immigrant grandparents, she didn't have any lasting ties to a particular place unless it was back to their village in Italy. And it was hard to feel connected to a place you'd never been.

"It's a good thing, too. Don't know how a ranch can make it if there's a mortgage to pay on top of everything else." He sighed and pushed himself out of the chair. "Thanks for listening, Missy. I gotta get back to the barn now, but sometimes I just need someone who's not rushing here and there."

"Anytime, Samuel. You know where to find me."

Maddy watched him leave, having a hard time believing he was pushing seventy. He still seemed as strong as his sons.

She thought of each of them, so different, and wondered what Seth was like. Brave, definitely. Driven like Adam, probably, or he wouldn't be in the military.

She looked around the office—the daffodils on her small table, trophies here and there, and Adam's books and binders filling the shelf closest to the big desk. She stood and perused the rodeo pictures on the wall: bull-riding, bronc-riding, roping, posing with a huge bull on a halter. It wasn't clear who was doing the riding, but it was definitely a younger Adam with the prize bull. Proud, grinning like she'd never imagined.

She'd only seen the serious side of Adam—determined, impatient, even angry—but never an outright smile. Did he still have one in him?

5

A dam grumped his way into the office early the next morning, his ankle throbbing and his mood as dark as ever. He couldn't believe they'd cut off his boot last night. His new twelve-hundred-dollar Luccheses. They had just sliced through the leather and wrenched it off.

Of course, that they still had to wrench after cutting it meant that there'd been no way to get his foot out otherwise. But dang, he loved those boots!

After the initial sharp pain had worn off, he'd spent a sleepless night of aching. It didn't matter—he wasn't going to spend the day sitting in the recliner playing Rest, Ice, Compression and Elevation. He had work to do, even if it meant limping in an Ace bandage. In tennis shoes. *Tennis shoes*!

Adam scrawled notes across the lease proposal, studied the solar well information, and muttered at his father when he came in. Maddy arrived after putting Mia on the school bus, but he couldn't manage much more than a polite smile for her, either.

Dad laughed. "Told you that you should have taken the day off. Ice will help that more than anything else, and maybe spare the rest of us your moaning and groaning."

"What happened?" Maddy asked.

"Oh, Grumpy Bear here sprained his ankle yesterday, but doesn't want to admit how much it hurts."

Maddy looked at Adam, concern in her eyes. "Do you need anything? Mia's pillow is still here if you want to put your foot up."

Adam ground his teeth. If one more person gave him one more piece of unwanted advice... "I'm fine." He looked down at his papers, but he felt her still watching him. When he finally looked up, she was focused on her computer again.

Good. Maybe they could have a normal morning.

And then Lacey came rushing in. "I missed the bus, so Uncle Dirt's going to take me down and then do the grocery shopping. But can you watch the bird for me? Bread and milk every hour or so." She set a bag and an open shoebox between him and Dad. "Thanks, Adam." She kissed his cheek and ran out the door.

Dad raised his eyebrows. Adam stared at the scrub jay with a splint on its wing. Maddy came over and hovered. "Oh, wow," she said. "Lacey takes care of hurt animals?"

Adam let out a long sigh. "She tries. Mostly they die anyway."

"She did keep that rabbit alive until its leg healed," Dad said.

"And it probably got eaten by the next coyote," Adam replied shortly. Then he saw the look on Maddy's face. "I'm sorry. I'm out of sorts right now, or I wouldn't have said it so badly. Even if it's probably true."

Maddy reached a finger to the bird and stroked its head lightly. "Maybe this one will get lucky."

She returned to her desk, and they settled down to work. The phone stayed silent, only two ranch hands came in with questions, and Adam was finally able to accomplish something.

His phone timer dinged, pulling Adam away from a dry discussion in *Beef Production* on the pros and cons of fall calving. With relief, he pulled bread and a canister of milk from the bag Lacey brought.

"Come on, bird," he murmured, dipping a pinch of bread into the milk and then touching it to the bird's beak. "You know you want some." He dribbled a little milk on it, tapped the soppy bread gently on it, but the bird didn't respond.

"Maybe he wants a female voice," Maddy suggested, moving to stand by Adam. "Can I try?"

Adam nodded to the slice of bread, and she did the same things he had, to no avail.

He stroked the bird's head with the back of his finger. "You can't get well if you don't eat," he said softly. "Come on, just try."

"Aww, you do care," Maddy teased.

"Just don't want it to die on my watch," he muttered, trying not to notice the warmth of her body next to him. "Here, I'll open its mouth and you squeeze a drop of milk off that bread. Just a drop."

He gently pried the jay's beak open, and Maddy got a drop down its throat. It pulled away, but when she dabbed the bread against its beak again, it opened slightly.

"He's eating," she whispered. "It's working."

It really was. Adam's spirit lifted—just because he was a realist didn't mean he couldn't be excited about saving a life. Or about the touch of Maddy's hand against his, giving him a zing he hadn't felt in years.

He wasn't sure how he felt about that—about her—so he

focused on the feeding. They got four more drops of milk into the jay, then let it rest on Lacey's bed of tissues.

Maddy returned to her desk, and Dad gave Adam a pointed look. Adam retreated to the boring article, but couldn't help being distracted by Maddy—especially those two vertical furrows on her brow that appeared when she was concentrating. And those crazy curls. And the softness of her voice when she'd been cooing to the bird.

He jerked his head up at the sound of "Mamma Mia" playing. Maddy's ringtone. Who would put "Mamma Mia" on her phone on purpose?

"Hi, kiddo…I know, sweetie. I miss you too…I'm glad you had a good time…Yeah, can you put your mom on?" Her voice lowered, but the office wasn't so big that Adam could stop listening.

"No, I don't know when I can come home. You know the situation…What I wouldn't give to see the twins joking around right now…I know, we had to pull Mia out of a bull pasture the other day."

Then Maddy froze and looked around the room. "Hang on," she said into the phone and walked out the door.

Adam was taken aback. "What was that all about?"

Dad shrugged. "Maybe she doesn't want to tell about that episode with us in earshot."

"No," Adam mused. "She said she couldn't go home. I wonder why not?"

"None of our business, son. Let her have her privacy."

Adam pursed his lips and returned to the article, but the mystery of Maddy stayed in his mind.

MADDY TROTTED down the building steps and ducked behind the homestead. No one would overhear her here.

She'd nearly done herself in. Her sister Sophia had mentioned how one of her son's dates had gone wrong and ended up in a broken window. Nothing horribly bad, but Maddy had just blurted out about the bull pasture episode. Why did a person always need to relate something similar in their own lives? Especially when that person was trying to fly under the radar?

"Okay, I can talk now," Maddy said, perching on the back porch of the house.

"Bulls?" Sophia squeaked. "Where are you that Mia got in with bulls?"

"Uh…" Caution was better late than never. "Near a ranch. Far away from Denver," she finally said.

"Are you even still in Colorado?"

"Of course." As much as she'd needed to run, she wasn't desperate enough to cross half the country.

In fact, she'd been here less than a week, but she felt safer than ever, despite the run in with Adam over the bull pasture. Just how much caution was necessary? Was there *anything* she could share with her family?

"Actually," Maddy said slowly, "we're over on the Grand Junction side. I can tell you that much."

"Wow, so far." Her sister was silent a moment. "Well, not so far. I've got the map pulled up, and it's only a couple hours' drive. Do you think we could meet somewhere in between?"

It was Maddy's turn to be silent. Finally, "I can't. I can't trust that Brock wouldn't be following you. You know what he's like. And they can't—" She cut off before she said too much about the Blacks.

Sophia sighed. "He's such a piece of work. Anyone else

would think you were over-the-top paranoid, but I remember what your face looked like that one time."

"I'm not paranoid," Maddy whispered.

"I know that, sis. And I know there was a lot more that you didn't show us. But…" A teasing note came into Sophie's voice. "Just who is *they*?"

"They?" Maddy stalled.

"Yes, *they*. You said 'and they can't—'"

"Oh, that. I mean the ra—place that I work."

But Sophie was no slouch in picking up details. "The ra —? A ranch? With a bull pasture?"

"Umm…" Maddy searched her mind for a possible evasion, but found only a distraction. But truly, what could it hurt? She didn't have to give any identifying information. "Yes, but I don't know for how long. Adam came back from a trail ride just as we were getting Mia out of the pasture, and he really lit into us."

"Did he get violent?" Sophie asked, a protective note to her voice.

Maddy sent her mind back. Adam hadn't tried to hit anyone, hadn't even threatened it. And actually, if she'd come riding into a dangerous situation, she might have blown her stack, too. "No, he just yelled a lot, especially at his brother who had no responsibility at all for Mia. But still…"

Sophie's tone changed completely "I'd yell too, if someone put themselves in danger but didn't actually get hurt. And his name is Adam, huh? What's he look like?"

"Sophie! I'm not interested in men right now!"

"Avoiding the question?" Sophie teased. "Curiouser and curiouser."

Maddy heaved a sigh and caved in. She knew Sophie wouldn't let go. "Adam has dark hair and eagle eyes and a frown to make you back up a step. His brother Caleb is actually better looking—blond with broad, broad shoulders. Well, they're both covered in muscle, being ranchers and all. But Caleb is nicer."

Sophie chuckled. "How fascinating, sis. Your voice describing Adam is different than describing Caleb. I think you might have a thing for Adam-who-cares-enough-to-get-mad."

"I do not! He's the last person I'd want to get involved with!" Although Maddy *had* seen a different side of him with the bird. She shoved that out of her mind and changed tacks. "Besides, you're the one looking for a new guy. Have you had enough of Sad Sam?"

Sophie snorted again. "Oh, he's long gone. Let me tell you about Richard…"

By the time they hung up, Maddy was laughing. But Sophie's earlier words echoed.

Adam and her? Her sister was delusional.

6

M addy returned to the office, her phone in her hip pocket and a serious look on her face. Adam tried to watch her without being obvious, but she stared at him.

"What?" she asked.

"Nothing." He shook his head and returned to his own work. Not that moving their calving season was anything he wanted to consider, and this guy's writing didn't get any more interesting, but it wouldn't do to just keep watching her.

Was she someone he might want to date? Did he really want to date anyone? He'd have no time at all until the rest of the calves were born, and his days would still be overloaded after that.

On the other hand, ranch work shouldn't fill his entire life.

Adam sent a glance her way, just a quick one. He was glad that her desk wasn't facing the wall, that he could see her face and not just the back of her head. But it was taking a lot of effort to get his own work done. He put the article aside and pulled out the breeding reports from last year.

He studied which cows and bulls produced calves with the highest weight, who had problems, how many heifers they needed from this group for replacements. His senses tingled —someone was watching him.

He glanced at Maddy, whose eyes were focused, whose fingers were flying on the keyboard. Nope, not her.

He looked at Dad, who didn't drop his gaze quite in time.

"What is it?" Adam whispered, leaning forward across the double desk. Dad had given a pointed look earlier—he'd better not say anything about Maddy now.

Sure enough, Dad glanced over at her. Then quickly back and down. "Nothing. Wait, there is something."

Adam raised his eyebrows. Dad pushed some papers across to him. Adam looked at scribbled diagrams and math problems, then back up.

His father's blue eyes clouded over. "I can't make the numbers come right. I add them and add them, and it's never the same."

Adam chuckled. "Gotta move into the 21st century, Dad. Try using the calculator."

But Dad shook his head. "I did. I still can't figure it. We have six hundred acres in hay, right? And about two tons per acre?"

Adam ran a hand through his hair. "No, Dad. Once the cows and calves are up at the summer pasture, we'll have about 1200 acres in hay. About three tons each for the first cutting, and one for the second, if we get a second."

His father nodded, but didn't look convinced. "Another bout of senior-itis, I guess." He shrugged and waved his hand at the papers. "You figure it out."

Adam shifted his foot, ignoring the throb in his, and set the papers on his side of the desk. He used a spreadsheet to plan the hay required to carry the cows through winter. And why his father thought he needed to calculate it now, he had no idea.

It worried him occasionally—this wasn't the first time Dad's thoughts didn't make sense—but it wasn't important now. "Actually, Dad, I do need to talk to you about the pastures. It's time to take soil samples, isn't it? Or did you do that already?"

"Already done," Dad said. "I sent them in last week."

If he had, they should have gotten the results by now. Adam frowned, making a mental note to call and check. Before he could say anything else, his father shoved his chair back and stood.

"I've got to look in on Caleb," Dad said, not meeting Adam's eyes. He walked out at a steady pace, but somehow his footsteps didn't carry the energy they used to.

Adam tapped his pencil. It sounded loud in the quiet room.

"Is he okay?" Maddy asked. Her brown eyes were warm with concern. "He seems sad."

Adam shrugged. "Just a little off his feed, maybe." He wished he could put his finger on what was wrong. Maybe nothing. Maybe it was his imagination.

"How's your ankle feeling?"

He tamped down the growl that wanted to come out. "Fine. No problem." If she was going to hover over every little hurt, he not only wouldn't be dating her, he wouldn't be sharing an office with her for very long.

It was time to see how repairs were going. "I'll be back in time to feed the bird again." He labored to his feet and strode out the door, not limping a bit. He didn't give in to his ankle until he'd closed the door behind him.

🐎 🐎

AFTER A LONG DAY of work sorting out tax information, Maddy collapsed on her sofa and pulled Mia into her lap.

"Did you have fun today, sweetie?"

"Yup! Did you?"

"Of course!" Maybe not fun, but satisfying, anyway. Except for the time she'd spent puzzling over Adam. He'd been studious sometimes and almost ADD at others. Both patient and frustrated with his father. And surprisingly gentle with Lacey's hurt bird.

That was what surprised her the most—that a guy who could gallop in and yell like he did could have the patience to coax a wild bird to eat. It made her smile inside.

She tuned back in to hear Mia say, "... thinks it's time to plant, Mama. Can we plant something?"

Maddy nodded. "I saw some flower seeds around somewhere. But we'll have to look."

An hour later, they had sweet pea seeds in three soil-filled paper cups, all lined up on the kitchen windowsill. They cleaned up the mess, scrubbed their hands, and it was time to start dinner.

"I'm making Nonna's spaghetti sauce," Maddy said. "Do you want to help me?"

Mia made a face. "Not really. I want to draw some sweet pea flowers."

Maddy was never sure if Mia didn't like to cook, or if her daughter was just entranced by many things at once. She nodded, and while Mia colored at the table, Maddy began the sauce. Nonna always simmered it all day, and Maddy never had time. At least it didn't come from a jar!

She hummed while she worked, smiling when she realized what she was doing—she hadn't felt calm enough to hum for a long time.

She startled at the knock on the door, though. She set her

spoon down slowly and peeked out the curtain. Lacey stood on the small porch, shifting from foot to foot.

Maddy opened the door. "Lacey. We didn't get to meet properly before."

"I know, right? I was soooo late for school yesterday. And Dad wouldn't let me come over until I got my research paper finished—who needs to know about the causes of the French Revolution anyway?—but I finally got it done. And then he said you needed some downtime right after work, and I needed to feed my bird, but is it okay now?"

The girl bubbled over with exuberance, and Maddy opened the door wider to welcome her.

"Ooh, it smells good in here," Lacey said, sniffing. She tucked a lock of long, blonde hair behind her ear. "What are you making?"

"My grandmother's spaghetti sauce." Maddy scooped a bit in a small spoon. "Want to tell me what you think?"

Lacey blew to cool it off first. "Oh, that's yummy! I wish I could cook. I can make a pretty good peanut butter fudge, and my cupcakes aren't bad, but that's about it. I try to watch Uncle Dirt, but nothing seems to sink in. And it's not like I had Mom around to show me. Did I say how glad I am you're here? There's just too much testosterone on this ranch, with only me to balance it out."

Maddy chuckled—four brothers and all those ranch hands, with only one girl? Lacey's assessment was spot on. And then there was Uncle Dirt. "I still can't get over that nickname."

Lacey laughed. "He's not dirty or anything. He's just been on the ranch forever. He's says he's older than dirt, so when I was little, I started calling him that. Everyone else does now, too."

"That's what your dad said. And he's your cook?"

"Well, he is now. He used to be out with the herds, I guess, but he got his leg busted pretty badly. So he helps with some ranch stuff and does all our cooking. Except for my fudge!"

"Sounds like an interesting guy." Maddy tasted her sauce and added another pinch of oregano. Just right. "What else have you tried to make?"

Lacey made a face. "I tried a soufflé that ended up about as flat as a slice of bread, and some chocolate cinnamon cookies that just tasted weird." She pulled out a kitchen chair to sit on. "And then last year I watched a YouTube video and tried making a Yule log."

Maddy raised her eyebrows. "A Yule log?"

Lacey gave a rueful smile. "Yup. It's a chocolate cake roll with frosting inside, and once it's all rolled up, you decorate the outside with more frosting so it looks like a log. Except mine looked more like a fat worm covered in lumpy dirt."

"Oh, it couldn't have been that bad."

"Those were Adam's exact words. And he was right. See?" The teenager pulled up a picture on her phone and showed Maddy.

It did look like a fat worm with lumpy dirt.

"Well, yeah, but he didn't need to say that. Besides, brothers never like their sister's cooking." Maddy chuckled. "Did it taste good?"

Lacey shrugged. "Mostly, but a little, I don't know, metallic-y? Uncle Dirt said I probably mixed up teaspoon with tablespoon and put too much baking soda in. But I *like* cooking. It's fun and something different to do when the ranch is shut down in the winter."

Maddy gave Lacey a speculative glance. "Winter's about gone, but would you be interested in doing some cooking together? I'll teach you some dinner stuff, and maybe we can learn to do Yule logs together."

The girl's eyes went wide. "Really? You'd do that for me? It's so nice to have another female around. I get tired of the guys sometimes. No one to talk to who understands."

Maddy smiled. She still wasn't used to being on her own, and she desperately missed her family. Lacey would fill a void in her life, too. "So what grade are you in?"

"Junior. Only one more year of high school to go!" The teenager sighed dramatically.

"Not so thrilled with school, huh?" Maddy could commiserate—she wouldn't want to go back to being a teenager for anything.

Lacey shrugged. "School's okay. I see my friends, and I like math. But it seems like everything has to wait until I'm grown up."

"Like what? What do you want to do with your life?"

"Adam keeps asking me that." Lacey frowned. "The thing is, I'm not sure. Sometimes I want to go to vet school because I like helping injured animals—that scrub jay is going to be okay, I think. But I think it would be cool to be a nurse, too, and help people. And sometimes I just want to work on the ranch the rest of my life." She got a gleam in her eyes. "But maybe if I learn how, I'll be a chef!"

Maddy grinned. "Okay then." She turned the sauce down to simmer and filled a kettle with water. "First lesson is how to *not* overcook pasta."

7

Adam almost slept through his alarm. He'd been out on the three a.m. calving check, and the last cow had finally dropped her calf. Last except for Number Fifty-Two, and she was always late. *Thanks, Lord,* he sent up as he wandered bleary-eyed into the usual early morning commotion.

Micah was yawning, Jesse was telling a joke about a rodeo rider and a beauty queen, Wes and another cowboy were discussing the cows that hadn't calved yet, and Ty leaned against the wall with his eyes closed.

"That's good," Uncle Dirt said after Jesse's punchline, "but did you hear the one about the cowboy and the dachshund?

Adam groaned in advance, and Wes, who'd been there a year or two and should have known better, took the bait. "No, what?" Wes said.

"He wanted to 'git a long little dogie!'" Uncle Dirt cackled.

"That joke is almost as old as you are," Adam broke in.

"Of course," the work-worn man snorted. "I wouldn't have my name otherwise."

The cowboys were still chuckling, more at Uncle Dirt himself than the joke.

Adam looked at them—good men, all. Mostly, anyway. He wouldn't be surprised if Ty's eyes were bloodshot from drinking last night. "All right, there's a lot going on today. It's still muddy, so those of you on horseback, be careful of their legs. Don't need any pulled muscles." Or sprained ankles where someone would actually cut your new boot off. At least it wasn't throbbing so much today.

He gave out assignments, naming some cowboys to be on daytime calving duty, and six more to take the night shift rotation through the week. He finished with, "Ty and Wes, it's your turn for mucking out stalls. Start with the calving barn—disinfect and spread fresh straw—then head over to the stables once Caleb has the horses out in the pasture."

All the hands took even turns with this most unpalatable job, and Wes groaned predictably. Just as predictably, Ty cussed.

Adam looked at him sharply. "You got a problem with that, Ty?"

Ty glared back at Adam. "No. I just think you could hire day workers for that." He spat on the floor.

"If I do, you'll be the first day worker on my list, and that's where you'll stay," Adam warned. "Get some rags from the kitchen and clean up that mess of spit before you go."

Ty tilted his hat back down over his eyes, but remained silent.

"You want us back on the fencing, boss?" one of the ranch hands asked.

Adam shook his head. "The rest of you are with me. We'll be assessing the yearling heifers and I'll need you in the pens out there. Luis, you take the Gator out with the vaccines and some grub for lunch. Wes, we probably won't be back until late, so you make sure the evening chores get done."

Dad elbowed him. "You sure you ought to be on a horse with that ankle?"

"My ankle's fine," Adam growled. He didn't need anyone hovering over him, Dad, Maddy, or anyone else.

Dad's eyes narrowed. "Didn't look like it yesterday. You push too hard, it'll come back to bite you." Then his expression changed. "You got any jobs left for an old man?"

Adam was shocked he'd ask. "Aren't you coming with us?"

Dad grinned. He seemed relieved for some reason.

"You too, Micah? Or do we have machinery that needs your TLC?"

"I'm in," Micah said. "The tractors can do without me for a day."

ADAM BLESSED his grandfathers once more as he saddled Mister. If they didn't have the land they did, they'd have a lot of cows living in mud. As it was, there was room for large pastures so the cows could spread out. The heifers born last year, the ones they were keeping as replacements, were at the east end of the ranch where there was another hay barn and corrals.

They rode in easy camaraderie, sometimes chatting and sometimes silent. The sound of horses breathing, leather creaking, hoofbeats settling in the dirt—they all gave Adam that feeling of rightness. The sun warmed his shoulders, and he thanked God for a beautiful day. And for an easy ride, not stressing his ankle any more than necessary.

Micah spoke up. "I didn't think you'd ride out today."

Adam heaved a sigh. "Like I told Dad, my ankle's fine."

Micah gave him a long glance. "You know, the rest of us *are* capable of doing things without you. Including getting the heifers vaccinated and checking their weight."

"I know. It's just…" Adam's voice trailed off. He didn't know how to put how he felt into words, this drive to make sure everything went properly, and he wasn't sure he even wanted to. Eventually, he gave up. "I needed to get out anyway. Too much time behind a desk does not a cowboy make!"

"You can say that again."

"Too much time behind a—"

"I got it, I got it." Micah groaned.

Adam gave a chuckle, but his mind had flitted to his office…and Maddy at her desk. She'd be having a quiet day today by herself. He was relieved that she was going to get the taxes done, but he wondered what she'd be doing next. He realized he really didn't know what an accountant did besides pay the bills and do the payroll.

He ought to ask her sometime. It wasn't right that he was half-running the ranch and didn't know what all the employees' duties were. And if he could manage to talk to her outside, perhaps he'd get to see the sun glimmer in her hair again. He wondered if she'd felt the same quiver as he had when they'd touched.

He gave a sharp shake. Any conversations with Maddy needed to be business-only. No glorious hair, no zinging touches, just business. He had no energy for anything else. Yet.

They found the yearling heifers split into two groups, one scattered across a hillside and the rest throughout a broad gully. The men moved their horses into a lope and circled them widely, then slowed to herd them toward the pens.

Mister walked eagerly, and Adam inhaled deeply as they

followed the stragglers. The air felt warm, the breeze was slight, and there was no place he'd rather be than riding in these mountains, pain or no pain.

Micah pulled his horse to an abrupt stop, shading his eyes with his hand and peering into the distance. "Is that Dad facing off with that heifer?"

Adam squinted. They were far ahead and he couldn't make out facial features, but the horse was definitely Cobbler. "No one else rides a Paint like that; it has to be Dad. I'm going to go help."

"No, don't," Micah said sharply. "He's doing fine."

Adam sat back in his saddle. Mister's muscles relaxed, but that was more than he could say for himself. Dad was working an angry heifer by himself. Adam's whole being wanted to assist.

But Micah was right. Dad was an experienced cowboy. He'd been wrangling cattle since long before Adam was born —he really wouldn't like being thought incapable of doing his job.

And he wasn't. Adam watched as Dad sat deep in his saddle, telegraphing signals with just his knees and his seat and letting Cobbler use his well-developed instincts to block the young cow. At one point, she backed and whirled, taking off up a hill. Dad gave chase and loosened his lariat. He gave a quick flick of the wrist to catch her, Cobbler sat back on his haunches, his weight against the heifer's movement, and she dragged to a stop.

"Brilliant," Micah said.

Adam grinned without taking his eyes off Dad. "He'll be riding us into the ground when he's ninety. You know, sometimes he does something that makes me worry he's having problems, and then I watch him like this and my worries disappear."

An hour later, they had the yearlings in several large pens, ready to vaccinate. The cowhands relaxed in their saddles, chatting while their horses dozed in the sun. Dad seemed in deep conversation with Jesse.

"Luis, you got the grub?" Adam called.

'Sure do, boss." He hefted an ice chest out of the Gator.

The other cowboys dismounted, dropping their reins to the ground. With the horses taught to ground-tie, they wouldn't wander off. The men gathered around Luis, grabbing thick roast beef sandwiches and single-person apple pies. Adam joined them, trying to limp as little as possible.

"Mmm," Dad said, grabbing a bite while he settled on the ground next to Adam and Micah. "Sure am glad Uncle Dirt's doing our cooking these days."

Adam nodded. They had a housekeeper come in once a week, but since Aunt Sarah left a few years ago, Uncle Dirt had taken over the cooking.

"He's saving some for us tonight, right?" Jesse said, folding his long body next to Micah.

"Of course," Dad said. "I think he's cooking kitchen tonight."

"Huh?" Adam's head shot up.

"Uncle Dirt," Dad said. "He's cooking steaks for us."

"But you said…" Adam's voice trailed off. Just because his father had mixed up a word didn't mean Adam had to point it out. He gave what he hoped was a reassuring smile. "Steak sounds good."

By late afternoon, six tired cowboys headed back home. Adam had kept a close eye on Dad, but no more strange words had shown up. Maybe it really was worry over nothing.

He put it out of his mind and concentrated on Uncle Dirt's juicy. And unexpectedly wondered what Maddy would be having for dinner.

⎯⎯⎯⎯⎯⎯⎯⎯⎯⎯⎯⎯

8

The next week dragged for Maddy. When her eyes crossed over expense deductions, she'd shift to catching up invoices and then back again. All while being hyper-aware of Adam's presence when he was at his desk and his absence when he was out on the ranch. The conflict of her unexpected attraction to him added to her complicated life left her feeling like she was on a spinning carnival ride.

Mr. Black was mostly out doing ranch chores, but when he was there, he either sat quietly at his desk or told her stories of growing up on the ranch. "It was simpler back then, Missy," he said.

And then there was the scrub jay.

Lacey brought it in each day before school. Adam coaxed bread and milk down its throat when he was in, and Maddy took over the task when he wasn't. Each time Adam fed the bird, she wondered if he'd ask her to help. Wondered if she'd have the same reaction to his touch. He hadn't needed her help again, but it was obvious that her attraction to the cowboy was growing.

Maddy had been alone in the office all morning, her eyes glued to the last submission screen for their tax return, but now she sensed a presence behind her. Adam or Mr. Black?

Her heart raced. Adam? Would he look exhausted this morning, or would his eyes sparkle when he said hello?

A chair creaked, and she knew it was the senior Mr. Black. And again had to tamp down her disappointment.

A few minutes later, the older man said, "I'm sorry to disturb you, but could you help me for just a minute?"

"Of course, Mr. Black. What do you need?"

He waved his hands in protest. "Oh no. None of this 'Mr. Black,' remember. I answer to Samuel."

"Right, Samuel." He was kind and not overbearing—she liked him. She scooted over in her chair. "What can I help you with?"

"It's these tax papers," he said. "The quarterly payments look different from last year's. I want to make sure I'm doing them right."

"But...wouldn't I be doing those?" With the annual tax return almost done, the quarterlies were next on her list.

"Sometimes," he said rather insistently. "Sometimes I do them. Depends on who's busiest. But they're due now, and see here?" He pointed to an open box. "It says to put the prior year's credits, but we didn't have any credits. We still had an amount to pay."

Maddy put a smile on her face and a gentle hand on his arm. "Mr. Black, Samuel, there are credits, they just aren't what you think they are. And you're actually looking at the January payment, not April. Let me pull what I've done so far and we'll check it."

She turned toward her desk, but jumped when she saw Adam's hovering figure.

"Sorry. Didn't mean to startle you." Adam's voice was a low growl.

Her heart pounded in surprise. Was he angry about something? Or still in pain from his ankle? Maddy glanced down and wondered if his cowboy boots made it ache more.

She looked back up at him. "Your dad had a question about the tax worksheet. And…there's more." She motioned him out to the hall.

"Samuel's fretting about the January quarterly payment. I know that one got paid on time. I'm not sure why he's so worried about it." She paused, trying to calm her pulse. Trying not to react to his closeness. His aftershave. *Stop it, Maddy. You're acting like a teenager!*

She took a shallow breath. "I've also found a few discrepancies with invoices and payments not matching up, and it makes me wonder what how accurate your old accountant was."

Adam ran his hand through his hair. He stared into space, then finally looked back at her. "Dad's just got a lot on his mind and gets mixed up sometimes. But tell me about the discrepancies."

Maddy led him back into the office, changed computer tabs and showed him the highlighted lines. "There were only a few to begin with, and then it's like she overpaid almost every invoice for several months."

He grimaced and studied the numbers on the screen. His expression changed from curiosity to concern to anger. Finally, he spoke. "She was embezzling. Look—the feed store, the vet, and three out-of-town suppliers, but never the electric bill."

Maddy squeezed her eyes shut. Of all the despicable things to do… An accountant was supposed to safeguard the truth, to be trusted both with a company's innermost secrets and their finances. How could anyone give up their integrity for such a relatively small sum?

She finally looked at Adam, who was muttering to himself. She stiffened—was he going to lose his temper again?

But he only straightened and spoke louder. "Mrs. Evans seemed to change in her last couple months, acted a little differently, especially since she gave her notice. I thought it was just because she was leaving to retire somewhere warmer, but I guess there was more to it than that."

He ran a hand through his hair again, tousling it delightfully. Maddy smacked the thought down—she did *not* need to think of him that way.

Adam finally spoke again. "I thought there was nothing I hated more than someone lying to me, but I guess lying *and* stealing is worse."

"Do you want me to do a full audit?" When would she get her own office back? How long would she have to sidestep around this awkward attraction?

Adam pinched the bridge of his nose. "Yes, please. Let's see exactly what damage she caused, and then we can decide what to do."

Maddy nodded. She looked over at Samuel and whispered, "What about your dad?"

"I'll talk to him," Adam said just as quietly. "Let me know when you've got some answers." He turned to go, then stopped in the doorway. After a long minute, he turned, his tired eyes a warm cobalt blue. "I never did apologize properly for my tirade that first day. I shouldn't have let go like that. It was just…" His voice trailed off.

"Just that there was danger," Maddy finished. He'd already apologized to Mia, so she wasn't expecting this, but it was nice. She had never in her life had an apology after someone yelled at her. Not from a grown man, anyway.

She didn't quite know what to think. She wasn't sure she could trust him not to lose his temper in the future, but… Apologies and aftershave were a heady mix.

9

Maddy and Lacey had just slid a large pan of lasagne into the oven Saturday afternoon when Micah's voice rang out. "You over here, Lacey?"

The teenager rolled her eyes. "Brothers!" she muttered. She went to the door anyway. "Yes, Micah dear? Checking up on me *again*?"

Maddy heard Micah snort. "Sure. Not like I have anything else to do all day, right? No, I just wanted to know if you want to…what am I smelling? Tomato sauce and cupcakes?"

A pause, then, "Oof!"

Maddy grinned. It sounded like she wasn't the only one to slug her brothers occasionally.

Booted footsteps sounded on her floor, and Maddy turned around to see Micah pulling his battered cowboy hat off. He held it against his chest and looked hopeful. "You guys have been cooking?"

Maddy shrugged. The table was covered with cinnamon honey roll-ups and a butter pecan cake, not to mention all the pots and pans littering the kitchen. "Turns out Lacey and I have a kitchen hobby in common."

"Mama makes lasagne and Lacey makes treats," Mia piped up.

"Mm, mmm," Micah said. "Are you sharing, or are you going to eat it all yourself?"

"We're sharing." Maddy smiled.

Lacey spoke at the same time. "Only people who work get to eat."

"Hey, I work!" Micah protested.

Lacey smirked. "Not anything to do with making treats. I'd think if someone wanted a piece of cake, they would be willing to pitch in on the cleanup."

"Sheesh!" Micah said. "If you were six years old again, I'd send you to your room for being disrespectful."

"If I were six years old, I wouldn't be using the oven," Lacey retorted.

"I'm six years old!" Mia added.

Maddy watched the banter with delight. They reminded her so much of her own family, and it filled an empty space in her heart.

"I'll tell you what," she put in when she got a chance, "Micah, you can help me wash up while Lacey gets the plates and cuts the cake."

"You're on!" Micah tossed his hat onto the couch and rolled his sleeves up.

"I get to rinse!" Mia said, pushing a chair to the sink.

Micah told a brief story of Lacey when she was little, and Lacey retaliated by sharing some of Micah's more exciting teenage exploits. Like the time he took the four-wheeler out when he was grounded, and when he'd eaten a whole pie by himself in the middle of the night.

"That's not fair!" he cried, snapping the dishtowel at her.

The teenager dodged easily. "That's what Caleb said when he found out you'd eaten it all."

Maddy declared the kitchen clean, and Micah dropped the teasing to grab a plate. "Butter pecan cake? Never heard of it."

They settled on the front porch, the spring breeze chilling them despite the sun, and dug in.

"Mmm," Micah said. "Tastes just like the ice cream without the cold. Didn't know you could cook like this, sis."

Lacey blushed. "This is the first good thing I've made from a real recipe. Maddy helped me."

Micah nodded at Maddy, his mouth full again. When he swallowed, he said, "I think we'll have to keep you around."

"Keep her around for what?" Caleb said, striding up the driveway with Wes.

Micah pointed at the women with a fork. "Lacey and Maddy have been cooking."

Maddy smiled a welcome. "It's on the table—help yourself."

They returned in a moment, each with a plate in one hand and a dining chair in the other. As they settled, Caleb said, "We were gonna hang out at Wes's cabin until evening chore time, but this is even better!"

"What? No hot date tonight?" Lacey teased.

"Nah, Susie's out of town, Caitlyn's mad at me, and Ronni has a new boyfriend."

Maddy's eyes goggled, but Micah just laughed. "Don't worry. You'll catch one someday, Bro."

Caleb slapped his cowboy hat at him. "Look who's talking!"

They ate and talked and laughed, telling old stories and new jokes. The warm afternoon gave way to a late-day chill. Micah got quieter as the others chatted, but Mia snuggled in

Lacey's lap, and Maddy felt more at home than she had in a long time. Maybe she ought to cook dinner for everyone on the weekends.

"What time are your evening chores?" she asked.

Wes shrugged, but Caleb spoke up. "It depends on the daylight. For the horses, we bring the mares and foals in for grain just before sundown. The others stay in the pasture. It changes day to day for the cattle."

"If they're all out on the range, or in the home pastures with good grazing, there aren't really any evening chores," Micah said. "Just all-day chores, unless we break for something. If we've got them in for some reason, then it just depends."

"Do you guys get much time off?"

Wes snorted, then lowered his head again. He seemed a quiet sort of guy.

Micah smiled ruefully. "Only when Adam lets us. Meaning, not as much as we'd like."

"Speak for yourself, bro!" Caleb put in. "I work the horses on my own schedule."

"Yeah, but you still get roped in for branding and stuff. Get it, *roped* in." Micah smirked.

Caleb rolled his eyes.

Lacey groaned. "Geez, you guys are lame. You probably still say 'Up and at 'em' when Adam shows up, don't you?"

Maddy smiled, then stopped as another deep voice spoke.

"That's better than 'Up and at 'em, Adam Ant,'" Adam said.

Maddy tried to quiet the sudden bouncing of her heart. Why should it be bouncing, anyway? She was a grown woman with responsibilities.

"What is this, hide out at Maddy's?" he asked.

Caleb leaned back, stretched his boots out in front of

him, and clasped his hands behind his head. "Nah, we're just soaking up some relaxation and good food."

Adam scowled. "Are you saying I'm not relaxed?" He glared at his brothers, then grinned. "I guess the shoe fits sometimes."

"Sometimes? Hah!" Lacey said. "Lacey do this. Lacey do that. Lacey, did you finish?"

"Yeah, but not all the time," Adam protested. "Now, did I hear something about food?"

Maddy stood, ready to show him into the cabin, but Micah forestalled her.

"Wait a minute," Micah said. "Didn't *someone* tell me a man has to work for his food?"

Lacey laughed. "He can wash the plates after."

Inside, Adam dished himself up a large serving of cake. Maddy had been having such fun listening to the others; she hoped Adam didn't put a damper on it.

"I actually came out to ask you about financial stuff," Adam said, picking up his fork, "but now that I think about it, it can wait until Monday." He took a bite and moaned in delight. "This is incredible! I'd hire you to cook for us, except it would hurt Uncle Dirt's feelings."

Maddy grinned. "Actually, I only did the lasagne that's still baking. Lacey gets the kudos for the cake."

Adam's eyebrows went sky high. "Really? Lacey made this?"

"With a little help. She's been trying things off YouTube videos, and this was a regular recipe we found online. But she's pretty good, you know."

"I have a hard time remembering she's not a little girl anymore."

Maddy looked out the open door to where Lacey sat. The teen wore a light coat of mascara but no other makeup, just fresh-faced natural beauty. Her sweater showed off her slender curves, and her determination to master something by herself was impressive. "She's just about grown up, Adam. You'll probably want to start changing the way you think of her. Like, yesterday."

Adam made a face. "I'm used to the others being full adults, but Lacey...if she's grown up, that means I'm *old*."

Caleb chimed in from the doorway. "You *are* old, bro. And you guys are being very cozy in here together. You going to come out and join us, or shall we leave you *alone*?"

Maddy's eyes widened—they'd only been talking, and not very long at that! She glanced at Adam. He was actually blushing. She'd never thought cowboys blushed.

She grabbed another chair and headed out to the porch, Adam following. She set the chair where there was space, but Adam slapped Lacey's leg and jerked his head sideways. She moved, and he took Lacey's place—right next to Maddy.

She tried to relax as the stories started up again, but a sense of confusion built inside her. Was Adam possibly attracted to her? And if so, how did she feel about it when she was trying to tamp down her own attraction?

She shook her head. She wasn't a giddy teenager anymore. She was a single mom with a messed up life and secrets to keep, and no way would a relationship fit in her life right now. Especially with her boss! She put the thought away and determined to enjoy the evening.

And enjoy it, she did. She discovered Adam could laugh as readily as his brothers, that he enjoyed teasing back, and that the family had a lot of love flowing between them. *Who are you, and what have you done with the old Adam?* she thought.

"So can we expect treats on a regular basis, Lacey?" he asked. "Just what kind of work will you want in return?"

Lacey twirled her fork in her fingers. "Oh, nothing too bad. Somebody could take over cleaning the bathrooms, somebody else could groom my horse after I ride..."

"O-ho!" Caleb cried. "A rider who doesn't have to care for her own mount? Never!"

"Okay then, how about somebody cleans my tack for me?"

Micah waggled a finger at her. "We're too old and experienced to let you get away with that. I'm thinking more like licking the beaters so they don't need as much washing."

"But there are three of us and only two beaters," Adam said with a twinkle in his eye.

By the time they had progressed from sharing out the beaters to possible bribery, Maddy was doubled over in laughter. *I needed this, Lord—thank you!* And then she sniffed. "The lasagne!" she gasped, leaping out of her chair.

She dashed into the kitchen, remembered to grab pot holders, and slid the bubbly dish out of the oven. Not burnt, thank goodness.

"Lasagne?" Adam said. "You mean there's dinner after dessert?"

Maddy grinned as she sprinkled the last mozzarella over the top. "In about fifteen minutes," she said.

Caleb brought plates in. "Too bad it's time for evening chores," he said. "But maybe we can do this again."

"Sure," Maddy agreed. "Weekday or weekend?"

"Doesn't matter," Caleb said.

"Weekend is better," Adam said at the same time.

Caleb grinned and shouldered his brother. "Some of us aren't limited to Monday through Friday business."

Adam shouldered him back. "Some of us don't have demanding evening chores," he answered smugly.

Caleb looked from Adam to Maddy and back again. "Right. You just want Maddy all to yourself."

Adam raised his eyebrows. "And if I do?"

Maddy caught her breath.

Caleb just shrugged. "Time to go, boys," he said, leaving the cabin.

"Hey, send Dad out if you see him," Adam called after.

Caleb lifted an arm in acknowledgement. Lacey caught Maddy's eye and winked, touched a finger to Mia's button nose, then left with the others.

Maddy's senses were on alert, supremely conscious of Adam beside her. His presence didn't seem to bother Mia, but this was *not* what she'd expected when she'd invited Lacey to come cook with her.

10

A dam watched his brothers, his little sister, and his ranch hand walk away. Maddy stood just inside the cabin door, helping her daughter out of her jacket.

He was physically aware of Maddy's presence, even if her attention was elsewhere. He could smell her perfume or whatever it was giving her a slight floral scent. His nerve endings seemed jittery, probably because he had no clue how he'd ended up here.

Sure, she was beautiful, and something inside him responded to her personality. And perhaps he had daydreamed a little the other day, but that was all. He really shouldn't even be there now—he should be checking the state of the pastures, and making sure the youngest calves were doing well, and...

His jobs seemed never-ending. They *were* never-ending, if he included checking on his father. That was something else he needed to think about more. But right now, he was standing next to a lovely woman who made him think of things he'd not allowed himself to think. Who made him feel strong and protective and butterfingers all at once. And who just happened to have a scrumptious dinner ready. If the Lord had set this up for him, maybe he shouldn't argue.

He wiped the table after Maddy put the last slice of cake away. She gave Mia silverware to put out.

"What can I do?" he asked, then stopped, realizing how rude they'd all been. She hadn't invited anyone over; they had each just stopped in and made themselves at home. Which was probably fine for cake, but what gave him the right to assume he was welcome for dinner?

Adam looked at her, puttering in the kitchen, seeming as happy as could be. He didn't know her well enough to read her moods, though. "Maddy? We sort of barged in on you, invited ourselves like you were…"

"Family?" she finished, looking over at him. "It feels good, like I'm accepted."

"Of course you're accepted. We all like having you around." How could she think otherwise?

She smiled softly. "I've been missing my own family, and having all of you here felt just right. And I would enjoy it if you stayed for dinner."

Their eyes met, and Adam felt like he was falling into them. Liquid chocolate, luminous warmth. Inviting, yet still reserved. He wanted to step forward, to kiss her, to see what those lush lips tasted like.

Whoa, that was unexpected. He stepped back quickly. Even if a kiss were a possibility, it was too soon. Way too soon.

"So, do you have an Italian family stashed back at home who taught you to cook? Or did you figure it out from YouTube like Lacey?"

Maddy grinned, her eyes lighting up. "Mom hates cooking, but my Nonna had me on a step stool beside her when I was little. You ought to see her—short and round with tight gray curls, waving a wooden spoon all over while she talks. And heaven forbid you show up and say you're not hungry!"

Adam laughed. He could picture Maddy looking just like that fifty years from now. "My grandma wasn't so flamboyant. She was soft and round and gave the best hugs. And made the best oatmeal scotchies."

"Oatmeal scotchies?"

"Oatmeal cookies with butterscotch chips. Everyone else liked chocolate chip cookies better, but those were my favorite. When she made them for me, I felt like I was her favorite grandson ever." Funny, he hadn't thought of that in a long time. Too long. He made a mental note to put some flowers on her grave in the family cemetery.

"Did your mom take after her, or was she like mine—a total non-cook?"

Adam paused. Mom wasn't someone he talked about a lot, but it wasn't like they kept her a secret. "She did like to cook. I was too young to care about dinner stuff, but she loved baking bread on Sunday afternoons. I'd come in from riding and slather butter all over. I think I usually ate a whole loaf by myself."

He hadn't thought about Mom's bread in a long time. He looked up at Maddy. "She died when I was seventeen. Killed by a drunk driver."

"Oh, Adam, I'm sorry. That's—"

There was a knock at the door. Maddy wiped her hands and opened it, and Adam's father stepped in. He rotated his cowboy hat in his hands like he was nervous. "My boys told me to come on down," he said, "that you had some scrumptious cooking going on."

"I'm happy to have you, but won't Uncle Dirt mind?"

Maddy said. She gave a quick glance at Adam, who smiled and shook his head. They'd talked enough about Mom, anyway.

Dad's shoulders relaxed at Maddy's welcome, and he grinned. "Nah, he said it left more for him to eat. Sure does smell good in here."

Maddy took his hat and hung it on a hook. "If you two will fill the water glasses, Mia and I will finish the salad."

Adam pulled four glasses down from the cabinet Maddy had pointed to, handing them one by one to his father.

Dad looked between him and Maddy with raised eyebrows.

Adam elbowed him slightly. This sense, this electricity that he was feeling with Maddy—the last thing he needed was for his father to get in the middle of it.

Maddy sprinkled sliced olives over the romaine and grated the parmesan, while Mia carefully placed cherry tomatoes around the edges. Adam and his dad set the water glasses around.

Maddy pointed them to chairs and brought the lasagne to the table. Adam fidgeted through an awkward moment as they settled, and then even more when little Mia said grace.

"Dear God, thank you for our food, and please bless that nobody will get mad. Name of Jesus Christ, Amen." Mia lifted her head quickly. "Can I have an extra big piece?"

Adam glanced at Maddy, whose face was flushed. What had they been through that Mia would pray for no one to get mad? Did Maddy have a hidden temper? Or was it her ex?

"After all that cake you ate? I'll be surprised if you manage a regular piece," Maddy answered. She dished up a small square and passed it to her daughter, never lifting her eyes to the others.

"I'll take one of those big pieces, if it's all right with you,"

Dad said, sending his plate Maddy's way. "This just like my Daisy used to make, although yours might be more authentic."

Good for Dad, changing the subject and easing the tension around the table, although Adam didn't remember his mother ever making homemade lasagne. He carried the conversation on. "What else did your Nonna—is that your grandmother?—teach you to make?"

Maddy relaxed some more as she described various Italian dishes. Adam took a bite and decided it was the best lasagne he'd ever had. More than that, his heart warmed to know that Maddy was no longer embarrassed.

They told stories of silly things they'd done when they were young and laughed out loud at some of Dad's antics as a teenager.

"You picked up a whole car and turned it sideways?" Mia asked, eyes wide with awe.

"Sure did, little one. Me and three other guys. The doofus couldn't drive it out, not with it nose and tail against the other cars. We got in trouble later, of course, but it was worth it."

Maddy turned to her daughter. "But if you do anything like that, you'd be in so much trouble it *wouldn't* be worth it, right?"

"Right, Mama," Mia sighed. "Can I be excused now?"

Mia went off to read, and the talk shifted to the long-term aspects of the ranch—calves, pastures, markets. And ranch hands.

Wes was reliable in anything they set him to. Jesse was revealing himself to be a whiz with the horses, and Caleb would like to pull him to the stables permanently.

"Don't know if I want to give him up," Adam said. "We'd have to find someone to replace him with the cattle."

"Give Ty a little more responsibility?"

Adam frowned. "I wouldn't trust Ty as far as I could throw him."

Dad shook his head. "He just needs to come into his own, son. People will live up to your expectations, you know."

Adam threw his napkin onto his now-empty plate and shook his head violently. "Ty will never make a good ranch hand. He's lazy, he drinks, and he vanishes anytime he can."

He knew his voice was caustic, but he hadn't expected Maddy to startle and draw back. "Sorry," he said in a softer voice. "Ty just pushes all my buttons."

"You don't give him much chance to do anything else," Dad pointed out. "Besides, we don't want to bore Missy here with talk about employees."

Adam glanced at Maddy's confused face. He must seem like two different people to her. But she was almost two people to him.

There was Maddy, the detailed accountant and loving mother. And there was the Maddy who cringed at displays of temper and protected her daughter. Her ex-husband must have been pretty bad.

Samuel put his napkin on his plate and stood. "It's been a fine evening, Missy. Thank you."

"I enjoyed it very much," Maddy said. She began to pick up plates, and Adam hurried to help.

"Are you a church-goer?" he asked. "Would you like a ride tomorrow?"

She paused and then looked up. "Sure, thanks. I've missed for a couple weeks now, and it feels weird."

Adam's hand brushed hers as they put plates in the sink at the same time. He heard her quick intake of breath at the same time a feeling of excitement ran through him. Maybe there was something here, something that might grow. Did he want it to? "Tomorrow morning, then."

Maddy nodded, but didn't look up.

The stars were brilliant and the air chill as Adam and his father walked silently home, wrapped in their own thoughts.

11

The *Three Ms*, Maddy thought, sitting in the back seat of the truck's club cab Sunday morning. Her, Mia and Micah. Too bad it was Samuel sitting up front with Adam.

Not really—it was probably a good thing she was back here. She kept being wishy-washy with her feelings about Adam. The attraction was getting stronger, even if neither of them had actually said anything out loud, but the complications in her life weren't going to go away. They did, however, seem to be settling down. It had been more than two weeks since she'd left Denver, and the ranch itself felt protective, like it had folded her into its life and wouldn't let any harm come to her.

She sat silently for the first few minutes, not trying to be nervous around him, just soaking in his closeness and considering the possibilities. Adam was the perfect example of a girl's dream cowboy—rugged and worn but still as handsome as ever. He wasn't conceited, just sure of himself, confident in his abilities and his place in the world. It showed in his walk and his speech and was one of the things that made her heart beat faster.

There were times, though, that his grumpiness at something verged on temper and put her on edge. It wasn't like when she was married to Brock—Adam was only her boss, after all—but she didn't like feeling hesitant around him.

And then Micah spoke. "I'll bet this is nothing like your California cities, is it?"

"Uh, no. Very different," she agreed cautiously. She hadn't wanted any connection back to Denver, so she'd asked Samuel to say she was from southern California. Now, looking out the window for something to comment on, she hoped it wouldn't come back to bite her. "We sure don't have mountains like these."

Adam glanced at her. "Isn't Los Angeles right up against the mountains?"

Was it? Maddy's tongue grew thick. "Um, yeah, but they aren't as big as these. And you can hardly see them for the smog."

"Did you spend a lot of time at the beach? Sometimes I wish I had an endless ocean instead of the mountains," Micah said.

"We've never been to the beach," Mia piped up.

Maddy managed not to put her hand over her eyes at her daughter's innocent words. "Not much, anyway," she said. "It still takes a long time to get there, and we were always too busy."

"Son, you don't need to ask a billion questions," Samuel said. "It's not like you're going to see the beach anytime soon, anyhow."

She caught Adam's eyes in the rearview mirror, but she couldn't read his expression.

"What happened to that tree?" she asked, glad to find something different to comment on. The trunk was split, but both sections had green leaves.

"Lightning-struck," Samuel said. "Long time ago, from the look of it."

"Good thing it wasn't last year," Adam said. "Last summer was way too dry, and lightning could send a fire our way real fast."

With that, the men's talk shifted to past fires, helping fight them, how close they got, whether the planes should drop water or fire retardant. Relief coursed through Maddy's body as she sat back and listened. If she'd had to go on about California…Adam wasn't one to forgive a lie easily, and she didn't want to lose his respect.

She watched him through the mirror, his eyes on the road, his face animated as he talked. With time to actually look, she noticed smaller things. He had a scar running through one eyebrow—what had caused that? Had he come close to losing his eye? And another scar just below the brim of his hat. She couldn't see his mouth, but—

Adam's eyes met hers in the mirror. She dropped her gaze immediately, fighting the heat that quickly engulfed her face. Caught drooling over a handsome man. She didn't think she'd raise her eyes to him the rest of the day.

He finally pulled into a gravel parking lot next to a quaint white church with a tall steeple and a few stained glass windows. Maddy's soul sighed in recognition, and even with missing her first Sunday through moving exhaustion, she wondered why she hadn't made the trip down on her own last week. The men stomped and brushed any remaining dust off their clothes before escorting her to the door.

"Howdy, Pastor Rich," Samuel said, taking his cowboy hat off and extending his hand. "Fine morning, isn't it?"

Pastor Rich, dressed in boots and new jeans like the Blacks but with a light blue shirt and a preacher's white collar, shook hands. "Looks like you've gained a couple, Samuel."

Samuel grinned. "This is Maddy Ricci—" He turned back to her in consternation. "How do you say your name, again?"

"Maddy Ricciolino," she said, stepping up to shake the pastor's hand. "I'm the new accountant at the ranch. And this is my daughter, Mia."

"Pleased to meet you, Maddy, Mia. I look forward to seeing you here often."

The men traipsed into the church and settled into a pew that seemed to be their regular one. Maddy sent Mia in first, then followed. Fitting together on one bench only worked if they squeezed, and she wouldn't have survived being scrunched next to the guy who'd caught her watching him.

Still, it looked like Adam had hung back so they could sit next to each other, which should make her feel better, but still…how embarrassing! She squeezed Mia's hand and focused on the service instead.

The hymns were new to Maddy, but she enjoyed the traditional feel of the service. She soaked in the organ music, but Pastor Rich's sermon about integrity made her squirm. Hiding her background and her real name wasn't being honest and upright in all things, now, was it? But what else was she supposed to do?

In the rec room for refreshments afterwards, the guys scarfed up donuts and coffee cake. Maddy was pouring a glass of punch when Pastor Rich approached.

"How are you doing out there with all the Blacks?" he asked, his eyes warm with humor.

"They're good guys," she said. "Caleb reminds me of my brother. And Samuel is great." Great at keeping her secret, but she didn't need to mention that, especially after the pastor's sermon.

"And Adam and Micah?"

"Micah is quieter than the others, I think, but Adam…" Maddy paused, not sure how much to say. "Let's just say we started out with my daughter getting into the bull pasture by mistake."

Pastor Rich roared. Heads turned, and he lowered his voice. "I'll bet that didn't go over so well."

"No, it didn't." Maddy smiled. "He's a nice guy in a lot of ways, but it left me a little wary of him, to be honest."

But Pastor Rich shook his head. "Adam cares greatly, takes responsibility for everyone around him. And if something is outside his control, he'll worry that he can't fix anything bad that happens."

Because of losing his mother? That tidbit had Maddy reconsidering. "So…he's afraid of things going wrong?" Which explained the bull pasture episode, but not his complete antagonism toward Ty.

"I'd say more that he's afraid of not being able to make things right. It's like when—"

Adam strolled over just then, and the pastor changed the subject quickly. "Everything going okay at the ranch, Adam?" he said. "Got all your calves born?"

Adam stood between Pastor Rich and Maddy. "Yes, thank the Lord. Except for one cow who's notoriously late. I got my first full night of sleep a couple days ago."

Maddy listened to them talk, trying to reconcile the two sides of Adam Black: the polite Adam she saw here and at the office with the one who blasted his temper that first day and had shown it a few times since.

She could see why he'd been angry about Mia. And dinner last night had been more relaxed than she'd expected. That might have been because Mr. Black had shown up, but... no, Adam had helped and chatted like any other friend.

Perhaps he *could* be a friend, although she didn't think she'd want to cross him as her boss. And all those thoughts of how attracted she was to him? He made her heart race, and she suspected he might feel the same. So should she focus on friendship, or let the possibilities happen as they would?

She looked over to where Mia was talking animatedly with an eight- or nine-year-old girl. Her face was lit, her hands were waving—whatever the conversation was, Mia was definitely at ease.

Maddy was grateful. Besides the trauma of witnessing Brock's abuse, and being shoved once herself, it was hard for the little girl to leave her friends behind. And her family. If she could make a friend here, they could settle in at the ranch with glad hearts.

Thank you, Heavenly Father. A place to settle is just what we needed. And if starting something with Adam would cause problems, please keep me away from it. Just, please, guide me to know what to do.

Two hundred divided by twenty-five did not equal six. Adam shook his head in exasperation—if he couldn't do a simple math problem...

He looked across the office at the reason for his distraction. Maddy was all business today, scribbling notes as she plowed through the backlog of work. He smiled at the little furrow on her brow and the way she tapped her pencil against her lips.

Adam had hoped she'd sit next to him at church yesterday, but she'd put Mia between them instead. Had that been simply manners, or was she not interested in him at all?

He could have sworn she and Pastor Rich had been talking about him, though, even if they had changed the subject when he approached.

"Hey, Maddy?" But his phone rang before he could say more. By the time he finished with the details of an upcoming veterinary visit, Caleb had come in and was talking to Maddy himself. Explaining invoices, it sounded like.

"What'cha need, Caleb?" he asked.

CHERISHED BY THE RANCHER

His brother looked up, pushing back that lock of hair that always fell over his eyes. The one that girls liked to touch. "Just poking my head in," Caleb said. "But you were busy and Maddy's got questions, so..." He shifted his attention back to Maddy's upturned face.

Adam would have pouted, but grown men didn't pout. Still, she could have come to him with her questions. Except he hadn't been very nice when she'd come to him the first time. Downright rude, he figured now.

But that didn't mean Caleb needed to step in.

Adam tried to tamp down the rising frustration, tried to concentrate on numbers again.

Caleb pulled a chair over to Maddy's desk, evidently settling in for a long consultation.

Adam fumed. Tapped his pencil. Glared at his brother.

Finally, he pushed himself up and stalked out to the equipment shed. He wasn't getting anything done, and he didn't need to watch his brother flirt.

Micah was in the middle of changing the oil on the hay spooler.

"Hey, Bro!" Adam called. "I gotta get out of here for a bit. Need some time on a horse. Want to go check the fence progress with me?"

Micah jerked up and hit his head on the tractor cover. "Sheesh, give a guy some warning, would you?"

"Aw, your head's so hard we could pound fence posts with it. Want to come?"

"Sure, just let me finish this, or we won't be able to feed tonight."

Adam watched his younger brother unplug drain lines, tighten bolts, and generally bang on the machinery. Micah had always been the kid who loved tractors as much as the animals, for which Adam would be eternally grateful. He didn't have much mechanical aptitude himself, and the ranch would be sunk if they had to pay somebody to keep the equipment running.

As they walked to the stables, Adam had to remind himself that Micah wasn't a kid anymore. At twenty-nine, Micah was only two years younger than Adam. He'd been married and divorced, with a small son to show for it, even if the family didn't get to see the boy much.

How hard it must be to have fallen in love and made a baby together, and then have nothing to embrace now. Micah kept to himself even more these days than he used to. Kept his pain to himself too, no complaining or whining, just doing his work and keeping his head down.

No, Adam thought, Micah definitely was not a kid any longer. None of them were.

ADAM LET Mister have his head as they crossed the home pastures. He put Maddy out of his head and mulled over the ranch hands and who worked well with whom.

Micah interrupted his thoughts with a jarring, "So have you noticed that Caleb keeps finding reasons to be around Maddy? I think he likes her."

Adam's fist tightened on his reins, and Mister jerked at the irritation.

He suddenly felt like he had a rock in his belly. He didn't have any real claim on her. Maddy could have her pick of any one of them. Why not Caleb?

Micah was still talking. "He brought the tractor back when she was going home one day. He was almost drooling. What was it Mom would say when we were little? Twitter-pated."

Adam couldn't seem to get any air into his lungs. Mister slowed as Adam's muscles went rigid.

Micah twisted in his saddle to look back. "You coming, or what?"

Adam kicked Mister harder than he needed to. "Or what" was right. Dinner with Maddy, even with Dad there, had been the most enjoyable evening he'd had in a long time. He enjoyed sharing the office with her, seeing her focused on spreadsheets or looking up something she didn't know about ranch business. The more he got to know her, the more he wanted to know more.

In truth, Maddy seemed like everything he'd wish for in a woman. She was pretty and confident, had a killer smile, loads of patience with her daughter, and integrity in her work.

He had to admit there was a proprietary feeling running through him already, but he really had no right to it. He'd never made a move, and she hadn't given him any overt signals that she was interested. But still…there had been looks and just something he could sense.

Could he have been mistaken? Was she interested in Caleb instead?

He clamped his lips against the thought, urging Mister into a lope. He'd do better to concentrate on getting to the crew working on the cross-fencing than examining his feelings. He liked them stuffed in a tidy box and put away.

Micah caught up to him, laughing. "So. You don't like the idea of Caleb and Maddy, huh?" He got a wicked gleam in his eye. "Maybe you've got a thing for her yourself! Is that the way the wind blows?"

Adam scowled and pushed Mister into a hard gallop. They breezed along the fence line, the wind blowing at his hat. Micah caught up, and they raced across the field like they had as youngsters, finally pulling up at the gate to the next pasture.

Micah slapped his hat against his thigh. "Hah! Can't outrun me as easily now!"

"We're not teenagers anymore, in case you haven't noticed."

"Nope, we're grown men who should be honest with each other. So tell me about you and Maddy."

"There is no me and Maddy," Adam growled. "And if there were, you'd be one of the last to know." Then another thought struck him. "But as long as we're talking honesty, why aren't *you* looking at her? Or anyone else, for that matter?"

Micah's laughter dropped away. "After Selena? You've got to be kidding."

"You've been divorced more than a year. Isn't it time you moved on?"

It was Micah's turn to scowl and grunt. "I'm not actually crazy, you know. Not a glutton for punishment, either."

Adam closed the gate behind them, and they rode on in silence.

Finally, Micah glanced his brother's way. "Selena's pretty nasty right now. Every time it's my weekend to have Jacob, she vanishes into thin air. I go all the way into Grand Junction, and she makes a point not to be there."

"How old is he now? Two?"

"Two and a half. And let me tell you, it sucks to have a kid you love and not be able to be with him. I haven't seen him since his birthday—he probably wouldn't even recognize me now."

"You talk to your lawyer about it?"

Micah shook his head. "He'd bring it all before a judge, she'd get slapped with contempt of court and maybe land in jail. And I won't do that to the mother of my son, no matter how much I don't like her."

Adam had no comfort of his own to give. All he could say was, "God will get you through this."

"And use it to make me stronger," Micah finished in a sing-song voice. "I know. Dad keeps reminding me."

They crested a small rise and could see the Gator and the four-wheelers where the ranch hands were working.

"Looks like good progress," Micah said, tilting his hat to block the sun better. Then he turned back toward Adam. "And what about you, big brother? You're the oldest, but you've never been serious about anybody, not really."

Adam put a grin on his face. "Maybe because I saw all the trouble you guys landed in." It wasn't really true, but it would do for now. That answer was all he was going to give. He didn't need to mention he might be ready for more.

He'd gone on dates, sure. Even had a girlfriend or two, but no one who'd felt like she belonged in his life. He'd been focused on the ranch, of course, but surely if you met your soulmate, the feelings would be strong enough to push other things down the priority list. A surface-only relationship seemed like a waste of time.

Maddy's face flashed in his mind, and his heart thudded again. He'd only known her for a couple weeks, but he was certainly feeling more already than with anyone he'd dated. Maybe he'd just been waiting until the right person came along.

Unless she was interested in Caleb.

Adam forced that thought away as they rode down the slope.

"Hey, Boss," Jesse called out, ratcheting the come-along to tighten the wire.

Luis hammered barn staples to fix the smooth top strand

firmly to the post, while Ty held the rest of the roll steady. He seemed steady himself, and Adam was glad to see he wasn't drinking. Two other hands were farther down the fence line, coiling the barbed wire they were taking off.

"How's everything going?" Adam asked.

Jesse nodded, then relaxed as Luis put in the last staple. "We'll finish this stretch today, top and bottom strands and the vinyl pieces for visibility. You want us to go up the north side tomorrow?"

Adam nudged Mister, turning so he could see all that had been done. Well-spaced, well-done, as he knew Jesse would have it. "Looks good. And yeah, I think so. North side next, west after that."

Jesse pushed his cowboy hat back to wipe the sweat off his forehead. "Sure, Boss. Break time, guys," he called.

Adam and Micah rode back along the newly re-done fence, but Adam's thoughts were elsewhere. Like wondering what Maddy was doing right now.

13

The next morning, Adam's mind wouldn't stay put as he gave out ranch assignments. He talked about the fencing project, but thought about Maddy's little check marks next to a list of numbers. He sent Jesse to work with Caleb, and thought about Maddy and Lacey cooking. He kept Wes back to help Dr. Sue when she came to look at some calves with scours, but his mind flicked to Maddy caring for her young daughter.

Man, he had it bad. And Micah was right. The thought of Maddy and Caleb made Adam burn with jealousy. If he was interested in her, he needed to do something about it.

When the ranch hands had left, Adam returned to his office and flipped a pencil in the air. Over and over and over, until he realized that as much as he wanted to see Maddy, he couldn't keep flipping it for another hour until she came in.

He wandered outside to where Lacey had set the scrub jay free last night, its wing seemingly healed. Now he checked for feathers on the ground—a telltale sign that a predator had gotten it.

The ground was clear, though. Adam breathed a sigh of thanks, but searched the nearby area anyway. It all looked clear, and he made a note to congratulate Lacey on her nursing, maybe do something to celebrate.

He wondered how long it would be before she rescued the next wild animal, and what it would be. Another bird? A rabbit?

Adam let his mind wander about this soft-hearted sister of his. Eventually, with a smile and a shake of his head, he headed back. Maddy should be arriving soon.

Inside, he could hear the small sounds of her settling in for the day, but he found himself stalled in the hallway. She was here —good. He wanted to talk to her, to maybe find out how she felt—also good. So why weren't his boots moving him forward?

Because Adam didn't want to mess this up; he didn't even know exactly what he wanted. And he didn't like not knowing. He ran through phrases in his mind, possible ways she'd react, what he might say next. Nothing he imagined dispelled the uncertainty.

Fine, then. He wasn't one to drag his heels over what might happen. Once it happened, he'd know how to handle it. Right?

"Oh, hi, Adam. I was just getting started," Maddy said, her curls swaying as she looked up. "It's going to be nice to work on something besides taxes."

He nodded. He opened his mouth to say something, but nothing came out. Nothing even came to mind. He stopped his hand from fidgeting with his belt buckle.

"Is there something you need?" she asked.

"No—yes. Have you found any other damage Mrs. Evans did?" Adam cringed inside. So much for not acting like a tongue-tied teenager.

"A little." Maddy pulled a file drawer open, riffled through the papers, and pulled out a clipped set. "I've haven't had much chance to look, though."

"I know, I was just wondering." He stifled a sigh, wondering how he could take charge of so many things and still be dumbstruck now.

Blast it, he wasn't used to not accomplishing what he set out to do. "Would you like to go out on a trail ride this afternoon?" he blurted.

Maddy's eyes sparkled. "Really? Out on the range?" Then she dimmed. "But I don't really know how to ride. I haven't been on a horse since I was a kid."

Adam smiled softly. At least he hoped it looked soft and encouraging, not weird or stalker-ish. "We'll do some practice stuff here, and we won't go far. Promise."

Her sparkle returned. "Then I'd love to. But I'd need to be back to meet Mia off the bus."

"Oh." Dang, the best laid plans... He lifted his hat and ran a hand through his hair. "Actually, we have a Skype call with my youngest brother at noon every Tuesday, so I can't leave until maybe one."

"What's that I hear?" Dad came in. "Something about the school bus?"

"I was going to take Maddy out on a trail ride, but there's really not enough time between our call with Seth and when Mia gets home," Adam said.

"Nonsense," the older man replied, sending a knowing look Adam's way. "I can take care of Mia. If that's all right with you, Missy."

Maddy's gaze went from one to the other, and Adam wondered what she was thinking.

She finally nodded. "I think she's met you enough times

that it would be fine, Samuel." She looked back at Adam. "So I'll take you up on that trail ride, cowboy."

Adam's heart gave some quick, light beats. Tongue-tied or not, he'd managed it. He tipped the brim of his hat. "Why don't you grab some lunch around noon while we're talking to Seth, and then we'll head over to the stables?"

She smiled and nodded, then turned back to her work. Adam settled at his own desk, but not before he saw his father smile and nod, too.

MADDY SAT in the large kitchen eating the roast beef sandwich Uncle Dirt had made for her, trying to quell the jitters running riot through her body. Adam was taking her riding. She was a little nervous to be getting on a horse again and actually going out on the trail. But even more, it was Adam.

Adam, who made her heart beat faster when he walked into the room.

Adam, whose serious face made her want to make him laugh.

Adam, who carried two different people inside him. Which one was real?

She listened to the murmurs and laughter coming from the other room, Adam's deep voice booming out like his father's. It warmed her, but also made her miss her own large, boisterous family. On the other hand, in the short time she'd been on the ranch, she'd become more relaxed than she'd been in the last five years. Knowing she was well out of Brock's way gave her more peace than she'd expected. As long as she kept her secrets, she and Mia would be safe.

The first time Brock had hit her, she'd been more shocked

than anything. She'd broken his family's heirloom, so she could understand him giving into a gut reaction. Not that that excused it, but still...

Their arguments had become more frequent, though, with Mia retreating to her room at the first sound of raised voices. Brock threw things against the wall, progressing to throwing them at her. She dodged successfully, until he started twisting her wrist instead. He knew just where to leave bruises that wouldn't show.

Back then, her family didn't know why she'd filed for divorce; she couldn't let go of her pride enough to admit that she hadn't walked away the first time he'd hurt her. But when Brock wouldn't let her go, when he came charging into her mother's house, shoved Mia into the wall, and grabbed Maddy by the hair, it was no secret anymore.

Police, hospital, pictures, the whole rigamarole was embarrassing. And the restraining order didn't help. When Brock violated it by breaking her door down and punching her, the judge put him away fast enough. Just not long enough.

He was released on the one-year anniversary of their divorce, but he hadn't learned anything. Threats, stalking, a note using Mia as leverage—Maddy couldn't chance it anymore.

She had tucked her tail and run, staying in a motel in Grand Junction until she lucked into the Black Rock Ranch's newspaper ad. She blessed Samuel once more for agreeing to keep her secret, as well as for hiring her. The only way Brock would find her here would be for someone to tell him, and nobody knew.

She ached for her far-away family, though. Nonna, her mom, her sister especially. The girl-talk, the crowded kitchen on Sundays, letting her niece put make-up on Mia, listening to her nephews tease each other...

She somehow pushed an over-chewed bite past the lump in her throat. The juicy beef had lost its appeal, and she set both her memories and the sandwich aside to examine the large room. She had never been here early enough to join the cowboys at breakfast, but she understood that Uncle Dirt cooked up quite a spread to keep them going all morning. And sometimes all day.

Two large, worn trestle tables and their benches combined with the barstools at the counter to be able to seat everyone. The six-burner range was spotless, as were the long counters. If Uncle Dirt hadn't been a neat-freak when he was a working cowboy, he certainly was now. She wondered if he'd let her and Lacey come cook in here sometime—there was certainly more room for complicated things than in her own small kitchen.

She opened drawers and cupboards until she found the plastic wrap and stored the remains of her sandwich in the fridge for later. The men finally finished their call from Iraq, and Caleb said he was heading for the barn to get the horses ready.

Maddy tensed again—was she really ready for this?

Adam came in and perused her outfit. She knew her jeans and long-sleeved shirt were suitable, but her tennis shoes?

"That won't do," he said, smiling as he shook his head. "Let's see what we can dig out for you."

She followed him to the basement, her previous thoughts making her a little hesitant. Adam began pulling boxes and totes down, opening and closing them until he said, "A-ha!" He pulled out various sizes of cowboy boots, some worn and scuffed, some almost new.

Maddy looked at the grin on his face, so very different

from Brock. His eyes sparkled with the satisfaction of his quest. She smiled back—Adam was a man of honor, the total opposite of her ex-husband.

"These are the ones we outgrew," he said. "Even with four of us, some of them never got more than a few weeks' wear. There's sure to be something here to fit you." He motioned her to an old chair and backed away.

Wondering about his perception, but grateful for it, Maddy tried on several pairs until she found some comfortable ones. "Okay?"

"Perfect. Let's go," Adam said. He almost jogged to the front door, clearly eager to hit the trail. She only hoped she wouldn't slow him down.

Or embarrass herself.

AT THE STABLES, Caleb greeted her cheerily. "Hiya, Maddy! I've got Chester here ready to go for you."

"I thought you'd get Big Blue out, not Chester," Adam said.

"No go. Blue's lame in the right front—Dr. Sue and Wes looked at her after the calves. Not sure what happened, but she shouldn't be ridden," Caleb answered. "Chester is just as calm, though. And a bit more Maddy's size."

Adam smiled slightly over at Maddy, as if he weren't sure about her suitability for this.

Chester was a short sorrel gelding with a wide white blaze down his face. Maddy stretched her hand out to him to let him sniff, the way her childhood friend had taught her all those years ago. She had gotten to ride occasionally through those third- and fourth-grade years until her friend had moved away.

She probably didn't remember anything correctly, but

Chester looked friendly enough. He whuffled at her hand, and she wished she'd brought something to offer him.

Adam stepped sideways to her and held out a carrot piece. Maddy took it, offered it to the gelding, and grinned when he took it gently and started crunching.

"Adam said you haven't ridden in a while?" Caleb asked.

"Not since I was a kid. You'll have to start at the beginning with me."

Caleb chuckled. "No problem. Everyone has to start somewhere. Chester's a good old guy, pretty obedient, doesn't pull too much. Let's get you up and check your stirrups."

"You've got Lacey's show saddle—we thought it would fit you better," Adam added.

Old adolescent, picked-on feelings rose suddenly. "Why, because she has a big rear end, too?"

Adam took a step back. "What? No!" He motioned to the big roping saddle on his bay. "You wouldn't be very comfortable in one of these. Too big and not enough padding."

"Oh." Maddy felt her face flush. But was it really her fault that everyone in the world focused on how slender a woman was? She was half Italian, her family gatherings centered around food, and she'd given up fighting her body shape years ago. Evidently she hadn't given up on being sensitive about it, though. "Sorry. I didn't mean to …it's just…"

Adam held his hands up in defense. "I may not have learned much about women, but I do know not to make comments about size!"

Caleb laughed. "Way to put your foot in it, bro! Keep talking and let's see what else you can come up with."

"Yeah?" Adam's smile had a dangerous twitch to it. "Might I remind you of your failure to say no to Cassie McLeod?"

"But that was…I only… Oh, never mind. You guys have a good ride." Caleb handed Chester's reins to Maddy and walked away with hunched shoulders.

"What was that?" Maddy asked, turning to pet her horse.

"Oh, just brother stuff." Adam chuckled. "A girl who wanted to glom onto him, and he couldn't convince her he just wasn't interested."

Maddy heated inside. 'Interested' was a word that had been on her mind lately. She knew without asking that Adam was interested in her. She could tell from the way he looked at her, the things he'd said. And that was a delicious feeling, even if she didn't know if she wanted to respond.

She said a silent prayer for safety and not to look too stupid. Adam helped her gather her reins in her left hand, then gave her a leg up. Swinging her leg over the saddle was harder than it looked, and she felt lucky to not have popped a seam during the stretch. Once she was settled, Adam shortened her stirrups, reminded her to sit up, and gave her a refresher in steering and stopping.

Chester walked where she wanted and stopped when she told him, and she breathed a sigh of relief. Quick answers to prayers were wonderful, and she hoped it would continue.

Adam mounted smoothly, looking like he'd been on a horse his whole life. Which he probably had. She wondered what it would have been like to grow up out here with livestock and wild mountains instead of in the suburbs. She'd never know, but Mia would. At least for a little while.

14

Instead of following the river, Adam led the way across a pasture (empty of bulls, thank goodness). He pointed out the black granite boulder on a hill that, along with the family name, had become the ranch's brand. He told stories of the ancestor who went mining for gold, silver and lead, only to make his fortune in beef.

Maddy paid attention as best she could, adjusting to her horse's movement and marveling at the joy in Adam's face. She'd never seen him like this before.

Adam maneuvered Mister to stand close enough to the gate that he could open it without getting off. Then he somehow got his horse to sidestep and pivot, so that he swung the gate open and ended up on the other side of it.

Maddy shook her head in amazement. That was something her friend had never tried. She nudged Chester forward, and Adam moved Mister to close the gate once she was through.

The man might have a temper he tried to keep hidden,

but he also had to have a lot of patience to teach a horse to respond that well.

They walked across the rest of the grass to a trail that led through the trees, and Maddy savored the sense of relaxation and freedom. "The trail's going to narrow soon. Want to try a jog-trot?"

"Uh…sure?" Mandy answered slowly.

"Don't kick him, just squeeze your calves against his belly. You can either stand in your stirrups and hold his mane or the saddle horn for balance, or you can just sit a little deeper in the saddle. He's got a pretty smooth gait, so I'd suggest sitting."

She tightened her legs against him, but he only walked faster.

Adam chuckled and nudged Mister into a slow jog. "He doesn't want to be in the lead."

Sure enough, when Maddy squeezed again, Chester began to jog. She yelped, bounced a time or two, then settled into his rhythm. "Hey, this is okay!" she called to Adam.

He looked over and grinned. "You're doing great. You can hold the horn if you need to, but don't forget to sit up. You're all hunched over."

They jogged for a moment, then Adam pulled back to a walk. Maddy sighed in relief as Chester slowed automatically.

"Have you always ridden?" she asked once she caught her breath.

Adam shrugged. "I think Mom had me up on a horse before I could walk. At least, I don't remember learning how."

"Did you start on a big horse, or did you have a pony first?"

He chuckled and shook his head. "Grandpa gave me a pony when I was three. Called him Two Bits because that was all he was worth."

"Two bits?"

"A quarter. As in, 'Shave and a haircut, two bits,' you know."

"O-kaay."

"He was a stubborn Shetland, used to put his head down and run for the barn. I couldn't pull him up for the life of me, just had to hang on and hope he didn't rub me off against a fence post."

Maddy's mouth dropped open.

Adam grinned. "You can guess how excited I was when Dad got me a Quarter Horse/Welsh pony cross when I was six. *Much* better behaved."

"So what happened to Two Bits?"

His grin stretched wider. "He was duly inherited by Caleb and then Micah. I think Dad figured he would teach us determination. He'd slowed down some by the time Seth got him, and Seth was smart enough to drop one rein and haul on the other, turning him in a wide circle. I don't know why the rest of us never figured that out."

The trail became narrow enough that they had to go single file. It began rising, and Maddy clung to the saddle horn as they climbed.

"Loosen your reins, and he'll make his own way," Adam called back.

She did, trusting Chester a bit, but trusting Adam's knowledge of the horse even more. Sure enough, Chester kept his nose almost in Mister's tail and stepped evenly up the slope.

"So," Maddy said when she could concentrate on something besides the powerful horse underneath her, "Seth is your youngest brother?"

Adam twisted to talk to her, his gelding still climbing

upwards. "Yes, poor guy. I think we all picked on him. He's off in Iraq now. Third tour of duty."

Oh. What was an appropriate response to that? 'I'm sorry' would sound inane. 'I hope he's safe?' No, Maddy didn't think there was any job over there that was safe.

"You must be proud of him," she finally said. "I'll add him to my prayers."

Adam looked forward for a moment, then turned again. "Thanks, and we are proud. Nobody wanted him to re-up the first time, let alone the second, but he felt like he needed to. Band of Brothers and all that."

Maddy thought about that, about how she would feel if her nephews decided to not only join the military, but to *stay* in.

"I hope I get to meet him sometime," she finally said. "You guys must be pretty strong, too. It takes a lot of courage to serve, but it takes a lot to stay home and support them, too."

Adam was facing forward again by then, tall and straight in the saddle. Maddy couldn't tell how he'd reacted to her words, but she didn't regret them.

"It gets really steep right here," Adam called back to her. "Stand in your stirrups just a little and let yourself tilt forward. That will free up his back so he can climb easier."

She did, keeping one hand on the saddle horn and one in his mane. She clenched the reins in her fingers and was glad she didn't have to steer him as long as Mister was in front. She rocked back and forth a bit, trying to keep her balance while he took uneven strides. He lurched at the top, and she pitched forward onto his neck. "Ooof!"

"Yeah, that last bit can be a little rough," Adam said, sitting oh-so-naturally in the saddle at the top.

The top. It wasn't the actual top of the mountain, but the wide meadow was filled with wildflowers poking through patchy snow and overlooked the whole valley. The Ouray River sparkled below. The bulls clumped together like a mass of ants, the mares were equally tiny, and the foals frolicked like minuscule pixies.

"Wow, you can see the entire ranch!" Maddy exclaimed.

Adam chuckled. "Not really, just the home pastures." He waved his arm to the side and behind. "Our acreage covers a lot of these mountains. The cows and calves are up here for the summer." He pointed across the valley. "The Manning Ranch leases a lot of the land over there, and the Lazy S takes the mountains on the north side of the valley."

"Lease? It's not all yours?"

He smiled. "We're not *that* rich. We've got about 4,000 acres of our own, which I'll admit is a good bit, and then we lease about 50,000 more from the Bureau of Land Management."

She soaked in the view, turned to look at the mountain range behind her, and inhaled the crisp air rather greedily. "You don't get this in Den—Los Angeles," she said, shaking inwardly at her slip. No matter how nice Adam was being, she had to stick to her story. "Especially not in the suburbs. I mean, you can see the mountains, but the air pollution is pretty bad." She should be safe with that. Denver could be bad, but LA was worse. At least from what she'd heard.

Adam shook his head. "I don't think I could stand city living. I need my animals, my mountains and the freedom to range."

Country life was growing on Maddy, too. She loved the incredible view up here, but she liked the "home acres" on the ranch, too. It was generally quiet, and she liked the connection with the natural world. The farm tractors made noise, but nothing like rush hour traffic at home. Or the fumes! Of course, staying away from the animals meant she didn't often smell anything other than dirt and hay and fresh breezes.

"So have you always been a city girl?" Adam asked, breaking her reverie.

She had to stay as close to the truth as she could, but still keep Denver out of it. "Spent all my time at the restaurant or the office or my favorite stores if I wasn't home."

"Not much shopping out here," he said.

"No, but that's what I wanted. No chance for—" She mentally slapped herself again. Why was she suddenly forgetting?

Adam wasn't going to let it go, though. "No chance for what?" He shifted in his saddle so he could look straight at her.

She couldn't evade those piercing blue eyes completely, and decided she could say just a little. "No chance for my ex to find me. He's...he's a pretty nasty person."

Now Adam looked truly concerned. "I got the feeling maybe he abused you."

Maddy didn't want to explain anything else. Too much turmoil that would come along with it. She shrugged. "I finally left."

She watched Adam's fist clench until his knuckles were white.

"It's okay, it really is," she reassured him. "He didn't do any permanent damage, but I'd just as soon he not find me. And I'd appreciate it if you didn't go spread it around—I don't like people pitying me."

Adam looked away and took a deep breath. And another.

When he finally turned back, he seemed calmer. "Did you know we've got bald eagles nesting on the ranch?"

"Really?" Maddy looked around, scrutinizing the pine trees. "Where?"

"They're one ridge over." He pointed, then eyed her speculatively. "It makes a long day, but if you keep coming out with me, you'll be able to handle that ride before long. Hopefully before they leave."

Riding with Adam. The thought warmed Maddy through. "How soon is that?"

"Another month and a half or so. They fledge in May or June, and once the eaglets are in full flight, they leave. But the parents usually come back in January or February to lay a new set of eggs."

Maddy stifled her disappointment. Watching bald eagles soar always seemed so…romantic? Patriotic? Empowering? So many things, and she still couldn't come up with the right word. Maybe just that they gave her a sense of majesty, even on television.

She shifted in the saddle, stretching a little.

"We'd better head back," Adam said. "You're really going to be sore tomorrow."

Her tired muscles agreed, and she knew that they'd be far worse the next day. A hot bath would be in order after Mia was in bed.

They rode back, with Maddy clinging for all she was worth during the steep downslope. When they leveled out and she could relax again, she realized just how comfortable she felt with Adam.

True, he was a serious guy, but he'd opened up enough for her to know him a little better. She'd shared rather too much of herself, but so be it. It was enough to begin a friendship.

And those intense blue eyes of his! Her heart pounded as she remembered the way they sparkled with humor or darkened with concern. She could spend a long time looking into those eyes.

15

Sometimes Adam wished he could clone himself several times over, and calf-processing was one of those times. He, Wes, and Uncle Dirt were bringing the remaining cows and calves to the pasture closest to the homestead. He'd sent Micah and a crew up to check on the newest mamas and then the water supply in the high pastures. Dad was down in Grand Junction, picking up the vaccines, syringes and insecticides they'd need for this second go-round, and Caleb had consented to leave his horses for a day or two to help. Not that Adam had given him much choice.

That all still left Adam with a long to-do list before branding.

He shoved his hand farther into his heavy leather glove, turned Mister to the left, and slapped his rope against his thigh. "Move along, now," he called to the cows. The sturdy calves trotted alongside their ambling mothers. Sometimes they'd run ahead, leaping and playing with each other, but even at two months old, they knew this was different from the few pasture rotations they'd already had.

If they only knew. They'd finish these few days with ear tags, a BR brand on their haunch, and most of the males would be minus a few important parts before they headed up to the summer range.

Uncle Dirt suddenly took off after a wayward cow, her calf bawling as he tried to keep up. The old man didn't head her as quickly as he might have in the past, but he still had it in him, gimpy leg or not.

With the cows and calves settled into the front pasture, Adam rode to check the water. By the time he got back to the homestead, all his plans had fallen apart.

He'd just finished tying Mister to a fence post when he saw Micah helping Ty limp to a pickup. "What now?" he muttered.

Luis approached from behind him. "Ty came in moaning and groaning, but I think he really has sprained his ankle. Not sure how, but Micah's taking him down to Urgent Care."

"Figures it would be Ty," Adam groused.

"And Jesse just puked over behind the equipment shed. He's looking sort of clammy and green."

If Adam were a cussing man, now would be the time for a blue streak. Instead, he just blew out his breath and sent a prayer up for help. They'd have a hard time branding and everything if they were short two people.

Dad, Wes and Caleb were supposed to help him at the chute. Micah, Ty and Dax were to be pen riders, with two others in the curve of the chute moving the calves along. Luis and Jesse would get the cows through the tick dip, and Lacey would help if they hadn't finished by the time she got home from school. A little short on hands, but they could have done it.

Now, without Ty in the pen and Jesse at the dip, things were all haywire. Luis couldn't handle the dip by himself, and two riders in the pen would be hard pressed to keep things going. But they needed the remaining cowhands to bring in the next herd from the pasture.

Could Adam hire someone from the Lazy S to help for a day or two? How many hands could they send over?

He untacked Mister and turned him out to pasture. Back in the admin building, he paused before he started down the hall. Was it possible…could Maddy help? She certainly wasn't up to riding the pen, but she could switch out the vaccination syringes and needles. And if Wes helped in the pen instead of at the chute, and if he moved Dax over to help Luis, they could manage.

Good. He hated to be beholden to the Lazy S.

MADDY DRESSED in jeans and the old boots Adam had found for her, thankful the boys hadn't always had big feet. It would be foolhardy to do this in tennis shoes. It was probably foolhardy for her to be doing this, anyway. She was a city girl, not a ranch hand!

She walked Mia down the driveway to catch the school bus, listening to the lowing of the cattle as they approached the homestead. The men had the cows and calves all penned up close. It looked like they were separating the calves away from their mothers, and she had a moment of feeling sorry for them. She knew it was only temporary, but still…

"Can I pet the calves when I get home, Mama?" Mia asked, skipping along beside her.

"I don't know, honey. They're getting shots today and might not feel very good." That was the one part of it her daughter could understand.

After Mia boarded the yellow school bus, Maddy

straightened her shoulders and walked back to the barns. She could do this.

The noise was tremendous. The calves were bawling for their mothers; the cows were bawling right back. Metal gates clanged and cowboys shouted, but under it all was an organized set-up.

"Over here," Adam called, motioning her next to the smallest chute. A table sat close by, with a cooler and a box of medical needles on it. A red Sharps box and two gun-shaped devices puzzled her.

"That's how we inject the vaccines," Adam explained. "Your job is to take the empty vaccine tube out and replace it with a new one, and to switch the old needle out for a sterile one. The old vaccine tubes go in the trash can, the used needles go in the box. Then it will be ready for the next calf."

"Vaccinations, got it," Maddy said. She could do this.

She eyed the cattle milling in the pen, and Adam explained that too. "The cows will get dipped in a pesticide to keep ticks and other nasties away. The calves will come into the chute one at a time, get vaccinated, branded, tagged if they still need that, and the males will get castrated."

Maddy blanched. "With a knife?"

Adam raised his eyebrows as he nodded. "It's actually more humane than banding, in my opinion. Hurts for a minute, then they scamper away. A lot better than spending a month aching from a rubber band cutting off their circulation."

"Hah!" Maddy muttered. "You haven't gone through it yourself."

Adam chuckled. "No, but when animals don't feel good, they quit eating. And the calves who get banded tend to be off their feed for about a month, so that's a good clue."

Whatever. Maddy was just glad she wasn't working at that end of the chute.

The business of the day began with shouts of "come on up there" and more clanging of metal gates. At first, Maddy didn't have time to think about anything but getting the vaccine and needle changed in time for the next calf. Once she got the hang of it, she had time to watch a bit.

There were cleverly hinged openings in the chute stall to let the men give the shots and get the branding iron in to the right places. She was surprised that the branding iron was electric. Nothing like the coals and long irons she had expected.

She was more surprised that most of the calves just stood there for all of it—getting their other ear punched with an additional ID tag, having a hot iron pressed against their hide for a few seconds, and even getting castrated. A few wiggled some, and all of them shot out of the chute as soon as it was opened.

They bucked and galloped, eventually finding their way to the paddock where their mothers were.

Maddy focused on keeping the vaccination guns restocked, but she managed to watch Adam, too. He was in his element, his movements swift and sure, keeping watch over the others while he did his own work. She admired his skill and concentration, and his determination to have a smooth running operation.

He was so very different from Brock. His personality, what was important to him, even his work ethic. And while she still cringed inwardly if she heard him yell at someone, she trusted it was for good reason, not out of viciousness. Not that she ever wanted him yelling at her again, but since she wasn't crucial to the ranch management, they should be fine.

The last calf came through, got prepped for the summer range, and ran back to his mother. Adam wiped a hand across his forehead, and Maddy leaned against the table.

"Done!" she said. "I'm more tired than I thought I'd be."

"Done?" Adam grinned. He looked over at his dad. "You want to tell her, or shall I?"

Samuel took his cowboy hat off to rub his hair, then settled it back on his head. "That's just the first hundred, Missy. There's another hundred to go today."

"And more in another month," Adam added.

Maddy groaned. This was hard work, and if she was tired from doing nothing but switching out vaccines, the men must be exhausted.

They didn't look it, though. The riders slouched casually in their saddles, sharing jokes. Luis and Randy were splashed with milky residue and their mud boots were, well, muddy.

Samuel motioned toward the barn. "There's a fridge with some water bottles in there, young lady. Want to bring a few out?"

By the time she came back, the noise had diminished—the finished cows and calves were being herded to a new pasture. Maddy could see another herd ready to come in. Just how many ranch hands did Black Rock have? Had she not noticed them in the cabins, or did some of them live off the ranch?

The rest of the day passed in a blur. Empty the shotgun, put a new cartridge in, twist off the needle, put a new one in. Calves coming in and going out, some bawling, some quiet.

They broke at one point, going in for stew and sandwiches. Uncle Dirt handed her a plate and shook his head ruefully. "It's gettin' so beautiful here I'm going to have to leave so I don't spoil it."

Maddy laughed. She knew he was joking, but being called beautiful warmed her throughout. It had been a long time.

She dragged herself to a seat at one of the long tables, but was almost too tired to eat. And there would be calves and more calves all day long.

She felt movement to her right and looked up to find Adam nudging Luis down so he could squeeze in beside her. Her pulse fluttered and any appetite she might have had was truly gone now.

Adam's hands were clean to his wrists, but his face still had smudges on it, one of them right along that chiseled jaw she'd been admiring earlier. Maddy thought about reaching up to wipe it clean, then forced her hand to stay in her lap. The last thing she needed to do was give him an intimate touch.

She wondered what his skin would feel like. Rough with stubble? Rough from the wind and sun and snow? It certainly wouldn't be soft.

She glanced at him again, only to find him watching her. She suddenly found her stew worthy of a detailed examination.

"Not hungry, Adam?" Caleb called down the table. "Or have you found something you like better than food?"

Heat rushed up Maddy's face, and she didn't dare look up. She could still feel Adam's gaze, though.

"You tend to your business, little brother, and I'll tend to mine," he said decisively.

Maddy heard Adam's spoon clank against his bowl and relaxed enough to take a spoonful of stew herself.

Would she like to make him her business? On one hand, her life was complicated right now, and likely to remain so for a while. On the other hand, if they were to start dating...she risked a glance over to Adam, who was now intent on his food.

She didn't know if there was enough between them to begin a relationship, but she would like to know him better. What did he like and not like about the ranch? What dreams did he have? Was there an ex-wife in the picture somewhere?

16

Maddy almost gasped at the last thought and pushed her mind to think about Mia instead. Being new at school was hard, but especially when it was almost the end of the school year. Mia seemed to be adjusting, though, and talked a lot about girls named Kiley and Elsa.

"So what do you think about ranch life?" Adam's question penetrated her thoughts.

"Um…the fresh air? Up in the mountains anyway—it doesn't smell so good down here today."

Adam chuckled. "That happens when you get a hundred cows and calves in a close space. Does that mean you liked our trail ride?"

"Oh, yes!" Maddy blushed at her own exuberance. "It was a whole lot nicer than riding in a dirt pasture when I was nine." She paused, then pushed forward. "What do you like best about being a rancher?"

"Me? I guess I never thought about it much. I like the time on a horse, even in the snow. And taking care of animals.

And, I don't know, just knowing that I'm doing my part making this ranch work."

She smiled. "I don't hear much about paperwork in there."

Adam shook his head. "No, that's just something you gotta do before you get to the good stuff."

"And those solar wells you're talking about? Is that good stuff?"

Adam's eyes lit up as he talked about using modern technology to do a centuries-old job better.

She liked seeing him excited. So far, other than the trail ride, he just seemed to keep his nose to the grindstone, not taking much pleasure in anything. It was good to know he had a lot of job satisfaction.

"...and it's pretty cool to get to work alongside my brothers, even if they're horribly annoying sometimes." Adam looked over at Caleb with a grin.

"My brother's in Seattle," Maddy said, "but I have nephews —twins—who do enough wrestling and teasing to fill the gap."

"Your family sounds pretty close. Don't you miss them?"

Maddy sighed. "Like you wouldn't believe. But we talk occasionally and that has to do for now."

"For now? This is temporary?" Adam frowned into his plate.

"I hope not—I love it here. But there are cars and planes for visits, right?"

He looked at her with puzzled eyes. "How'd you get way out here, anyway?"

"I had to get away from my ex, remember?" she kept her voice low.

Adam looked pensive. "So this might really be temporary. You'll go back if he stops causing problems."

Maddy shrugged. "I guess. I haven't let myself look that far ahead—it seems pretty impossible." And with her temporary status, any relationship with Adam would be pretty impossible, too. She was surprised at the disappointment she felt.

Chairs scraped and boots scuffed on the floor—the men had finished wolfing down their food and were headed back outside. Maddy rose to follow, wishing she could have a longer rest. But it was probably easier to get it all done and collapse later than to take a bigger break now.

A million calves later, or at least what seemed like a million, Maddy looked at her watch. "I'm sorry, Adam. I have to go. Mia's bus will be here in a few minutes."

He nodded as he pressed the hot brand against a calf's haunch. She could see him counting in his mind before he released it. "We'll work it out. Thanks for your help."

"If Lacey can watch Mia, I can come back."

Adam grinned, his tired eyes sparkling again. "I'll look forward to it."

She'd look forward to it, too. And then, "Oh. You'd probably do better with Lacey helping here, wouldn't you?"

"Well, maybe," Adam said, "but I'd rather you came back."

Her heart fluttered again as she gave a small wave and left. Maybe things weren't so impossible.

But it wasn't to be. Mia got off the bus and promptly threw up. Maddy groaned. She'd never minded changing dirty diapers, but vomit did something to her, and she struggled to keep her own stomach settled.

"It's okay, sweetie," she told Mia, who was starting to cry. Maddy swiped a hand across Mia's brow and frowned at the fever she felt. "Can you walk to the cabin, or do you want me to carry you?"

Mia smiled weakly. "You said I was too big to carry."

"That's right, I did. And you probably are. I could carry you a little way, though."

Mia shook her head. "I feel better now. I can walk." She leaned on Maddy as they went, though.

She settled the six-year-old in bed and gave her some fever reducer. "You sleep for a little while, sweetie. I'll be right here."

Maddy left Mia's bedroom door open and tried to quiet her kitchen clatter as she searched for the ingredients for minestrina. It was Nonna's go-to whenever anyone felt off color, although sometimes Maddy made it just because it tasted so good.

She had small pasta shells that would work instead of *ditaloni*, and fresh mozzarella, parmesan and olive oil were standard ingredients in her kitchen. Twenty minutes later, she was inhaling a bowl of it while her daughter slept.

ADAM CAME by later that evening, freshly showered but looking exhausted.

"Here," Maddy said, fixing him a bowl of minestrina.

He took it gratefully and sank onto the sofa. "Thanks, it smells heavenly."

"Wait 'til you taste it," she said with a grin.

"Ohhh, mmm," was all she heard for a bit. Finally, Adam swallowed without another bite immediately ready. "That's really awesome. I could marry you for this."

Maddy's mouth dropped open. Adam's eyes widened. His spoon hovered over the bowl.

"I—um—" he stammered. "I didn't mean for that to come out."

She gave a nervous laugh. "That's a good thing, because we hardly know each other."

Adam's face was thoroughly red. He broke eye contact and busied himself with a few more mouthfuls. He paused, then put the bowl down and looked at her. "I would like to get to know you better, Maddy."

It was Maddy's turn to blush. Hadn't she just been having those same thoughts? She took a short breath and answered quietly, "Even with everything I told you? That my ex-husband is after me?"

He looked at her and nodded, and she wondered just what he was thinking. Did he wish she would say something else? Did she pass muster?

"How's Mia feeling?" he said, finally.

"About Brock?" What kind of connections was Adam making? "What does that—oh, you mean being sick." Maddy's own stomach unclenched. "It's just a bug going around—she'll be fine in the morning."

"I'm glad. Jesse's still miserable." He picked up the bowl again, practically inhaling the last of the minestrina. "I shouldn't have eaten all this—I'm going to start gaining weight if I spend much time with your cooking."

"Not if you keep working like you did today."

Adam chuckled. "Yeah, branding days will wear you out. And I've been spending too much time behind a desk."

"Did you get all the calves done?" Maddy leaned against the counter, trying to stay relaxed. Not easy, when there was a gorgeous cowboy sitting on her sofa and loving her food.

He shrugged. "From the first time heifers, yes. Two hundred and four. There'll be seven or eight hundred more from the experienced mamas, but they're not old enough yet. Then we'll drive them up to the summer range."

"Sounds like fun after all the branding. Here, let me take that." Maddy carried his bowl and spoon into the kitchen. "When do you think you'll go up?"

He didn't answer.

Maddy turned to see Adam's eyes closed, his head drooped forward.

She just looked for a moment. His face had softened in sleep, his rough hands relaxed on his jeans. How did he make it through the long, tough days—and nights—of ranching?

She admired him, definitely had feelings for him. But she wasn't sure how he could fit into her life, or her into his. And she wasn't into flings.

After a moment, she perched on the couch and reached her hand to touch his jeans. "Adam? You really ought to go home and sleep."

"Hmm?" He opened his eyes slightly. "Yeah, you're right." With a groan, he pushed himself upright. "I'm sorry, I don't usually do that."

His face was still soft, and Maddy smiled. "You've earned the right to rest. And I imagine you've got a load of other work tomorrow."

Adam nodded and settled his hat on his head. "Thanks for the comfort food. And the couch." He smiled ruefully. "Maybe next time I'll be better company."

He paused, looking like he wanted to say something else. His eyes met hers, his hand started to lift toward her, then he stopped mid-gesture. He looked past her, tipped his hat, and turned to go.

"Thanks again," he said from the doorway.

Maddy stood silently and watched him walk away.

17

Maddy looked out the window at the snowflakes falling lightly Saturday morning. She hoped it wouldn't last —it was the end of April, after all. But the daffodils had finished and the tulips were in full bloom. Spring was definitely here.

Mia was still sleeping, so Maddy slipped into her coat and out the door to inhale the crisp air. The mountains in one direction were blurred by opaque clouds; when she turned, the ridges opposite rose sharp against blue sky. Green pines up to the tree line, rocky above. Cattle grazing in the pasture, not concerned about any change in weather. Green grass, blooming flowers …Colorado was certainly one of God's most beautiful creations, and she offered a quiet prayer of thanks.

Back inside, Maddy showered and settled with a cup of coffee and a breakfast burrito. Sometimes even an Italian girl wanted something else. She clicked her phone to read the news, but the first thing she saw was a text notification. Her heart seemed to freeze mid-beat.

You're mine. Don't forget it.

Her hand shook, and she sloshed hot coffee across her fingers. Stifling a cry of pain, she put the coffee cup on the table and dashed for the sink, streaming cold water over the burn.

The pain eased, and Maddy forced long, deep breaths into her lungs. Her body still quivered. How had Brock found her out here?

Her breathing sped up again. The room closed in.

Wait—it was just a text. He obviously had her phone number, but not her location.

But how? The only one she'd given it to was Sophie, in case there was an emergency at home. Her sister would never share it, and Maddy had blocked the number from showing up on caller ID.

Shallow, quick breaths. The police. She needed to contact the police. Surely sending a text like that was violating the restraining order.

She snatched the phone from where she'd dropped it, began to dial 911, then stopped. If she called the police, she'd have to tell them where she was. Wasn't that a danger in itself? Brock had friends in the Denver police, and they could easily be on the lookout for reports of her.

She sank into a chair and rested her head in her hands, trying to calm herself. *Dear God, help me know what to do. Guide me in a safe path, for Mia's sake, if not for mine.*

Maddy stayed with her head bowed while she listened for sounds from Mia's room. Nothing. At least she could call the cops without Mia listening in. She tapped the phone to life again.

Call your lawyer, came the thought.

Of course. Mr. Wilkins would keep things confidential; her location wouldn't have to show up on a police report.

She brought up his cell number and dialed. He wouldn't care that it was Saturday.

Fifteen minutes later, she sighed in relief. The attorney now had a screenshot of the text, he would alert the authorities, and she would get a new burner phone. He had also given her strict instructions not to mention this to anyone except Samuel, who already knew. Without knowing how Brock had gotten her phone number, he wanted everything kept super tight.

Holding back wouldn't be a problem for Maddy—she'd never want to lay her problems out for the world to see. She set her phone down, grateful also for the way Mr. Wilkins's steady voice had calmed her churning emotions. *Thank you, Lord, for sending me to the right person. Thank you so much.*

"Mama?" Mia appeared with bleary eyes and a rumpled Moana nightgown, reaching her arms to be pulled into her mother's lap.

"Good morning, sleepyhead." Maddy cuddled her close, breathing in her little girl scent. This child was her life, and Maddy would do whatever it took to keep her safe. To stay safe herself.

Maddy jumped at the knock on the door a few minutes later, her trembles coming back despite herself. She put Mia on her chair, motioning *shh* as she went to the door. "Who is it?" she said, just loudly enough to penetrate the thick wood.

"It's Adam. You said you wanted to come out to feed sometime."

Maddy swiftly unlocked the deadbolt and opened the door. "Yes, we'd love to." Dang, she still sounded shaky. She turned to Mia, taking the chance to catch her breath and calm her nerves again. "Go get dressed, honey. Don't forget to brush your teeth."

When she turned back around, Adam was leaning against the doorway, looking as handsome as ever. He might not be as tall as his brothers, but he was solid muscle. Muscle that could protect her if Brock ever did find her.

She forced the thought away. She was too well hidden—under an assumed name, she could be anywhere in the state. Or out of the state. She'd get a new phone number and be safe.

Besides, Adam craved honesty. He'd either hate her for lying, despite her lawyer's instructions, or he'd become over-controlling to protect her. She didn't want either of those or to become an object of pity to everyone around. When this was all over, she'd find the right time and tell him the whole story, but not now.

Brock's stalking left her on edge, despite her prayer and the attorney's calming tones. Mia bounced with excitement as they headed for the equipment barn, but Maddy couldn't manage to keep any enthusiasm in her voice. Better to stay silent than make it obvious she was nervous.

Once more, she gazed at the mountains around her, at the ranch she was learning to call home. She knew she was safe; she knew Brock couldn't actually find her.

ADAM LED the way past the hay barn. He smiled at Mia, skipping alongside, holding her mother's hand. The girl was so full of joy and anticipation that it even made Adam look forward to this everyday task.

He glanced at Maddy, who was quieter than normal.

Actually, her face looked rather somber. "You have a lot on your mind this morning?"

"Me? No, not at all. Just thinking about…being out here. Will it keep snowing, do you think?"

"I hope not—it's supposed to be spring! The weather app says just an inch or so, but we know how accurate that is." Adam smiled at the thought of a southern California gal getting comfortable in snow.

They turned behind the barn, to where the tractor had one round bale loaded and another ready to go on its tines. Maddy stopped cold.

"What is *that*?" She pointed, her mouth staying slightly open.

"It's a hay spooler." Adam chuckled. "An un-spooler, actually, but we don't call it that. It lets the bale unroll and gives the cows a nice long line of alfalfa to eat."

Maddy, still holding Mia's hand, walked all the way around the large tractor. "You're not taking us on that, are you? There's no place to sit!"

"Sure there is. Up here with me!" Sure, the tractor cab wasn't meant for two people, let alone three, but the seat was wide and Adam had put a blanket in the cargo space for Mia to sit on.

"I guess," Maddy said slowly. "As long as we're not perched on that giant hay bale. Or hanging onto the back of the tractor."

He was a bit disappointed that there wasn't a gleam in her eye at the thought of sitting close with him, but he'd take what he could get.

They squeezed in, and the old tractor finally started. Adam didn't know if it needed some of Micah's TLC, or if his nerves had messed something up. He hadn't had a woman sitting next to him like this since, well, longer ago than he could count.

They chugged to the first gate, and Maddy climbed down to open it. He watched her move—fluid and graceful, totally unlike the ranch women he knew. Was that her Italian heritage? Or had she had ballet lessons, one of the perks of city living? He knew she'd be just as graceful dancing in his arms, and he wondered when he could invite her into town for an evening.

Back in the cab, she nestled against him without being quite so stiff. He put an arm around her soft shoulder, and she glanced quickly up at him. "Gotta help you stay on the seat," he said. But she didn't seem to mind and he reveled in her closeness.

A hundred acres on, the cows and calves began to follow them. Adam pushed a few levers, and the bale lowered and began unrolling behind them. Mia giggled and stood up in the back to watch the cattle gather. "The babies are so cute!" she shouted.

"Quiet voice, Mia," her mother reminded her.

Mia clapped a hand over her mouth, and Adam smiled. He hadn't been around kids much, but Mia was teaching him that patience worked wonders with a child who wanted to please.

"They're not really tame," Adam said. "I don't think they'll stand still for you to pet them."

Mia's face fell, then her eyes lit up again. "Do they have names?"

The bale ran out. Adam stopped the tractor and switched the tines to the extra bale, then held out a hand to help Maddy down. No matter that she'd climbed down by herself earlier. She took his hand with a soft smile, and he felt the thrill through his whole body.

Mia jumped into his arms, and it surprised him how comfortable he felt holding her. "Do they have names?" she repeated.

"No, but do you see those tags in their ears? They have numbers on them, and if we need to get a particular cow or calf, that's what we use to make sure we have the right one."

"Not as easy to tell apart as Mister and Diablo, huh?" Those were Maddy's first words to him in fifteen minutes.

"No," he said, "but if a herd of horses is all sorrels, you'll have a hard time telling them apart, too. Unless you know a particular one personally." Adam remembered being twelve and going out to get his mother's sorrel mare, whose only white marking was a small star. He hadn't realized that the other three sorrels were solid except for small stars, too. He got teased for a long time, not just for bringing in the wrong horse, but bringing in a *gelding* instead.

He chuckled and shook his head, but Maddy didn't respond.

Mia did, though. "Can I name them?"

"Name what?"

"The baby cows!"

Oh. There were probably a hundred calves right here. "Um, sure, if you want to. And if you can tell them apart," he added.

Mia clapped her hands and jumped until Maddy put a hand on the child's shoulder. "That one is Barbie, that one is Skipper, that one is Tiger 'cause he has a sort of striped tail, that one is Maui, that one is Moana…"

She was still naming them after he'd taken the wrap off the bale. Adam couldn't remember when he'd been so charmed by someone so young. And so impressed that she could find joy in such little things. "She's great, isn't she?" he said quietly.

Maddy started. "What? Oh, yes. She is."

Adam watched her for a moment. "Is everything okay, Maddy?"

"Of course!" she said immediately. "Why wouldn't it be? Everything is fine!"

Except he could tell it wasn't. She seemed brittle and wary, not to mention distracted.

"If you ever need to talk to someone…"

She shook her head. "I don't. I won't."

"…it's kind of isolated out here. I just want you to know I'd keep anything you say confidential."

Maddy blinked at him. "Thanks," she finally said. "But it's under control. Oh, look, Mia got one to let her pet him!"

Adam almost swore. He hadn't even noticed the girl walking away. No wonder she'd been able to slip into the bull pasture so easily.

This was okay, though. Their moodiest, most protective cows weren't in this group, and if a calf stepped on Mia's foot…well, she'd learn the way any kid on a ranch did.

He'd wondered what the ranch would be like with children, if Micah could ever bring Jacob out here. All he had to do was look at Mia to see. He liked having her there, something he never thought he'd feel.

And then there was the way he felt when he looked at Maddy. Even with something troubling her, or perhaps especially with troubles, her presence made Adam smile. She brought out all his protective instincts—Lacey would say he was going all caveman—and a curl of warmth spiraled up inside him.

This ranch needed children, a new generation. It needed Mia and Maddy. *He* needed Mia and Maddy.

The thought caught him by surprise. He hadn't *needed* anyone in a long time. He really liked Maddy, though. There was a connection growing between them, and it felt right and good.

So what was he going to do about it?

Nothing now, other than be the kind of man that Maddy could share her troubles with. That, and spend as much time together as possible.

"C'mon, you two. We've got another bale to spread."

"What's it like seeing one born?" Maddy had asked on their way back from feeding the cows.

Now, at midnight, she was about to find out.

She'd taken Mia all the way into Grand Junction that afternoon, buying summer clothes for her growing girl, as well as a new cell phone, and going to a movie. She'd wanted to mail a postcard to her mother while she was far away from a Beaver Falls postmark, but Mr. Wilkins's cautions echoed in her mind.

Adam had knocked on her door while she was still reading before bed. "We've brought the last cow into the calving shed. I thought you might want to come."

Maddy checked on the peacefully sleeping Mia. Could she leave? There was nothing in the cabin to start a fire, and Jesse and Wes were in nearby cabins, anyway. Not that she was truly worried, just still a bit on edge. She slipped into her coat and pulled a knit cap down over her hair. "I thought the cows had their calves right out in the pasture."

He shrugged. "Mostly. If we have time, we'll pull in a cow

that's having problems. If it happens again, we'll sell her on. But this one has produced several champion bulls, so she's worth the extra effort."

Maddy followed Adam out the door. They stepped around the worst muddy spots as they walked companionably through the cold night, close but not touching. And Maddy wished they were.

Adam made her feel safe, but he also made her heart thrill. And she had a feeling he just might feel the same way. Then she scolded herself. Brock's text had shown that her life was still too unsettled for a romance, no matter how enticing the cowboy. Especially one who prided himself on his honesty.

She thought once again about telling him that Brock had contacted her. As much as her fear of Brock was well-founded, logic said that her worry of him finding her out here was ridiculous. Still, she could at least tell him she was using a false name.

Maddy was still figuring out how to word it when they reached the calving shed. It was spotless; the cement floor had been hosed down and straw spread thick for the cow to lie on. Except she wasn't lying down; she was on her feet and looking extremely uncomfortable. And Wes wasn't home in his cabin, he was sitting on an overturned bucket in the corner.

So much for telling Adam.

"Any change?" Adam asked, leaning on a rail.

Wes shook his head. "She's got a ways to go, I'd say."

Half an hour later, Maddy was shivering in the night air, but the cow had started to groan occasionally, and Maddy could tell she was pushing.

"Do cow labors take long? Anything like the thirty-six hours I had with Mia?" she asked.

Adam looked sympathetic. "If they did, they'd probably

be dead. It's usually only an hour or so from when we notice it. But who knows how long they're having contractions before then." He turned to Wes. "She is in some distress, though. Let's check the calf."

They pushed and prodded until the cow had moved to a metal contraption that held her head. Adam pulled on a clear plastic glove that reached almost to his shoulder, while Wes moved the cow's tail out of the way. Maddy watched in amazement as Adam reached in.

He felt around for a moment, then frowned. "It's got one leg bent back at the knee, and the other back at the shoulder. Gonna need some help here."

Wes jerked his head at Maddy. "If you feel like helping, you could stand by her head and just talk to her. She's not super tame, but your voice will calm her."

Maddy went around the headlock thing and stared at the cow. Her red and white hair was a little curly, with white whiskers around her mouth and nose. Her eyes seemed dull. "Does she have a name?"

"Nope," Adam grunted. "Just Number 52."

Wes pushed on the cow's belly in particular places, depending on what Adam said, while Adam shifted and pushed and pulled inside the beast. Maddy stroked the coarse whorls on the cow's face and murmured nonsense words.

After what seemed an interminable time, Adam stepped back and pulled the mucky glove off. "Got it. She should do okay now."

In an instant, with two pushes, the calf dropped out and landed on the ground. The cow stood tiredly until Wes came and released her head. Adam cleared the calf's nostrils for good measure, and they all backed away as the cow turned and started licking.

"Another bull calf," Adam announced proudly.

"Wow," Maddy said, amazed at the new—and wet—life. "That was really fast. Why didn't she lie down? Doesn't it hurt him to drop like that?"

"Nope," Adam and Wes said together.

"Seems most cows give birth standing up," Adam added. The two cowboys went to a spigot outside to wash up, but Maddy just stood and gazed.

A newborn calf with big, dark eyes and floppy ears, and a mother intent on licking every piece of it she could reach. Maddy had never realized that animal mothers were so loving. She supposed most of it was instinct, but she liked knowing that Number 52 cared about her baby and would probably protect it with her life if a predator came close.

With the mom still licking, the calf stuck out its two front legs and tried to stand. A few tries, and it was up. And then down again. When it managed to stay up, it tried to suck from between the cow's two front legs, but finally found her udder and latched on. The cow switched her tail contentedly and somehow kept licking the calf's rear end.

"You need a name, little one," Maddy murmured.

Wes cleaned up the afterbirth, washed again, and said, "G'night, boss."

Adam thanked him and came to stand beside Maddy. "Pretty incredible, isn't it?"

Maddy searched for words from her full heart. "It's awe-inspiring. New life from God."

They watched for a few minutes, Maddy feeling at home with Adam standing close. The peace of the moment and the warmth emanating from Adam opened Maddy's heart. She wished she could tell him her story, tell him who she really was. But she had trusted Mr. Wilkins with her life already—she needed to trust his advice now.

She let her mind wander from not being able to tell Adam

to Adam himself, and how he wasn't nearly as intimidating as when they had first met. She knew him better, had seen inside his heart just a bit, and she liked what she saw.

She wondered what she'd find if she really got to know him. What did he want out of life? How had he handled his mother's death as a teenager? Did he have a relationship with God?

The calf finished nursing, and its mother almost licked it over. It folded its front legs to lie down, and Maddy turned to Adam. "Look, its—"

"Do you—" Adam said at the same time.

They both stopped, waiting for the other to keep speaking. Instead, the silence drew out as their gaze met.

Adam's blue eyes were dark with fatigue, but there was something in them Maddy hadn't seen before. He began to speak, then closed his mouth again. That mouth that suddenly seemed so kissable.

Adam's eyes dropped to Maddy's lips, then back to her eyes. She wondered just what he saw in them—eagerness or apprehension? Or perhaps just an openness to possibilities?

She tilted her head just a bit, and he leaned closer. A whisper of his breath touched her mouth.

"Hey, Adam! How's the cow?" Caleb's voice broke the silence of the night.

Maddy jerked away.

Adam took a step back just as Caleb entered the calving shed. "She's fine," Adam said, almost growling. "And it's one in the morning—what are you doing up?"

"Couldn't sleep, thought I'd check. Hi, Maddy." Then he looked between them. "Oh, did I interrupt something?"

Maddy turned away, not able to stop the blush from rising up her cheeks. He could have easily walked in on them kissing.

"Only the admiration of new life," Adam said, a touch of nonchalance in his voice. "It's a bull calf."

"Good. Think we'll keep this one?"

Maddy could almost hear Adam's shrug. "We'll see how he's looking at weaning."

Maddy turned, her emotions back to normal. "I've got to get back," she said. "See you tomorrow."

Adam nodded to her, his eyes warm and inviting.

"And I'll make sure I announce myself before I interrupt!" Caleb called.

Maddy blushed again, but she was already heading out. The cool air and sparkling stars helped calm her once more. *What do you think, Lord? My life seemed too much of a mess for this, and I haven't dated since Brock. But could it maybe be a good thing with Adam? If it's possible, could You keep me safe and let me be happy at the same time?* She wanted to follow His will, and she found herself hoping this was part of it.

19

A dam ended his phone call and took a moment to admire Maddy's concentration on her work, not to mention her glorious hair and richly tanned skin. This was definitely a woman he'd like to spend more time with. The workers were almost done fixing her office, but he hoped they'd take a few extra days.

"Hey there," he said softly, not wanting to startle her.

She looked up with a smile. "Hey, Adam. I didn't see you come in. I've got the bills set up to pay electronically now, so you can check them anytime. And I've got some details on Mrs. Evans' doings."

"Yeah?" He pushed their almost-kiss out of his mind and sat down while she pulled up a spreadsheet.

"I've done January through November of last year. Everything was fine until some small overpayments in those last couple of months."

He rubbed his jaw, wondering how they could have been so wrong about the old accountant. "We didn't have any sort of precautions set up, did we?"

Maddy looked at him with those warm, brown eyes, and Adam thought he'd like to sink into their depths and forget business altogether.

"Unfortunately not," she said. "I'll let you know what else I find."

He nodded, but was reluctant to finish the conversation. "What do you think she was doing? Were the starting bits a trial run for later?"

She shrugged, her hair swaying as she turned back to the screen. "Maybe. Or maybe she just wanted some extra for Christmas presents."

"Except she kept going." Adam took the opportunity to admire the highlights in her curls until she looked at him again, and he jerked his gaze back.

"I'll know more in another few days," Maddy said, all business.

Dang. Had he mistaken her reaction the other night? No, he didn't think so. Maybe she was just very work-focused. He stood and moved the chair to its original spot. "I'm going into town and wondered if you wanted to get away from the computer for a bit."

"Yes!" She grinned up at him. "Well, not that I'm desperate to leave the computer behind, but if you wouldn't mind adding a stop at the store, there are some things I need to pick up."

Adam smiled. You could put a city girl on a ranch, but you couldn't keep her away from shopping. "In about half an hour?"

"Sounds good." Maddy turned back to the computer, her mouth still quirked up in pleasure.

Adam walked over to the stables and found his younger brother working a two-year-old. Caleb had an easy lope on the mare already, and Adam was once again amazed at the masterful way Caleb had with horses.

"Adam. What's up," Caleb called when he noticed him. He slowed the mare to a halt.

"Heading into town," Adam responded. "You got that list of grain you need?"

"In the tack room. And could you swing by Stevenson's and pick up a saddle for me? I dropped one off for repair a week ago."

Adam grinned. "What'd you do, run over it with a truck?"

Caleb shook his head. "Got careless and left it on the ground near Idiot Girl here. Stupid horse picked it up and threw it! Tore a strip out of the leather, too."

"Sounds like the horse wasn't the stupid one." Adam was serious now. "You haven't needed a minder for a while now. What happened?"

It was Caleb's turn to grin. "Remember Brenda Riley? She came by, and…I kind of got distracted."

"Sheesh, Caleb, you aren't a teenager anymore!" Adam's voice was sharp. "You can have all the fun you want with your girlfriends—"

"She's not a girlfriend, she just—"

"—but not when it impacts the running of this ranch. Grow up, would you?"

Caleb's eyes narrowed. "And just who made you my boss?"

"Dad, that's who."

"Since when?"

"Since he's getting tired and forgetful and can't do it all."

"Ohhh." Caleb drew out the word. "I get it. He didn't suddenly promote you—you're taking charge behind his back."

"I am not. I don't do anything he's not aware of. It's just…

dang it, I don't have time for this. I'll be back with your grain later." Adam spun on his boot heel and stalked away, the earthy smell of the barn giving him no pleasure. Caleb got to ride horses all day and dance with pretty women all night. He had no idea what it was like to have the responsibility for everything.

He entered the tack room and noted with satisfaction the bridles hanging neatly, the saddles lined up on their racks, the ropes coiled and looped just so. At least Caleb knew what he was doing in his own domain. When he paid attention, anyway.

The feed list was on the counter next to a package of Equiiox. Adam wondered which horse it was for, and if Caleb had discussed it with the vet or just ordered it online. Then he grabbed the list and tried to put the rest out of his mind. He had a quasi-date with a lovely lady and he didn't want to be preoccupied with problems.

"So where are we going?" Maddy asked as she used the step-side and the handholds to pull herself into the truck. It was a big truck, and she didn't have a lot of height on her, but she didn't give him a chance to help her up.

Adam buckled up and started the engine, the quiet purr making him smile inside. He liked his machinery running well. "The bank first—I have to pick up some papers. Then the feed store and the saddle shop." He steered down the long driveway and looked at Maddy before turning onto the road. "And then, if you're willing, some pizza? It's been a long time since breakfast."

Maddy laughed. "You're offering to take an Italian girl to an American pizza place?"

"I didn't think of that," Adam stammered. "Uh, there's also a burger joint and Sally's Diner."

She waved a hand at him. "No, no, pizza is fine. I really don't expect authentic pizza unless Nonna is making it."

"Are you sure? We can—"

"I'm sure. I hung out at Abbie's Pizza on Friday nights as much as any other kid in my high school."

Ah, here was his chance to get to know her better. "So what were you like as a teenager? What did you like to do?"

Maddy let a lock of hair curl around her finger. "Pretty typical, I guess. Hanging with my friends, going to football games, a party here and there."

"Cheerleader?" Adam could totally see her with pompoms and a short, sassy skirt.

"Hah! In my dreams! I wasn't one of the popular kids. Too nerdy, too fat."

Adam looked at her sharply. "You? Too fat?"

Maddy shrugged and kept her voice normal. "I call it curvy now, and I try to keep it under control. But in high school…yeah, fat."

"And teenagers can be cruel." Adam tried to remember if he had been one of the obnoxious kids who had teased others, but nothing stuck out.

"College was better—I wasn't needing to fit everyone else's expectations so much. And I had a supportive family who helped me realize you don't get to choose your body type, and that food is an integral part of life and love and family." She cracked a grin. "Especially if your Italian grandmother lives with you." She settled partly sideways and leaned against the door. "So what about you? Were you a jock in high school?"

Adam chuckled. "Our high school barely had a football team, and basketball was intramural at lunch. Now, if you count rodeo…"

"Big, bad bull rider?" Maddy sent a smile his way that could carry him a long time.

143

He smiled back, but shook his head. "I don't have that much crazy in me. Seth and Caleb did bronc riding, though. Me, I was pretty good at calf roping—skill and speed instead of danger."

Adam regaled her with rodeo stories the rest of the way down the mountain. He'd never really met someone from California, someone who didn't know at least the basics of rodeo sports.

Maddy stayed in the truck while Adam retrieved the papers Dad needed from the safe deposit box, and then Adam backed up to the feed store loading dock.

Maddy gasped as she got out. Square bales of alfalfa and straw lined one side of the covered area. The other held sacks of about thirty types of livestock feed. "Soybean meal? Beet pulp pellets?" she read. "I thought it would be oats and maybe corn for chickens."

Adam laughed. "There are more types of feed concentrations than you can imagine. Horses need different feed than sheep, and a working or breeding animal needs nutrients that retired animals don't."

"How do you balance it all?" Maddy asked, reading a few labels closely. "Protein content, energy, vitamins and minerals. You'd need a degree in nutrition to do this."

"Well, yes. That's what I went to college for."

She turned to him quickly. "You have a degree in nutrition?"

"No, ranch management and animal husbandry. There's more to ranching than just branding or driving cattle to summer pasture."

"Oh." Her mouth stayed in an O shape as she read the next label. Adam's heart sighed—he could stare at her expression forever.

"I never dreamed it was so complicated," she said. "It's not the carefree life that shows up on TV, is it?"

"Unfortunately not." Adam shook his head, both in answer to her question and to clear away feelings that were quickly becoming too strong. "And when you add two brothers and fourteen ranch hands to the twenty horses and eleven hundred head of cattle, it gets worse."

He gave his list to Curt, who worked the feed dock, and escorted her inside the building.

It wasn't a huge store, but there were a lot of ranchers around Beaver Falls, and it was crammed with most anything they would need. One side of the space was given over to tools—anything from hammers and pliers to tractor parts and batteries. The rest was split out by animal type, with a refrigerator for vaccines and other medicines that could be given without a vet.

Maddy wrinkled her cute nose at the smell of worming pastes and first aid ointments, but liked the aisle of halters, grooming equipment, and tack. "Leather smells so good," she said, holding a bridle close to her face.

Adam inhaled deeply. "Yup. Leather and wood shavings— enough to make any man happy." He had the feeling Maddy could make him happy even without leather and wood, but he kept that thought to himself.

"Black Rock, you're ready to go," came over the loudspeaker.

"I guess Curt has us loaded up. Ready for the next stop?" He offered her his arm in an old-fashioned gesture and smiled when she slipped her hand in and walked with him.

An hour later, they had picked up Caleb's saddle and stopped at the grocery store, then parked the heavily burdened truck in front of Sam's Pizza Palace. Adam helped

Maddy down and kept her hand clasped in his. He smiled inside when she didn't draw it away.

They sat across from each other at a booth, browsing a list of toppings and combinations. "Got a hankerin' for anything in particular, ma'am?" Adam said, putting on a drawl.

Maddy rolled her eyes at him, and he grinned back. "Are you a meat-lover guy or are you up to some less traditional choices?" she asked.

"Oh, I'll go for meat as much as the next guy. But this time, you choose."

"Something not so predictable, then," she said. "Chicken, bacon and artichoke in a white sauce?"

Adam blinked. Who would want those three things together on a pizza?

"Or is that not manly enough for you, cowboy?"

"Is that a challenge? You should know I don't back down from a challenge. Chicken and artichokes may be sissy, but I can eat as much of them as the next man. Or woman." He grinned at her and motioned for Tasha, whose hair was red this week. She'd worked there for years, and he'd even dated her for a bit, but it hadn't worked out.

"Hi, Adam," Tasha said, snatching quick glances at Maddy. "You haven't been in for a while. How ya been keeping?"

"Doing fine, Tasha, keeping busy. This is Maddy Ricciolino. She's our new accountant."

Tasha looked directly at Maddy now and grinned. "Nice to meet you, Maddy," she said. "It's about time Adam took up with someone classy. And I love your hair. Wish I could have curls like that."

Maddy turned a pretty shade of muted pink. "Thanks, but I can't claim any credit. It just does its own unruly thing."

Tasha looked at Adam, then back at Maddy, before

turning to her notepad. "So what can I get you? The usual meat-lovers, Adam?"

"No, a medium chicken-bacon-artichoke." Adam kept a straight face, but it wasn't easy. "With white sauce," he added.

Tasha stared for a moment. Maddy seemed to be holding back a snort. Tasha looked between them with narrowed eyes. "Chicken bacon artichoke, got it." She turned toward the kitchen. "A sissy special, Sam," she shouted.

"Uncalled for, Tasha," Adam muttered.

Tasha just wriggled her rear as she walked away. Adam cringed at what Maddy must think.

But the woman in question burst into laughter. "You'll like it, I promise," she said when she could speak again. "And Tasha…wow."

Adam fiddled with his water glass. "We dated a few years ago. Now she thinks she can treat me like, I don't know, like that."

"Maybe she still likes you," Maddy suggested.

He shrugged. "No reason to. I mean, she wasn't happy when I broke up with her, but there just wasn't anything there. I couldn't keep going out with her when I didn't care. She got over it eventually."

"Maybe she didn't."

"No, she did," Adam insisted. "She's been with Sam for two years now. Keeps tabs on everyone, though—has to share any possible gossip…er, news. Now, what about you? Did you ever break anybody's heart?"

Maddy sipped her ice water, and Adam gave her time to think. "Just Johnny Peterson. He kept after me and after me and I just couldn't take it anymore."

She sounded a little nonchalant to be talking about her ex, but Adam's hands fisted anyway. He struggled to keep his voice light. "A stalker? What did you do?"

"I finally shoved him in a mud puddle," she said, her eyes twinkling. "We were seven."

Adam laughed. He did like this woman. She was new to ranching, but she was feisty enough to deal with what she needed to.

A thought crossed his mind, one that hadn't in quite a while. If ever.

Besides the attraction that was growing, on his part anyway, was Maddy someone important in his life? Had God put her in his path?

He didn't know that yet, but he knew he wanted another chance to kiss her. One without his brother around.

20

Friday morning, Maddy went through the details of Mrs. Evans' discrepancies once more. This time, she noticed something new: the most recent bills were overpaid by two or three hundred dollars, but the November and December ones were rounded up an odd amount so that it came out an even hundred for the total payment. A $17.28 overpayment, so the check was exactly two hundred dollars.

Why? Surely the former accountant wasn't siphoning off such an odd amount. And so small.

Or was that because she didn't think anyone would notice?

Maddy sorted her list of vendors, invoice amounts, the amount paid, and the discrepancy. She added a few notes, but she'd need to go over all this with Adam.

The computer dinged again, but it was her personal email this time, not the business account.

Her mind needed a break by now, anyway. She answered one email from her sister, but the rest looked like spam. She deleted them one at a time, just in case. And then she froze.

I'M GETTING CLOSER.

Nothing other words, no signature, just the very generic and spooky email address of *YouRmine@yahoo.com*.

Maddy's heart pounded. She could feel the pulse in her hands, hear it in her head.

It had to be Brock. There wasn't anyone else who would send a message like that, no one else who would be getting closer.

She had bought a new phone with a new number right after his text. But how had he gotten her new email? Hired a hacker? Or threatened someone she loved?

She shivered, a hard, violent shake that ran up and down her spine. If he hurt her family...

No, if he hurt her family, the police would lock him away for good, and he wouldn't risk that just for them. But if he found Maddy herself, he wouldn't care about the repercussions. Would he just beat her up, or would he make good on his threat to do far worse?

But if he came here, surely Adam and his brothers would protect her. Brock couldn't take them all down together.

Except they weren't all here at the same time. If Micah wasn't making noise in the equipment shed, he was out somewhere with the cattle. Caleb was over in the horse barn. And Adam had his father to protect, too.

And even if Brock wouldn't go after them individually, they couldn't look out for her if they didn't know. That had to be enough for Mr. Wilkins' permission to tell them.

Maddy realized she'd started pacing the room, not even sure when she had gotten up from her desk. *Calm down*, she told herself, trying to slow her breaths. Brock wasn't here. He might never get here. And his cocky attitude wouldn't let him come after her without sending a frightening warning first. "I'm getting close" wasn't the same as "I'm coming now."

She had time.

She forwarded Brock's email to Mr. Wilkins with an explanation and request, then followed it with an actual phone call. The lawyer wasn't available, though, so she left a message with his secretary.

Fidgeting too much in her chair, Maddy tidied Mia's corner, straightened her desk, dusted the monitor and keyboard. Anything was better than just sitting and waiting.

"Going all clean-freak on us?" Adam was leaning against the doorjamb.

Maddy laughed nervously. "Just a lot of restless energy, I guess."

"Anything I can help with?"

She sighed. "I wish you could. There's…" She hesitated, Mr. Wilkins' instructions shouting in her head. "There's stuff going on with Brock, but I'm not allowed to talk about it."

"Ohh-kay." Adam's expression looked awkward, like he wanted to say something but was holding back. Well, that made two of them.

He came close to her desk and lowered his voice. "You know I'll keep whatever you say confidential."

Maddy nodded. "I know. It's just that…" If she couldn't tell, then she couldn't tell. She'd just have to deal with it. "Maybe soon. I'm waiting for a phone call."

Adam's eyes were somber. "I'll leave you some privacy. But when you're done, I'd like to see what you found about Mrs. Evans."

Maddy nodded. "I'm sure it will be just a few minutes, but I sent it all in an email."

She watched him leave, wishing this whole thing were over. Or had never happened in the first place.

Her phone chimed and she answered eagerly.

"I got your email, Maddy," Mr. Wilkins said. "I've already sent it on to the police. How are you doing?"

She shuddered. "Nervous. Worried. About what you'd expect. I mean, he could show up any time."

"He won't," Mr. Wilkins said firmly. "The sergeant said he was seen in a restaurant this morning. He may have gotten your email address, but he still doesn't know where you are."

Maddy dropped into her chair and let her body sag. Relief washed over her. It wasn't peace, but at least she didn't need to panic right now. *Thank you so much, Lord.*

"I appreciate it, Mr. Wilkins. I wish they could find something else to arrest him for."

"We're watching everything he does. We'll find something eventually. In the meantime, it's good you're out on that ranch."

"About that…I know you said to keep quiet about everything, but if Brock *does* show up, the guys on the ranch really need to know." Maddy held her breath. *Adam* needed to know.

"Maddy, we don't know how he got your phone number *or* your new email address. Which, by the way, you need to change again."

"I know, but—"

"Until we do, you can't trust anyone not to be the leak. Maybe it was inadvertently done, but it still happened."

He reminded her that while they were looking for the leak, Colorado was a big state, and Brock's chance of physically finding her was slim to none. He reassured her once more, then hung up.

Maddy stared at the pencils on her desk, lined them up from tallest to shortest, then again by color gradation. Finally, she took a deep breath and went to find Adam. She may not be able to tell him, but his presence would steady her nerves.

Except he'd been called away to check a problem cow.

21

W ith the ranch hands hanging out at Jesse's cabin in the late evening, the mountains forming a perimeter around the ranch, and Mia's giggles, Maddy calmed down about her situation. She had a new phone, a new email, and Mr. Wilkins was right—the chances of Brock finding her were slim to none. She really hadn't felt this protected since high school, when her brother offered to beat up a girl who called her names.

Back at work the next day, she was happily entering numbers for payroll when Adam knocked on the open door. "I had an idea," he said. His voice cracked a little, and she smiled to herself.

"Yeah?" She didn't look up from her numbers.

"You busy tonight?"

Now she looked up. Adam's t-shirt showed off his muscled shoulders, and he had a bit of a scruff on his face. *Be still, my heart.*

"It's going to be clear, which means chilly," he said, "but

we'll have a gorgeous night for stargazing. I could pick you up around nine-thirty?"

Stargazing. With Adam's arm around her to keep her warm? Except… "Sounds like fun, cowboy, but I've got Mia."

"We'll just be in the field behind the cabins. And you left her sleeping when the last calf was born."

Maddy frowned. "Yes, but I've felt guilty about that ever since. I shouldn't have left her. Even if the risk is minuscule, I can't do it."

Adam frowned. Then his eyes brightened. "I bet I could get Lacey to babysit."

But Maddy had an alternative. "We could stay close to the back door, and I could keep a window cracked to hear her."

Adam's smile spread across his face. "Great! I'll bring everything we need."

He left, and Maddy turned back to her computer. What would a person need for stargazing? She shook her head and tried to pay attention to her work, but the thought of laying on a blanket next to Adam, gazing up at the grand heavens, took over instead.

He really was all she wanted in a man, even though she hadn't been looking. He was a hard worker, a leader, and really cared about the animals and the people on his ranch. And while he was serious about work stuff, he could laugh at jokes, he allowed himself to be teased, and he teased back in return. He loved his family and…did she dare to think he might be coming to care for her?

She thought back to when the calf was born. Not just the feelings that whirled through her at his closeness afterwards, but his tenderness and care. If only Caleb hadn't shown up right then…

Maddy shook the luscious memory away. Right now, she

needed to finish the payroll so the ranch hands could have something to spend in town. They'd invited her to go with them one Friday night, but the bar-and-pool-table scene wasn't for her.

By the time ten o'clock rolled around, Mia was fast asleep cuddling her stuffed T-Rex, and Maddy had added fleece leggings under her jeans. It might be the end of April and well into springtime, but that didn't mean it wasn't cold at night!

Adam rolled up in his truck, even though it was only a five- or six-minute walk from the homestead to the cabins. He carried camp chairs and blankets from the pickup bed to the space behind the cabin, grinning all the time.

And oh, how that grin tickled her heart!

When he had everything situated the way he wanted, he put the tailgate up. He lifted a thermos in one hand and two mugs in the other. "Hot chocolate?"

"Ah, a man after my own heart."

Adam got a funny look on his face, and Maddy cringed inside. True, she'd daydreamed about following up their almost-kiss with a real one, but to be honest, she wasn't sure she was ready for another relationship now.

She marveled at how her feelings could go from anticipation to caution and back again so quickly. If something was going to grow between them, she was too unsure to be one to instigate it. "Come on in," she said as evenly as she could. "Let me check Mia one more time."

The child hadn't moved, other than to pull her T-Rex closer under her chin. Maddy opened the window an inch, grateful to whoever built the cabin for the smooth-gliding workmanship. At her old apartment, opening a window involved grunting and groaning until it finally went up with a bang.

She followed Adam out the back door, shutting the lights off as she went. They stood for a moment, eyes adjusting, and

Maddy marveled at the difference in what she could see. The trees were a darker shade of black, the starlight outlined the fence posts, and oh, the sky! Like she had never seen it before.

She wouldn't call it velvety-black—it was too crisp and sharp for that. Each star sparkled individually, some blue-white, some yellow. A few even pulsed. The Big Dipper was to her right, low in the sky, one of the few she knew how to pick out.

Adam led her over to the chairs, and she settled into a lounger that reclined. He tucked a blanket around her, his hands lingering on her arms. His eyes were soft and her heart fluttered, but he stepped away.

"It's a beautiful night for star-gazing," he said as he settled into his own reclining chair. "I don't come out often—morning comes too early—but I like knowing it's here when I want. I could never live in town."

"There's a billion more stars than I've ever seen before," Maddy said. She took her eyes off the panorama above and glanced at him, only to find him looking at her, not the constellation.

He didn't blink. Anticipation curled in her stomach.

She hadn't planned on giving her heart to anyone for a very long time, but then again, it had already been a long time since Brock had held even the smallest piece of her heart. Was she ready for this?

Unsure once again, she turned back to the night sky. "I know the Big Dipper, and I can pick out Orion's Belt, but that's all. How about you?"

She could hear the smile in Adam's voice. "See that big W over there? That's Cassiopeia. That's Perseus beside her, and below the Big Dipper is Leo."

She found Cassiopeia easily and even thought she'd be able to find it again. But Perseus? No way.

Adam leaned across the gap between them, which, come to think of it, wasn't much of a gap at all. He put his face close to hers, turned her head slightly, and pointed.

His breath warmed her cheek, and she could hardly see the stars for the jumble of feelings. She could smell his aftershave or shampoo or whatever, mixed with the ever-present smell of leather. His skin was slightly rough against her ear, but she didn't move. To be honest, she didn't think she could move.

"There, see it?" he murmured. "Those three small stars making a triangle? That's one knee. Then from his head and to the right is his sword arm. And that line is his arm with Medusa's head at the bottom. The other line of stars is his other leg."

Maddy nodded numbly, finding what *might* be Perseus. Or might not. She really didn't care right now.

If she leaned her head ever so slightly, they'd be cheek to cheek. If she turned, their mouths would be millimeters apart. Every nerve ending she had tingled with longing.

Did she want this? If he kissed her, there would be no going back to their still-growing friendship. And that might ruin the best thing she'd had in a long time.

Adam gently pulled her head around. His eyes held hers for a long second before he dipped his head, giving her a kiss that was both soft and strong at the same time.

He pulled away too soon, a question in his eyes. "Was that okay?" he whispered. "Should I have asked first?"

But her heart suddenly knew with certainty what her mind had been unsure of. She reached for him, pulled his head back to hers, and let him know that a kiss was just fine. Better than fine.

. . .

THEY LOOKED AT STARS, then back at each other, then back at the stars. Adam might have snuck another kiss or two in there. And Maddy might have snuck one back. But amidst the excitement and exhilaration and joy, came the persistent feeling that she needed to tell him. Brock, the stalking, Mr. Wilkins. Everything.

She sighed and sat up.

"What's wrong?" Adam asked warily.

Poor Adam. He wouldn't know what hit him. "Um, you remember when I said I couldn't tell you stuff?"

He nodded slowly.

"I'm still not supposed to, but I think you need to know." Maddy glanced at his lips, wondering if this would change how many kisses they'd have in the future. His eyes had turned dark with concern.

She sighed. "I guess I need to start at the beginning. You know I'm divorced. What you don't know is the whole story and what's happened since." She paused, swallowing with difficulty.

"I know he was abusive," Adam said softly.

Maddy nodded. "I wasn't going to stick around through it. Or put Mia through that either."

Adam scrambled to his feet. "Mia? He hit Mia? Dirty son of a low-down... Men like that shouldn't be allowed to exist. I ought to—"

He towered over Maddy, but she put a hand on his leg. "Names won't help, Adam, and no, he didn't hurt Mia. At least not physically. Except for the time she got shoved when she couldn't get out of the way fast enough."

She could see him rein in his emotions, but the tension didn't leave as he sat back down.

"At least it's over now," he said.

"Actually, it's not." Maddy worked the blanket with her

fingers. "He wouldn't give up. He kept after me, stalking me. I got a restraining order, but it didn't stop him. He went to jail, but came out threatening me even more. The police couldn't guarantee my safety, so I ran."

"Ah, and that's how you ended up in the middle of a mountain ranch."

Maddy glanced at Adam, glad to see the understanding in his eyes. He really didn't care about her history. She warmed as he stroked her cheek with the back of one finger.

"You could have told me before. It's no big deal, but at least you're safe here now." He kissed the corner of her mouth.

Maddy looked down and smoothed the blanket across her lap. "That's just it. I'm not. And I couldn't tell you before. From the beginning, I couldn't risk anyone letting it slip in town."

"I wouldn't do that!"

"I know that now, but I didn't back then. I worried that if it were common knowledge on the ranch, someone might let it slip. And then a week ago, Brock got some information, and my attorney gave me strict instructions not to tell anyone anything. And you don't like lies."

Adam drew her close and rested his forehead against hers. "It really isn't a problem, Maddy. You don't have to tell all the details of your private life."

Maddy pulled away. "Adam, when I ran, I left my identity behind. I'm not Maddy Ricciolino, I'm Maddy Johnston. And I was Maddy Bianchi before that. I didn't grow up in Los Angeles, I grew up in a Denver suburb. I've never seen the ocean."

Adam's brows drew together. "You're telling me you didn't just keep things private, you made up who you are?"

"Sometimes you have to do what you don't like." Maddy

had no other response. *God, please help me here. I need him to understand.*

He snorted. "Wait a minute. You had to give your real name and Social Security number for payroll."

Maddy stiffened, but forced herself to be calm. She didn't want this to turn into a big fight. "Your dad was the one who hired me. I told him everything, but asked him to introduce me as Maddy Ricciolino. It's my Nonna's maiden name.

"Adam, don't you see? I couldn't risk Brock finding me here. Which wouldn't be hard if everyone in town knew you'd hired a Maddy Johnston."

He frowned. "How much does he know now? Does he know you're here?"

"No, thank the Lord. But somehow he got phone number and now my email. He sent some threats, which is when I called Mr. Wilkins, who said not to tell anyone while he tracked things down."

Adam looked at her intently. "Listen, he can't find you with just those, but you need to get a new phone and change your email, and—"

"I already did," Maddy said. "When I registered Mia for school."

"Oh." Suddenly Adam's arms were around her, holding her in close, warming the chill that had settled over her. He couldn't make everything better, but if he were on her side, she could make it through this.

An eternity of comfort passed in a few minutes. Maddy lifted her head off Adam's shoulder. "Are we still okay?"

"Huh. You've got an ex-husband after you, and you've just announced you're not who I thought you were. I'm not sure that's the definition of 'okay.'"

"I've told you now."

He pulled her head back to his shoulder. "You have, and I

promise I'll keep you safe from the dirtbag. Whatever it takes. But geez, you told Dad and not me? And you've really never seen the ocean?"

She smiled, suspecting that telling only Samuel was a bigger deal than anything else. "I'll see the ocean someday. And remember, you can't tell anyone else."

And then Adam pulled her face up and met her with another kiss.

22

Adam worked at his desk Monday morning, not liking the arrangement. Maddy's office had been finished, the desk and shelves set up, and she had moved back in this morning. The partner's desk had been centered again, her makeshift computer area had been dismantled, and Dad's easy chair had taken its place. And it didn't look right.

He should be able to look up and watch Maddy working, or catch her glance, or something, anything. His desk time had become boring again.

He took a phone call, turning to look out the window while he listened. When he hung up, Maddy was standing in his doorway, clutching a handful of papers. His calculations for the solar wells vanished as memories of her story and their Saturday night kisses washed over him. He wanted to leap from behind his desk, take her in his arms, and simply hold her for the next hour.

But her face carried a troubled look, and he left thoughts of cuddling behind. "What is it?" he asked, ready to do whatever he needed to take away the worry on her pretty face.

"I think there's been a mistake," she said quietly. "I got an email from the bank saying that the checking account is overdrawn. I mean, the overdraft protection kicked in, but my balance doesn't show us being anywhere close."

Adam frowned. They hadn't expected any more irregularities in Mrs. Evans' bookkeeping.

"I printed the last few days of activity on the account—the overdraft would have happened recently—and found this." She thrust the paper out, one line highlighted.

"Check number 8356, paid on the 12th," Adam read. She had made a notation on the side: BLM lease. "But…"

"I know. You paid that at the beginning of February. Here's a copy of their emailed receipt." She handed that to him, too. "So I checked this one out, and it looks like your father wrote the new check."

Adam blanched. His father had turned over the day-to-day finances to him quite a while ago. And now he was writing twenty-thousand dollar checks? Adam's inclination was to storm off and confront his dad. Instead, he inhaled deeply, breathed out a prayer for calmness, and called the bank.

"We had enough overdraft protection to cover it?" he asked the bank manager.

"Of course. And if I hadn't thought it was legitimate, I would have called, I assure you."

Adam sighed. "I know, Tom, thanks. But can you set our account to require two signatures? And would you flag our account to call me if you get any checks over a thousand dollars that are not signed by me or Maddy Ri—"

"Madelena," Maddy corrected.

"Madelena Ricciolino," Adam continued, I'd appreciate it."

"I'm marking it as we speak," the bank manager said. "I

can set the two-sig requirement here, but you'll need to order new checks with room for both."

"Will do. Thanks, Tom." Adam ended the call and sunk his head into his hands. Finally he looked up. "See? You've been a good influence on me. I didn't blow my stack. And I think that deserves a reward."

She grinned, her face lighting up. "And what might that be, cowboy?"

He stood and walked around his desk. "Come closer and I'll show you."

Several minutes of tender kisses later, Adam said, "I need to go talk to Dad about this. Wish me luck!"

"Luck," she whispered, a soft smile in her eyes.

ADAM FINALLY FOUND his father over in the stables, working oil into reins that hadn't seen use in ten years. *Lord, help me know what to say. Help me remember it was just a mistake*, he prayed silently. Then he cleared the emotion from his face. "Hey, Dad."

"Adam! Taking a break from work for once?"

Adam gave as much of a smile as he could muster. "Sort of. Need to talk to you for a minute."

"Sure. Nice to know an old man is still needed."

"Aw, come on, Dad, you're not old."

His father chuckled. "Got a good few years on you, that's for sure. Only one older'n me around here is Uncle Dirt." Dad nudged him with his shoulder, then wiped the oil off his hands. "So what can I do you for? Need some advice on pasture rotation? Or is it time to decide about the wells?"

Adam shook his head. "I'll always want your input on managing the pastures, and the wells won't happen for a while yet. But…" How could he ask this without accusing his father of stupidity?

"Do you remember writing a check about a week ago? To the BLM for the lease this year."

"No. Yes. Well, I don't rightly know. I mean, I write one every year. Hard to tell if I just did one or if I'm remembering last year."

Adam nodded and leaned against the tack room wall.

His father reached for the bridles again, then stopped. "Wait. That lease comes up in February, doesn't it? So I wouldn't have been writing any checks now." With a look of satisfaction, he poured more oil on his rag and picked the reins up again.

"But you did, Dad. You wrote a check for $21,563 on May second this year. Maddy pulled up a copy. Your handwriting, your signature."

The older man stared at the wall in front of him, hands not moving, eyes not blinking. "N-no," he finally murmured. "I must have been sleepwalking or something."

Adam twisted the toe of his boot against the concrete floor, wishing he were anywhere but having this conversation with his father. His proud, hard-working father who never wanted help with anything. But the check wasn't the only problem his dad had been having. The episodes all swirled in Adam's mind, faster and faster, and the worry he had been tamping down for the last months forced its way to the front. He couldn't ignore it anymore.

He sent another prayer upward, then stepped to his father and put his arm around those lean shoulders. "Dad, it's not just forgetting names. You're doing work that's already been done, or doesn't need to be done. You've mixed up words, re-built a gate that was new, forgotten to feed, and now the check. And sometimes I think you get a bit, well, not confused, but not following the track of what someone is saying. I think we need to go see someone."

His dad didn't take his eyes off the wall, just kept shaking his head. "No. There's nothing wrong with me. Everybody makes mistakes. Losing words is just part of getting old. And so what if I work on something that's not important?"

He clenched the rein tightly in his hand and moved away from Adam's arm, then turned suddenly. "I'm not a useless old man you can just shut away somewhere! I made this ranch what it is, I raised you, this is my *home*!"

Adam stepped back, shocked. "Dad! Nobody said anything about you going anywhere!"

His father glared at him, paler blue eyes flashing. "Just you remember that, boy! You can't kick me out just so you can run the place on your own."

Adam took a deep breath. This was his father, whom he loved. "This isn't about the ranch, Dad. I don't want to run it by myself anyway. I don't think I could. I'm just worried about you. I want you to stick around forever, but I want you healthy and strong. I want you *with* us."

Dad's eyes had softened a bit, but he was still holding that rein for all it was worth.

Adam stepped forward, put his hand lightly on his father's arm. "Dad, we need to see a doctor. Maybe you've got a vitamin deficiency or something. I've heard that can cause brain fog. Or maybe a heart problem and there's not enough oxygen getting to your brain. It could be anything."

Adam had studiously avoided the "A" word, a specter hovering over every person with an aging parent. It wasn't something he ever wanted to face, but he especially wasn't ready to deal with it now. He never thought he'd be praying that his father "only" had a heart problem.

He moved his hand to cover his father's. "Would that be okay? Can I make an appointment?"

Dad blinked, keeping vulnerable tears at bay. He nodded, then stared blankly at the rein and his rag.

"Can I help you for a bit, Dad? It's been a long time since I've cleaned tack." Adam reached for another old bridle and began unbuckling the bit. "Got another rag?"

Dad smiled—a little quavery, but still a smile. "Sure," he said, handing him a rag from a pile on the counter. "Let me know if you need help."

23

Two days later, Maddy smiled to herself as Adam explained the improvements he wanted to make on their leased BLM land and the application procedures they required. She was turning into as much his assistant as the ranch accountant, but that was fine with her. As long as she could make notes, keep files, be as organized about everything as she wanted, she'd do whatever he asked.

Maybe even *without* a kiss as a reward. Although that kiss under the stars...that kiss, his acceptance of her situation, and then more kisses... only Adam was left in her head after that. It only took a glimmer of a thought to have her reliving it and the soft kisses yesterday.

"Maddy?" Adam's voice brought her back to the present. "Where'd you go just then?"

She only shook her head and tried to keep her face from flushing red. Back to business. "So you're allowed to put a fence and a building on government land?"

When they finished the lease discussion, Adam leaned

over her desk with a gleam in his eye. "Want to take a morning walk with me? No Mia, no brothers, just us?"

Maddy shot up from her chair without a second thought. "Why is it we live on the same ranch, work together, and still have a hard time finding time by ourselves?" She paused to stack her notes neatly and close her laptop. "Out along the creek?"

"There're some flowers blooming there now that I thought you'd like."

Aww. What a sweetheart he was. She grabbed her sweater just as Caleb came in.

"Adam, good. I think Dad has all the hands out doing something with the water troughs, and I've got a problem with a yearling." He turned and walked right back out.

Adam looked at Maddy ruefully and shrugged his shoulders. "Duty calls, I guess. Raincheck?"

She nodded, but her body sighed and sagged in disappointment. She was falling in love with Adam, which she shouldn't be after three days, but it was more than just his kisses and the touch of his hand on her cheek. It was all she'd seen of him in the last few weeks. But even with that, she really didn't know him well enough to see if they might have something real.

How could they succeed at together-time if the ranch always interrupted them? For that matter, did she want a future with a guy who always had his ranch taking precedence?

She shook her head, realizing that wasn't really a problem. Part of what drew her to Adam was his commitment to his family and the ranch. She knew he'd be just as committed to her as he was to them.

. . .

Two hours later, she wandered over to the stables. Adam was just heading into the tack room with a bucket while Caleb led a young horse with a newly bandaged leg out to a paddock.

"Hey, cowboy," she greeted Adam. "Got time for that walk?"

He smiled widely. "Sure!"

"Nuh-uh, Adam," Caleb warned. "It's almost noon. Seth should be Skyping anytime."

"Right. It's Tuesday." He turned to Maddy. "Want to come meet my youngest brother?"

It wasn't quite what she had hoped for, but she wasn't going to break up a Skype call from Seth. Besides, she'd heard so much about him that she wanted to see if the real-life version held up to the paragon his brothers had described.

"Does he call every Tuesday?" she asked.

Adam lifted one shoulder. "Usually. And usually about noon, maybe twelve-thirty. Dad's glued to the big screen where we have it come in. We all try to be there if we can, but it doesn't always work."

"What if he can't call?"

"If it's something local that's keeping him busy, he'll usually email to let us know. But if there's no warning, then he's probably gone out on patrol somewhere, and we all worry until we hear from him again." He took her hand as they walked back to the house.

"That must be hard, having him over there and in danger."

"Yeah, but his area's been quiet for a while—he's spending a lot of time in local construction. Working on a school right now."

Adam took hold of Maddy's hand when they left, and she marveled at how right his calluses felt against her soft skin.

She wondered if the family knew about their developing relationship. She wouldn't mind; she just didn't like to be the center of attention.

"Hey, you two!" Caleb called after them. "You're going to get razzed if you walk in holding hands."

So much for wondering.

Adam looked down at her, a smile broadening across his face. "You ready for this? They can tease something fierce."

It was going to happen sometime—they weren't keeping anything a secret. "I don't think it will surprise them," she said, squeezing his hand. "May as well get it over with."

Adam pulled her hand to his lips, then kissed her softly on the mouth. "Good for you," he murmured. "Let's go get 'em."

Samuel grinned widely from his recliner as they walked into the large family room. "About time," he said, blue eyes sparkling at their joined hands.

Maddy grinned back. Micah raised his eyebrows, but that was it. And Caleb already knew, so...no problem. No teasing, either.

Caleb dusted off his jeans as he entered, then sprawled in what must be his favorite chair. "We'll let the two lovebirds have the couch," he said.

Adam snorted. "So generous." He swept an arm out, inviting Maddy to sit. They settled with her close enough to smell his personal mixture of horses and aftershave. That was her favorite scent these days, and she took glorious breaths as she gazed around.

The furniture wasn't new—wood and worn brown leather, with blankets here and there—but was still comfortable. The room was dominated by a large stone fireplace rising up two stories, and Maddy couldn't take her eyes off it.

"Pretty impressive, huh?" Adam murmured in her ear. "Especially when you realize it was built a hundred and fifty years ago. The original Grandpa Black had a wife with a sense of grandeur."

"I'll say. And you're lucky she did."

While she was admiring the fireplace and browsing the books and pictures scattered around, Micah fiddled with his laptop and the settings on the wide-screen TV. Finally, a chime sounded and Micah clicked to connect.

Seth's face filled the screen. Dusty forehead, bright eyes, wide grin, and then a well-worn camo t-shirt. "Hey, guys! Great to see you!"

Caleb and Micah started talking at once.

"You look good, man."

"Busy dodging bullets?"

Adam watched eagerly, but seemed to be waiting until things calmed down. Maddy snuck a glance at Samuel. The older man's eyes leaked tears as he soaked up the sight of his youngest son.

"Come on, Dad, we talked just last week," Seth said when he noticed. "You miss me that much?"

Samuel shook his head. "Just so glad to see you."

Adam reached over to pat his father's arm. "We're cool, Seth. Lots going on here, but nothing I can't email you about. What's the situation over there?"

Seth snorted. "Gimme a break—you know I can't talk about that. But..." he waggled his eyebrows. "Who's that pretty thing sitting next to you?"

Maddy blushed. She'd swear Adam blushed slightly, too.

"This is Maddy Ricciolino," he said. "She's our new accountant."

"And Adam's new girlfriend!" Caleb shouted.

Seth slapped his forehead dramatically and gasped. "Adam has a girlfriend? A certain hot spot must have frozen over!"

Adam growled. "Watch it, Seth. You'll be home someday, and I have a long memory."

"Yeah, but you—you hardly ever date! I'm going to have to adjust my perception of my big brother. Like, totally upside down." He looked at Maddy. "All kidding aside, it's nice to meet you. How'd you ever rope Adam into a date? Because I *know* he'd never ask a girl himself."

"Actually, he did," Maddy said. "Although only after he'd yelled at me for my daughter going into a pasture—"

"A *bull* pasture," Adam interrupted.

"And after weeks of saying as little to each other as possible as we worked," Maddy finished with a grin.

"You have a daughter?" Seth was almost bouncing in his chair. "Kids at Black Rock Ranch—who woulda thunk? Maybe we'll get little Jacob here eventually and round it off. Whaddya think, Micah?"

Micah just scowled.

"If you guys are done with the dating and family stuff, I have a sweet little filly I want to tell you about," Caleb said.

"Me first," Samuel piped up. "You're safe, son? Still doing construction stuff?"

Seth nodded. "We patrol, but this town is pretty secure. And we've almost finished six classrooms. This kid named Aziz keeps challenging me in a soccer scoring match. And whomping me." He talked about the kids he'd met and some of the Iraqi men he was working with on the school. "Good people. It feels great to be helping."

Samuel spoke again. "Any idea when you're getting some leave? Enough to come home?"

Seth shrugged. "You never know. Maybe in a few months.

Man, I can't wait to get on a horse again. You should have seen me trying to use a clothesline to show kids how to rope!"

Sitting close on the couch, Maddy snuggled into Adam while the family talked for another fifteen minutes. She liked seeing them together like this, at least as much together as they could manage right now. They were all good people.

And Adam, the responsible, detail-oriented oldest brother who smelled so delicious, was the best of the bunch as far as she was concerned. Not that she was biased or anything, but she could spend a lot of time nestled under his arm.

"I LIKE SETH," Maddy said as they walked back to the Admin building.

"He really is a great kid." Adam slung his arm around her shoulders.

"Not a kid anymore—I think he's been through a lot. And those were some impressive muscles I saw on him."

Adam arched an eyebrow. "Oh? Better than mine?" He lifted his other arm and flexed.

Maddy elbowed him. "I'm going to guess that Seth works out with some hefty weights. But you know I love your arms. And shoulders. Ranch work has given you a pretty impressive set yourself."

"Impressive enough to let me put them around you and steal a kiss?"

Delight spiraled up inside her, and she lifted her face.

Adam lowered his head to hers and kissed her lightly, then deeper. She sank into it—every bit as wondrous as the other night. His arms carried a solid, secure weight that she treasured. She pulled back after a moment, then leaned in and rested her cheek against his. There was something oh-so-intimate about having her cheek touching his, and she soaked it in.

He pulled back with a smile and traced her lips with a gentle finger. Then dipped his head to kiss her again.

His cell phone interrupted them, and he stepped back to answer. A look of concern crossed his face. He ended the call and took her hand to walk the rest of the way to their offices.

"Problems?" Maddy asked.

"Nothing I can't handle. The Lazy S is bringing up an old boundary dispute."

He dropped her at her office door. "I'll see you tomorrow —this will probably take the rest of the day."

Maddy kissed him goodbye and settled at her desk again. Spreadsheets looked incredibly boring all of a sudden. The problem with falling in love with your boss is that you wanted to spend all your time with him instead of doing your work.

On the other hand, spending a few minutes kissing this incredibly handsome cowboy should be at the top of her to-do list every day.

24

Springtime had come to Black Rock Ranch in all its glory. Lupine spread white and purple blooms in wide swaths, and calves frolicked in the pastures. Adam could stand on the front porch, inhale the sweet, mild air, and bask in the moment forever.

At least he would, if he weren't tied to the desk so much. Calving season had been replaced by breeding plans, solar well development, pasture rotation calculations, and the still-mysterious embezzlement of Mrs. Evans.

On the other hand, the week had been filled with amazing moments. First, the time with Seth—he knew how lucky they were to be in communication at all. And then some stolen moments with Maddy, just as precious since there always seemed to be someone else around.

Now Adam heard unexpected voices in the equipment shed. He entered to find Micah hunkered down by a tractor's tire, Maddy looking over his shoulder, and two small hands holding a socket wrench.

"I can't get it," came Mia's voice.

Adam shifted so he could see better. Mia knelt between Micah and the tire, trying to position the socket over the lug nut.

Micah reached forward and nudged it into place.

Mia looked up at him with a grin. "Thanks, Mr. Micah!" Then she pulled the handle, ratcheted it back, and pulled it again. When all her small strength wouldn't budge it anymore, Micah covered her hand with his and pulled.

"There, all done," said Micah.

"We did it! We did it!" Mia shouted.

Adam grinned at Mia's delight. Maddy turned, saw him, and motioned him over. He flushed, but there was nothing better than a joyful family and a good woman to share it with.

He slipped an arm around her shoulder and bent his head to breathe in her sweet-smelling hair. "You're coming over for dinner tonight, right?"

She leaned into him. "Tonight? Gee, I'm not sure. I'll have to check my calendar."

Adam chuckled. "Your calendar, huh? The one that has *Adam* written on each day in big, bold letters?"

"Yeah, that one. But you realize that there's a lot of white space left, and you never know when something might come up."

"Right." He kissed the top of her head. "You let me know if it does. Otherwise, family dinner tonight. And maybe a walk afterward, if I'm still awake."

"Oh, I'll make sure you're awake, cowboy." Maddy looked up at him, her eyes filled with starry light.

My oh my, this woman could make anything seem possible.

• • •

DINNER THAT NIGHT started out beautifully. Adam's favorite, most tender roast, thick gravy, mashed potatoes, and those long, French green beans that Uncle Dirt did something fancy with.

"I just like experimenting," the old man said. "You never know, I might experiment my way into a million bucks."

"It's scrumpdillyicious, Uncle Dirt," Mia said.

Adam smiled at the swipe of gravy that lingered on the little girl's chin until Maddy wiped it off. "Manners, Mia," said his favorite single mom.

Adam passed her another napkin, catching Caleb's frowning glance along the way. He raised his eyebrows in question—did Caleb think he should stay hands-off with Mia?

Caleb just shook his head and took another bite. But he still had a funny look on his face.

They chatted through dinner—hay crops, horses in training, typical ranch stuff. They also teased Lacey.

"You still seeing What's His Name?" Dad asked.

"Which one?" Caleb laughed. "Gavin or Tyler?"

Lacey blushed. "Actually, Julio."

"Julio Esteban?" Caleb teased. "A bit out of your league?"

"Hey!" Adam elbowed him. "Give your sister some credit. Maybe Lacey is out of *his* league!"

"At least he comes from a ranching family," Micah said.

"Micah! I'm not going to marry him or anything," Lacey protested. "We're just going out."

"I thought you were dating Tyler?" Dad said, a little late.

There was a moment of awkward silence, then Caleb said, "Gotta keep up with the conversation, Dad."

While their father looked confused, Uncle Dirt stood. "If you'll excuse me, this little filly of yours and I have a special concoction for you to try."

Lacey followed him out. They returned quickly, Lacey proudly carrying a cake smothered in white coconut frosting.

"You made this?"

"Wow, Lacey!"

She beamed a smile that shone through the roof. "We spent all yesterday evening on it," she said.

"What?" Caleb cried. "There was cake last night, and we didn't know?"

"We've been practicing decorating techniques," Maddy whispered to Adam. Then she turned to Lacey. "So have you decided between being a chef or a rancher for a career?"

"Or a vet?" Adam added.

"Or a nurse?" Dad said.

Lacey ignored them until she had the cake triumphantly sliced and sitting in front of each of them. "I don't know. I want to be all those things. But I still have a year before college, so I don't have to decide yet."

Adam couldn't understand giving up all they had here to do something like cook or work in a hospital. How could she not want to be a rancher, or at least a vet?

His brothers teased her some more before the companionable talk turned back to ranch business. Until Lacey innocently said, "It's too bad about Mrs. Evans. She seemed so nice."

Adam froze. He'd only told Dad, wasn't going to tell anyone else until he knew the total damage.

"Mrs. Evans?" his father asked. "What's going on with Mrs. Evans?"

"I told you, Dad, remember? And how did you find out, Lacey?" Adam kept his voice even.

Lacey's eyes were wide as she looked at their father. "Dad told me, but how come he doesn't remember now?"

"I'll catch you up later," Adam said quietly.

"Would somebody please explain what you're talking about," Caleb growled. "Mrs. Evans?"

Adam sighed. "Maddy found some discrepancies, so we've started going through the accounts for the last year. It looks like Mrs. Evans was writing checks for more than we owed, and skimming the extra for herself."

Dad frowned. "Oh yes, that's right. And I'm sorry. I guess I shouldn't have turned it all over to her. It was just more efficient. And she seemed so honest."

Adam kept his frustration controlled, although it wasn't easy. If everyone would be upright and have integrity in everything they did, they wouldn't have to worry about sneaking around or keeping their lies straight, and they could be proud of who they were. And the rest of them could get on with a nice, straightforward life.

Honesty had been part of his family's code as long as he could remember, but sometimes they got sucked into problems. Amber, Adam's last real girlfriend, had spun him a story of how her grandfather had left her an inheritance, which was why she could afford nice things when her family really couldn't. When she got arrested for theft and forgery, she spun more stories to the police, eventually tangling her lies and including Adam.

He'd been shocked by her revelations, although it wasn't hard to show the police the truth and clear his own name. He still wondered why she couldn't have been happy being the daughter of a local butcher. Adam shook his head to clear it—it had been a few years now and shouldn't bother him anymore. Really, it shouldn't. He slowly tuned back into the conversation.

"Are we in trouble? Can you tell if it's a lot or a little yet?" Caleb was asking.

"About fifteen hundred, so far," Maddy said.

Caleb sat back. "Not horrible, but…dang."

"I'm actually hoping it gets to two thousand," Adam grumbled, despite himself. "That would make it a felony when we turn it over to the cops."

The room was silent for a few moments, then Micah spoke up again. "Any idea why she did it?"

Maddy answered. "We think it might have started with Christmas presents or something and then expanded from there. Retirement, maybe?"

"The why doesn't matter, just the what," Adam said. "You steal, you pay the price."

Micah gave him a long look. "Old Testament justice, huh?"

Adam shrugged. "It is what it is." He knew they didn't truly understand the impact, but it was simple. Order was necessary.

Dad disagreed, though. "Let's find out a little more before we judge her so harshly," he said, back in the conversation as if he'd never checked out. "You're always talking about how much technology can do, Adam. Why don't you see if you can find out what she's doing now? See if that gives us any clues."

Adam closed his eyes briefly, biting back the sarcastic comment that wanted to come out. He wiped his mouth and stood. "I'll do that, Dad. And it's my turn to check the cows." He gave Maddy a peck on the cheek, tousled Mia's hair, and headed out for some clear air where he didn't have to pretend to be soft and understanding.

25

After Adam's talk about integrity and lying during Friday's dinner, Maddy was more glad than ever that she'd already told him her story. He might be angry with people like Mrs. Evans, but Maddy was immensely grateful he'd understood her own need. She'd seen him clench his jaw in frustration too many times, and it was a relief to know that he made allowances for circumstances.

It was funny how well she could read him already. He had such depth in his eyes, and she could tell his mood from whether they seemed more emerald or olive. Of course, plenty of soft kisses and time gazing into those inviting eyes helped. Even if it had to be in quick snatches because someone always wanted him for something.

Maddy smiled at the thought and checked the clock in her quiet office. Sure enough, Adam knocked on her open door, then took his cowboy hat off and rubbed his hair.

"Long morning?" she asked, saving her work on the computer.

"Nothing that can't be made easier by the sight of you," he said with a smile.

"Great pick-up line, cowboy, except you don't need one." She took his hand and walked with him through the warm sunshine for Seth's Tuesday Skype call.

Inside, Samuel clapped one hand on her shoulder. "Good to have you here, Missy."

The banter between the brothers carried on—Caleb's hot date Saturday night, Micah talking to his tractors, and Adam and Maddy came in for some teasing. Maddy settled in, letting her mind wander to how she might send a message to her family. Maybe she didn't miss them as much now that she was involved with Adam, but they'd still want to know how she was. And despite having a new cell number and email address, she didn't want to go that route. Mr. Wilkins wouldn't like it, either.

Preoccupied as she was, Maddy didn't notice the growing tension in the room until twelve-thirty. Samuel was staring at the empty fireplace. Adam flipped a pencil through his fingers. And Caleb would tell a joke and then trail off through the punch line.

"What?" she asked. "What's wrong?"

Samuel began to answer, then hunched his shoulders and turned away.

Adam stilled his pencil and spoke. "Seth's usually connected by now. And he didn't send any emails to reschedule."

"Which means?" Maddy put her hand on Adam's back and rubbed gently.

"Which means he's probably out on patrol," Micah said. "And no one can tell us anything about it."

"Oh," was all Maddy could say. To not know how dangerous it was, or when he would be expected back...the family didn't even know when it would be time to worry. So the worry started now.

"Someone could at least tell us if he's around but busy," Caleb said, standing. He brushed his hands down his jeans. "I'm going to email Captain Carter."

Maddy turned to Adam. "Will the captain tell him anything?"

Adam shrugged. "If Seth is around, we'll probably hear from him first. If not, then all the captain can say is that he can't say anything."

Nobody else moved, though. Maddy wondered how long they would wait to see if Seth came on, but she wasn't going to ask out loud. All she could do was squeeze Adam's hand and wait with them.

Thirty minutes of brooding silence later, Caleb returned, grumbling and shaking his head. "Still no answer."

Adam sighed and got to his feet, pulling Maddy with him. "He's probably just on a local patrol. Let's try checking in tomorrow. Maybe earlier."

Caleb shrugged.

Adam glanced at Maddy, then said, "You ever get that other creep feeder done?"

She supposed he was just trying to change the subject, but Caleb glared at him. "Sure. What's it to you?"

"Just checking."

Caleb came closer. "That's what you like to do, isn't it? Check on everybody about everything. Like you can't trust anyone else to do their work."

"I do not," Adam huffed. "I just didn't know if we'd need to order more lumber."

Maddy stepped back as Caleb came within three inches of Adam's face. "If I needed more lumber, I would have ordered it. I don't need you telling me how high to jump."

Adam worked his jaw, obviously biting back some words. "I need to make sure this ranch runs smoothly. And if that means checking on people and projects, that's what I'll do. Whether you like it or not."

Maddy looked at the others. Micah was staring at his brothers, his mouth hanging open. Samuel looked back and forth between the two, but he seemed confused about the conflict in front of him.

Caleb poked Adam in the chest. "You're not the boss. You—"

"That's enough!" Maddy scolded, coming as close as her nerves would let her. "You guys are both stressed out about Seth, but you don't need to take it out on each other."

Caleb crossed his arms. "I'm just saying things I've wanted to for a long time. Adam needs to get down off his high horse so the rest of us can breathe."

Adam glared, but kept his jaw clenched shut. His fists clenched as well, his hands raised a bit. Just ready for a fight.

"Come on, Adam," Maddy said. "We're going back to work." She reminded herself that Adam was not Brock, that fist fights were not his normal way of solving problems. She ignored the brothers' tight fists and the knot in her stomach, and tugged Adam toward the door. "You guys will let us know if Seth calls, right?"

Micah met her eyes. "Definitely."

"Is Seth calling today?" Samuel asked.

Maddy had wondered before if something was going on with Samuel, but the confusion on his face now made it obvious. She had other concerns right now, though.

ADAM KEPT a lid on his temper while Maddy dragged him away. Across the yard, through the admin building, back to his office, where she was likely to read him the riot act.

Instead, she hugged him.

Little thing that Maddy was, it was amazing how much strength there was in her hug. Or how much strength he could receive from her hug.

He held her for a long time, her hands meeting around his back, her head on his chest. He rested his cheek in the curls on top of her head, blowing softly if one got too close to his mouth.

When Adam's heart rate finally slowed and his breathing became more regular, he pulled her around to his desk chair. He sat, tugged gently on her hand, and she settled comfortably in his lap.

He pulled her head close again. "Thank you," he murmured.

She looked up at him, a soft smile on that beautiful face. "Anytime, cowboy. But I sure hope that doesn't happen often"

He shook his head. "Hardly ever. I have to say I was surprised at Caleb. His accusation."

Maddy was quiet for a long moment, then she tapped her hand on his chest, a steady rhythm that anchored him. "Now that you're calm and hopefully thinking clearly, could there be any truth to what he said?"

"No, of course not. I know they can all do their jobs." But a voice in his mind said, *Then why don't you let them do it?*

The thought took him aback. He *did* let them do it. Didn't he? Caleb was just prickly about him checking on things.

Wouldn't you be prickly, too?

He tried to picture Caleb or Micah questioning him about renewing leases or making sure he got payroll out. They had discussed the solar wells and the new cross-fencing as a family, but Adam had pretty much taken the lead, told them what he wanted to do and why, and that was that.

If they came back with major concerns, of course he would listen. But if they were constantly checking to see who he had contacted about it or if he had ordered the materials... just how prickly would he get?

"Huh," he said aloud. "Maybe Caleb has a point."

Maddy's hand stilled, but she didn't look up. "You like to make sure everything will run smoothly," she said. "Being in control is part of who you are, I think."

"Maybe," he said. "I wouldn't say I'm a control freak—"

Maddy snorted.

"What? I wouldn't!" He let his hand play with her hair. "But yeah, I figure if I can see problems coming, maybe I can solve them before they get too far out of hand."

Maddy sat up with a gleam in her eye. "Head them off at the pass?"

Adam groaned dramatically. "Somebody's been watching too many old westerns."

He kissed her gently, amazed that a woman like her would be nestled in his arms right now. "Thank you again. Not just for in there, but here, calming me down, helping me think."

"Anytime, cowboy." She kissed him back, smoothing the back of her hand across his hair.

A moment later, his cheek still resting on the top of her head, Maddy shifted. "Adam? What's going on with your dad?"

He drew in a deep breath and let it out slowly. "I'm not sure. He'd like to convince himself it's normal aging, but he's definitely having memory issues."

She looked up at him. "Alzheimer's?"

"I hope not. But we have a doctor's appointment in the city tomorrow."

Maddy traced a pattern on the back of his shirt, then tipped her head up. "If you're going to Grand Junction, could you mail a postcard for me?"

Adam stiffened. "You're going to let someone know where you are?"

She shook her head adamantly. "No, just that I'm all right. And that's why I want you to mail it from down there —it can't be traced to Beaver Falls that way."

True. It would take a lot for someone to start in Grand Junction and find them way out at the ranch. Even Beaver Falls wasn't that close. "I guess I can do that."

"Thanks, cowboy." She snuggled in again.

He held her close, thinking of all the complications going on right now. Her problem with her ex, his dealings with the Lazy S, the leads he'd found on Mrs. Evans, trying new technology on the ranch, worries about Dad.

He sighed again, kissed her hair, and finally pulled away. There was still work to be done, and maybe it would take his mind off everything else.

"Come on, Dad, let's get this over with." Adam watched his father straighten his bolo tie and take one last swipe at his hair. What would he do if the doctor gave them the worst news?

"I'm coming, I'm coming," Dad said. "Old Doc Baker won't mind if we're a few minutes late."

"I'm sure he wouldn't," Adam said, ushering his father out the door. "But he's on vacation this week. And I figured since he wasn't around, we'd go into Grand Junction and see someone who specializes in people your age."

"Who? I don't want to see anyone else. Doc Baker knows me, even if I haven't seen him in ten years. This new guy better be good."

Adam prepared himself for the explosion. "It's a new gal, not a new guy. Dr. Susan Jacobs."

Dad whipped his head around. "A woman? No way. Nunh-huh. I'm not seeing no woman doctor about my private life."

"Dad, come on. It's not like you're going to have to strip

for a full physical." He motioned to the open truck door. "I'm sure she'll listen to your heart and take your blood pressure, and then just ask questions."

His father glared. "Oh, so now this is a quiz?"

Adam let out a long sigh, wishing Maddy were with them. She seemed to have a calming influence on everyone. "Dad, look. Something's wrong. You know it, I know it, and the good Lord knows it. So let's go find out what it is."

The old man's face froze in a grimace. He climbed into the truck, waving off Adam's hand of help.

Adam tried to make small talk on the hour-long drive, but Dad kept his stony silence.

They parked in front of the medical center. The foyer was deceptively inviting, and then it was the elevator and hallways until they reached the doctor's office. Adam's father remained quiet, but his face grew paler and tighter the closer they got.

Adam sent a prayer heavenward for strength and courage. *And if possible, Lord, for an easy answer to all this. Something we can cope with.*

Dad glared the whole time the cheery young nurse was taking his temperature and blood pressure. And then they waited.

Dr. Jacobs, when she finally arrived, was older than Adam and younger than his father. Her red hair showed a hint of gray and was almost as curly as Maddy's. She entered with an air of competence and a compassionate face.

"Hi, I'm Susan Jacobs," she said, extending her hand to each of them. "You must be Samuel Black, and you're…"

"Adam Black. His son."

"I'm glad you're here." Her smile was kind, and if his father didn't react, Adam's own tension eased a bit. She sat on a stool and studied her iPad for a moment.

"I understand you're having some memory problems," she

said. "It looks like you haven't seen Dr. Baker for some time. Why don't you tell me what's been happening?"

Dad looked at his hands, then his boots. "Can't remember names," he mumbled.

Dr. Jacobs scooted a little closer. "That happens to all of us, and is rather common once we get older," she assured him. "There are a lot of things that can cause memory issues, some of them relatively simple to fix, some of them not."

Dad mumbled something.

"I'm sorry?" Dr. Jacobs said.

"I said it's the 'not' that worries me," Dad said.

Adam put a hand on his arm. The connection seemed to help both of them.

Dr. Jacobs leaned closer, an intent look on her face. "I know memory problems automatically make people think of Alzheimer's or something similar, and those are frightening things. But perhaps there's another physical reason for the problems—there are several possibilities. And even if we end up with a dementia diagnosis, it's far better to know early than late. Right?"

Dad looked at the wall, but Adam latched onto her comment about other physical reasons. "What other things could cause this?"

Dr. Jacobs shook her head. "Let's check everything out, first."

A brain tumor flashed through Adam's mind. That would be even worse—was that why she wasn't getting specific?

But Dr. Jacobs had continued. "Mr. Black, besides forgetting names, what other problems have you had?"

Dad looked back down. "I go someplace to do something, and when I get there, I can't remember what I came for. More than the usual."

Adam spoke up. "A few weeks ago, he wrote a check for

a large bill, not remembering that we had made the payment in February. And then we were waiting to Skype with my brother in Iraq, and Dad forgot why we were there. Even though he was the one to remind us in the morning."

Dad's face turned red with embarrassment, but Dr. Jacobs nodded. "When did this start? Has it gotten worse lately?"

Dad shrugged, but Adam said, "I started noticing things about six months ago, but it's gotten worse."

The doctor nodded. "Do you get confused in the middle of a sentence or a conversation, Mr. Black?"

Dad shrugged again, but Adam thought back. There had been family times when his father had looked confused, and more times when he'd trailed off in the middle of a sentence. He told Dr. Jacobs.

"Do you ever leave something on the stove and forget it?"

Dad shook his head. "Don't cook anything."

"What about getting lost when you drive somewhere?"

"We're ranchers," Adam said. "There are three of us boys helping run things, plus ranch hands. It's usually someone else who runs errands."

Dad looked at Adam. "I took Cobbler out the other day, got an idea I should check the water levels up on the south range. And...and..."

"And you couldn't get home?" Adam tried to keep the worry out of his voice.

Dad's chin trembled. "I couldn't even find the pond. I've been riding up there for more'n fifty years, and I couldn't find the blasted pond!"

Dr. Jacobs broke the silence after a moment. "Tell me about your eating. Any changes in appetite? Or in what you eat?"

"Just regular stuff. Uncle Dirt does the food for all of us."

She raised her eyebrows at the name, but kept on with her questions. "What about sleeping? Any changes there?"

Dad's face brightened. "Yes! And that's what I figured this was from. It takes longer to fall asleep, but the main problem is…" He blushed. "Is all the times I have to get up in the night to use the bathroom."

Dr. Jacobs smiled. "That's pretty normal for a man of your age. Do you get back to sleep afterwards?"

Dad shook his head. "Not hardly a wink until sunrise. And then when I *should* be getting up, I sort of crash into sleep. Had to start setting an alarm."

Adam didn't have anything to say, just patted his father's arm in solidarity. Or comfort. Or something.

Dr. Jacobs made some notes. Finally, she spoke again. "We're going to do two quick mental exams. First, can you repeat these three things for me? Pencil. Car. Dog." She spoke each of them clearly.

Dad looked surprised. "Sure. Pencil, car, dog. What's with that?"

Dr. Jacobs just smiled and reached for a piece of paper. "Now I want you to draw a clock, and then put the hands to nine o'clock."

Adam watched, feeling like this was a kindergarten test that Mia would have no trouble passing. But when his father put two numbers wrong and had the minute hand showing nine-thirty, not nine straight up, he began to worry. *Please, God, no. Not that.*

Dad pushed the paper back to the doctor. "What's the big deal with a clock?"

Dr. Jacobs smiled. "Thank you, that was great. Now, what were those three items I had you repeat?"

"Uh, pencil…truck, no, car. And, um." Dad's face drew

tight as he concentrated. "Horse!" he finally called triumphantly.

"Good, thanks," Dr. Jacobs said.

"Good?" Adam was aghast. "That was good?"

His father gave him a puzzled look.

Dr. Jacobs turned to Adam. "Your dad did just fine. We need to assess where he's at before we know how to help."

The doctor spent the next twenty minutes asking simple questions about the date and season, where they were, and if he could repeat three words, followed by simple instructions like folding a paper and putting it on the floor, or counting backwards.

They talked some more, and then Dr. Jacobs said, "First, I think we need to get you some help for a decent night's sleep. Don't drink anything after eight p.m., and try some melatonin about half an hour before bed."

Dad turned to Adam. "See, I told you it was something easy."

Adam gave a half-smile. After those questions, he sensed that Dr. Jacobs wasn't done.

"I'd like to run some tests, though. Now, don't panic," she said as Dad blanched. "There are several physical issues that could cause memory problems—oxygen flow to the brain, a vitamin deficiency or even a previous stroke, in addition to the bigger issues like Alzheimer's. So let's find out about those first, shall we?"

Dad was silent, so Adam spoke. "Wouldn't we know if he'd had a stroke?"

"Not necessarily. TIAs—mini-strokes—especially can be silent. You might not know you had one except for the effects."

"Will tests show that up?"

Dr. Jacobs paused. "It won't show the stroke specifically, but if brain tissue is damaged, that will show in a MRI scan."

Dementia. Strokes. Permanent damage. Adam looked at his father, weather-beaten, worried, and the rock in Adam's life. *I can't do without him, Lord.*

Dr. Jacobs typed into her iPad, then looked up. "The lab requests will be waiting at the front desk for you. I'd like to see you back when those results are in." She stood, and the Black men stood with her. "It's been nice to meet you. Try not to worry too much."

"Thanks, Doctor," Adam said. "We appreciate it."

They went across the hall to the lab for the first of Dad's tests. Nine small vials of blood later, they headed back to the truck. Adam still felt the weight of the possibilities, but Dad's steps were much lighter. "See, I told you it wasn't anything to worry about! I probably just need more vitamins."

Adam nodded, not able to speak. Not after watching Dad's failure with a simple clock drawing. The only words he could get out were silent ones for the Lord. *Please, God, give us the strength to get through this. Help me be able to help Dad. And please, please, I know You know best. But if it's possible with Your will, could You please make it an oxygen problem, not Alzheimer's?*

27

With his dad settled in his living room recliner, Adam waited for the scheduler to call. He had the breeding schedule to figure out and a new study on pasture fertilization he should read, but he couldn't concentrate.

Would he need a power of attorney? It should be written while Dad was still competent. Or would Dad just sign the ranch over to the brothers completely? Or would he refuse to do anything?

Adam picked up a trophy on the desk, a crystal bull from winning Grand Champion a few years ago. He turned it over in his hands. Wished it were a crystal ball.

He hated to think of what Dad would become if he didn't have the ranch to run. What would he do with his time? Even just riding out, he'd have to have someone with him so he wouldn't get lost. Would one of the brothers do that? A ranch hand? Would they hire someone?

Adam put the crystal bull down, sat at his desk, and pulled the research article toward him. Fifteen seconds later, he was up and pacing again.

"Adam?" Maddy poked her head in. "Are you okay?"

He looked at her, this lovely woman with her own load of troubles. He didn't want to pile more on top of them, and it wasn't like she could do anything to help anyway.

"No, I'm fine," he said. "Just need to think."

"Okay," she said cheerfully. "Let me know if you want to talk it out. I've got another hour before Mia gets off the bus."

She left, and Adam strode back to his desk. He flipped to a clean sheet of paper in his notepad and started writing, bold strokes slashing across the page. *1. If Alzheimer's: A) Research treatments and therapies. B) Start looking for someone to be a companion. 2. If stroke: A) What changes to prevent more? B) Therapy to recover brain function. 3. If heart/oxygen-related A) meet with cardiologist...*

Just writing steps down put Adam back in control. If he could see a plan to deal with whatever outcome, they could get through this. They'd need outside help—the three brothers would have an extra load picking up Dad's work anyway. They could help with his care, but couldn't afford for any of them to give up ranch work.

His brothers. He needed to let them know what that appointment was like, the problems their father had doing simple tasks. But it was hard to think of sharing the burden if he didn't know the right direction to go.

Adam spent the next twenty minutes making notes and writing questions. The scheduler finally called and set his dad's MRI and other tests for Friday. Two days to wait, and then however long to get answers.

He leaned back in his chair, ran his hand through his hair and realized he really needed a haircut. He'd been too busy with his dad—and Maddy—to think about it. Ah, well, courting Maddy was worth looking messy a bit longer. But now he needed to gather his brothers.

He found Micah in the equipment shed, with Maddy and Mia watching him do something to one of the four wheelers. Just the sight of Maddy put a smile on his face. Probably eased some worry lines as well.

"You going to be here a while, Micah?" Adam asked.

Micah paused his wrench-turning. "Maybe another hour."

Adam nodded. "I'll go get Caleb—we need to talk."

He had to wait for his other younger brother to finish putting a well-muscled buckskin back in the pasture, but they were soon gathered in the equipment shed.

Maddy smiled at him, but turned to Mia and said, "Come on, kiddo. Let's leave them to their cowboy talk."

"No, stay," Adam said. "You probably ought to hear this too." He grasped her hand, grateful for the sense of security it gave him.

"We need to talk about Dad," he said, but he couldn't find the words to continue.

Caleb came to the rescue. "What did the doctor say? There's something to worry about?"

Adam nodded. "He...Dad couldn't...the doctor had him do some things, easy things, and he couldn't." He looked up at the rafters. "He just wasn't able, and she kept..."

His brothers just stared at him wide-eyed, but Maddy squeezed his hand and spoke up. "She, the doctor? She kept what, Adam?"

Adam closed his eyes, not feeling in control at all. "She kept saying he was doing fine, but he wasn't! He couldn't put the numbers around a clock right. He couldn't remember three words she'd told him earlier. He said...he said he's even gotten lost riding up to the pond!"

Maddy leaned into his shoulder. Micah leaned on the four-wheeler. Caleb didn't lean anywhere, just took a step back and said, "But that's, that's Alzheimer's. Dad can't have Alzheimer's."

"What's all-zimer?" came Mia's little voice.

"Shh," Maddy responded.

Adam told a deep breath. "Yeah, he can. It happens to people all the time. But she said it could also be some other things, anything from a vitamin deficiency to blood flow to the brain." Just speaking the alternatives aloud gave him a little control back. "She wants to run a bunch of tests. We did the lab work today, and the scheduler just called back. I'll take Dad back down on Friday for an MRI and some other stuff."

"Alzheimer's," Caleb repeated.

"Wait and see," Micah said.

Maddy looked up at him. "What can I do?"

Adam filled his senses with her warmth and caring. "Just be here. Be my anchor."

"What's an anchor, Mama?"

Adam smiled at her. "Something that keeps someone from just floating away in confusion. And your Mama's a very good anchor."

They talked a bit more, but it all came down to waiting.

EARLY FRIDAY MORNING, with twenty minutes before she needed to walk Mia to the school bus, Maddy set her concerns aside long enough to grin as she listened to her daughter. Mia was conducting an argument between Barbie and a triceratops. Barbie wanted to go to school with it, and the triceratops insisted that school was just for dinosaurs.

Her daughter was happy, the sky was as blue as she'd ever seen it, the sun was warming the cabin. Spring was here and summer on its way. *Thank you, Lord. And please be with Samuel and Adam through the tests and the results.*

She rummaged around in the freezer. Baking for therapy might be necessary sometimes, but baking for joy was delightful. By the time Adam and Samuel got back from all the tests, a triple-berry pie would be just the right reward for them. Even it it came from a bag of frozen berries.

She hummed as she mixed the berries with sugar and cornstarch. Barbie had won the school fight and was now making friends with a T-Rex. Maddy was rolling out the pie crust when her cell phone chimed.

"Maddy, I'm so sorry." Her sister's voice was high-pitched in panic. "I didn't—I can't—"

"Hold on, Sophie! Take a deep breath and start from the beginning." Maddy looked over to where Mia was now gathering dinosaurs and Barbies for recess.

"It's Brock. He knows where you are." Sophie gulped for air.

Maddy squeaked. "He has our address?"

"No, I don't think so. But he knows you're on a ranch, and he knows it's near Grand Junction. Mom knew that from the postmark on your letter. She—" Sophie sobbed, then tried again. "Mom was telling Mrs. Norris when they were having lunch yesterday—I've told her and told her she can't say anything, but I guess she forgot. And Brock's been following her. He was in the cafe already, and he got up and walked right past them. He even gave Mom a thumbs-up!"

Sophie wailed again, but Maddy was frozen in shock. There were plenty of towns between them and Grand Junction, plus a ton of ranches, but if Brock was so obsessed that he would stalk her mother, he wouldn't give up until he had checked every last ranch in southwest Colorado. She had to get out of here. She had to pack. She had to—

She couldn't even think. Couldn't swallow. Couldn't breathe.

She thought she'd run to the end of the earth, hidden here in the mountains, that even if Brock had found her online, he couldn't find her physically.

How could her mother have been so casual as to even tell her friend, let alone tell her in public? Didn't she realize the danger she'd put Maddy in?

The room closed in on her, the colors around her darkened. Her sister's babbling voice faded.

Breathe. She needed to breathe. She needed to keep it together for Mia's sake.

Maddy gasped, a smidge of air getting to her lungs. She closed her eyes and willed her body to relax, until she could draw one short breath, then another.

"Mama, what's wrong?" Mia's little voice held grown-up concern.

Maddy managed a longer breath and opened her eyes. "Come here, sweetheart," she said, opening her arm.

With Mia snuggled in, Maddy's chest relaxed and her heart rate began to slow. "I'll call you back," she said to the phone that was still in her hand.

She had to stay calm for Mia. She had to figure out what to do. She had to get herself together and make decisions. She needed to call Mr. Wilkins. She needed to tell Adam.

No, first she needed to pray.

Maddy settled both arms around Mia, ready to pray silently right there, but the child was done cuddling. "Mommy, recess is over for the dinosaurs," and she squirmed away.

Maddy glanced at the clock and managed a smile. "We need to leave in about five minutes, so it's time to clean up. I'll be in my bedroom for a little bit."

"OK, Mama." Mia moved her toys into her "classroom" instead of their toy bin, but Maddy wasn't going to fight it.

Her shaky legs got her to her bedside, where she dropped to her knees. *Dear God...* Her voice quavered. She took a deep breath and started again. *Dear God, please keep us safe. Please guide me and let me know what to do. I know You love us. I know all things are in Your hands. Please.*

She paused and waited for inspiration. Surely the Lord would point her in the right direction.

A warm peace filled her, a sense of God's arms around her, but no specific answers came. Did that mean they'd be safe if they stayed? Or was she just supposed to wait for an answer? She loved the feeling and was grateful He'd sent it, but she wasn't very good at waiting for His timing.

She sighed and stood. She kept the prayer in her heart, but she also knew that if she had no specific answers, that she needed to do the best she could and trust God to tell her if she was on the wrong path.

And that was the question, now that she was calm enough to think. What was the right path? Stay? Or start looking for somewhere else?

28

Late Friday morning, Adam paced the radiology waiting room while his father was getting an MRI. An hour in a noisy tube—Dad wouldn't be in a great mood when he came out.

He wasn't sure exactly what it would tell. A brain tumor would obviously show up. And Dr. Jacobs had said something about blood flow, so he supposed it would tell what parts of Dad's brain were working well. But an "easy" test like an MRI still wouldn't show Alzheimer's. His research had told him that the only 100% way of diagnosing it was looking at the brain tissue itself—after you were dead.

When Adam had memorized the magazines at one end of the room and the poster at the other and knew there were exactly twenty-six steps from wall to wall, he told the nurse he was going out to the main corridor.

She looked relieved.

How did anybody get through the waiting and the uncertainty, especially alone? He wished Maddy were there with him—she'd know how to distract him. She'd ask what

Micah was fixing, how Caleb's two-year-olds were doing, when they were going to brand the last set of calves.

She'd talk to him about the wells and cross-fencing, and the difference they would make. She'd listen patiently while he talked about soil tests and fertilizing the fields, or how they would know when it was time for the first cutting of hay.

Actually, it was amazing how much Maddy had absorbed since she came to the ranch. Adam tipped his hat back and rubbed his eyes. Was it really only a month and a half since she'd arrived?

So little time to account for such a big change in his life. He wished he could spend all his time focusing on her without the specter of Alzheimer's hanging over their heads.

He wanted to know what her favorite flower was, if she ever pulled April Fool's pranks, if she liked to dance. What had her dreams been in high school, even college, and was she living them? Well, other than a failed marriage—that wouldn't be in anyone's dream life. What were her dreams and goals now? Could she settle into ranch life forever, or would she head back to the city eventually?

A nurse opened the door and escorted his father to him. He looked pale and worn. "Do you know where you go next?" she asked.

Samuel looked expectantly at Adam.

"Yes, cardiology," Adam said.

The nurse gave them directions, and Adam guided his father through the multitude of corridors to the next set of tests.

Drained of energy, Adam parked the truck near the house and helped his father out. Compared to Adam's tiredness, Dad seemed exhausted. His face was drawn, and he'd had his eyes shut for most of the trip.

"Dad, you're back!" Lacey cried, greeting them at the porch. "How was it?"

"I think I'll just sit for a spell," Dad said. "My age is catching up to me." He kissed Lacey on the cheek and headed for the living room. "You call me if you need anything," he told Adam.

"Will do." What he wouldn't give to help his father past this, whatever *this* turned out to be.

Lacey gave him a worried look. "Is he going to be okay?"

Adam shrugged. "I hope so. Mostly, he's just tired. It's been a long day."

"At least you didn't have to try to do algebra while you worried about him—school was hard." Then she shrugged. "I'll stay with him while you go tell the others."

Adam nodded his thanks and trotted back down the steps. What he'd really like to do was go hold Maddy in his arms. But she'd be getting Mia settled after school, and he needed to check in with his brothers, so he wandered over to the stables for feeding time. He gave Mister an extra handful of oats and a behind-the-ear scratch, then went to help Caleb and Wes take grain out for the mares and foals.

"Creep feeder looks good," Adam remarked.

It was true—the trough had been sanded and repaired, and two new horizontal poles replaced the old, worn ones. The whole setup let the foals under for their extra feed and kept the mares out.

Caleb was on edge, though. "Why wouldn't it?" He gave him a look. "Don't you think I can take care of things over here?"

Adam was too tired for this. "Not at all, just saying 'good job.' No need to be so touchy."

Caleb huffed. "You do have a tendency to boss the rest of us around, you know."

Adam snorted, but he kept his defensive hackles down. "Yeah, probably. Comes with the territory, I think."

Caleb leaned a shoulder against the fence. "And what territory would that be? The oldest brother kind, or the second-in-command kind? Or could it be the I-have-to-be-in-control kind?"

"I don't always have to be in control," Adam protested wearily. "But there are a lot of working parts to this ranch, some of which I had no idea about until I started helping Dad more."

It was Caleb's turn to snort. "Tell yourself that if you want, Bro, but you were a control-freak when you were a teenager, too."

"Only compared to you. Some of your escapades about got you killed."

Caleb rolled his eyes. "Better than being a buttoned-up, old-before-your-time big brother who never knew how to have fun."

"I knew how to have fun. It wasn't your version, but it was fun."

"Hah! You couldn't ask a girl to dance if your life depended on it. You probably still can't, not even Maddy."

Adam sighed. He hadn't come out here to pick a fight with his brother, and that last comment had hit home. Caleb went dancing on a regular basis. Micah had too, until he and Selena had a baby. And Seth was driven to prove himself, which drew the girls to him big time.

So Adam hadn't dated much. And he hadn't taken Maddy out much at all—no movies, no dinners, no antique shopping or whatever girls liked to do these days. But what was he supposed to do about that? He had far more on his plate than his brothers did.

"Look," he finally said. "I came out to talk to you about Dad. We need a plan to manage his care, and—"

"We don't even know what that will take yet, Adam! How can we plan anything until we have a diagnosis?"

"I know, but we'll do better…" He stopped to correct himself. "*I* will do better if we have some ideas laid out. For one thing, we can figure out how to lighten his workload. Can we talk about it tonight?"

Caleb gazed over the mares, licking the last of the grain from their tubs, and the foals, who were still eating happily away in the creep feeder, safe from their mothers scarfing up their food. "I guess. But you'd better bring Maddy, too. You guys are getting serious and she needs to know what she's getting into."

Serious? They'd been a couple for a whole two weeks. Were they really getting serious?

Even without real dates, Adam didn't need to think long to know the answer: yes.

29

Maddy had spent the day praying. Working too, but always with a prayer in her heart or on her lips. Especially when Brock's angry face pushed into her mind. She had called Mr. Wilkins, who had called the Denver police, who had said they would "check on Mr. Johnston's whereabouts."

That gave little comfort, but her work and God's peace had still settled her. She didn't know how things would turn out, just that God knew her situation. She needed to deal with it however she could and trust Him to do the rest.

With His help, she set thoughts of Brock aside and got back to work, stopping now and then to say a special prayer for Samuel and Adam. Samuel's situation left her feeling completely helpless, sitting on the sidelines while someone she'd grown to care about dealt with a possibly serious issue, but she could always pray.

Maddy counted her blessings once more as Mia got off the bus. She wouldn't be able to spend as much time with her daughter if this were a full-time job.

The two of them watered their flowers in the hot sun—it was nearly eighty degrees today—and splashed each other with the hose. Mia showed off her somersaults, and Maddy read some funny Shel Silverstein poems to her. *Ickle Me, Pickle Me, Tickle Me too!*

They were still giggling over that one when Adam showed up. He walked slowly, and when he smiled at Maddy, it was with a tired face.

"Long day?" she asked, standing and brushing her shorts off.

Adam took her hands and leaned in for a kiss. "Like you wouldn't believe. And hey, kiddo, how are you?" He reached down and tousled Mia's hair.

"Want to see me do a somersault?" she urged.

"Sure. How about under that tree?"

He put his arm around Maddy, and they stood close while they watched Mia perform. Over and over and over.

"Want to talk about it?" Maddy asked softly.

"Not much to tell yet. Lots of tests, lots of waiting, and no answers yet," he said. He drew a deep breath and let it out. "We're going to talk about possibilities at dinner tonight."

"But you don't know anything," Maddy reminded him.

Adam sighed. "No, but I don't want us to be blindsided, either. It would be nice to have an idea of what to do for each possibility. And…" He paused to kiss her hair. "I'd like you to be there."

"Me? But this is a family thing." Maddy was comfortable around all of them, but still…

"Mm-hmm, I know," was all Adam said.

Mia came running up. "Were you watching? Did you see?"

"I counted *twelve*," Maddy said.

"You're a pretty good somersault-er," Adam added. "I think that calls for an Uncle Dirt-cooked dinner, don't you?"

"Yes!" Mia shouted, before dashing into the cabin.

Maddy waited until the door slammed, then pulled Adam over to lean on the porch railing. "It's been a long day for me, too," she began. "I don't think I've stopped praying since this morning."

"Thank you, that means a lot," Adam said.

She shook her head. "Well, for Samuel too, but mostly… Brock knows the general area I'm in. That postcard you mailed for me from Grand Junction? Mom actually told a friend of hers. In public. Where Brock just *happened* to be stalking her."

Adam sucked his breath in and closed his eyes. He squeezed her hand, then said, "We need to call the police here."

Relief flooded Maddy. "I was hoping you'd say that. Mr. Wilkins and the Denver police still say he'd never find me, but I'd really like someone here to be on the lookout for him too." She couldn't believe how much better she felt now that Adam knew. Adam, who was on her side. Who had never judged her for any of this.

He pulled her close now, looked deeply into her eyes. She could see love and concern in his. What did he see in hers?

"We'll keep you safe. You know that, don't you?" He brushed a lock of curls away from her face, then wrapped his arms completely around her.

Her own hands went up to his broad shoulders. He was strong through and through, this cowboy of hers, and her arms didn't even reach around him. Maddy tipped his cowboy hat off, ran her hands through his hair, then pulled his head down for a kiss.

Adam and the rest of the family gathered in the living room to eat Uncle Dirt's steak and chili instead of joining the ranch hands in the large kitchen. They'd moved the old table into the middle of the room, and all six Blacks, with Maddy sitting next to Adam and Mia next to her, fit easily around it.

The room was homey, the steak perfectly medium-rare, the chili spicy as only Uncle Dirt could make it. With the aroma of the food mixed with the ranch dust clinging to all of them, it should have felt as comfortable as a summer trail ride.

But Adam fidgeted. In his mind, he had pictured this conversation with just his two brothers. Including Maddy wasn't a problem—as long as he could keep his mind off *her* problems—but how could they talk about all in front of Dad? At the same time, how could they leave him out?

He wished he could just take Maddy for a walk. They could swing Mia between them—she loved that—and look at the calves still in the pasture while they ignored the news about Brock. Maybe they could even try counting the stars.

But that wouldn't solve anything, so Adam inhaled deeply, took a long swallow of soda, and spoke. "Dad, I know we don't have answers from the tests yet, but we thought it might be good to sort of, well, start talking about plans."

Dad glared at him. "I'm not going to one of those *homes*."

"That's not what we're thinking," Adam said. "But there's a lot of work on this ranch that you do—"

"I can still work," Dad retorted.

Caleb and Micah looked to Adam, but stayed silent.

"We know you can, Dad," Adam said. "But maybe it's time to—"

"I'm not going to wobble tingle sworn," Dad said.

"Huh?" Adam looked around the table to find the others in as much shock as he was. "Say that again, Dad."

"They darn suh you. Not sleep hound am sidee wife." Dad threw his napkin onto the remains of his steak and stomped out.

Adam sat, stunned, then shot into life. "Call the doctor!" He rushed after his father.

In his bedroom, the older man sat slumped on his bed. He looked at Adam with watery, confused eyes. "Ton bell, turtle."

Adam didn't know what his father had said. He didn't know how to fix this. He could only sit beside him. Put his arm around him. And wait.

Maddy came in after a few minutes. She knelt in front of Samuel and put her hands on his knees. "This is pretty scary, isn't it?" she said.

Dad nodded.

"To be honest, it's pretty scary for all of us, too. But help is coming and we'll get through it together. Would it be okay if we prayed?"

Adam gave a mental shake of the head. Why hadn't he thought of that? He squeezed Dad's shoulder while Maddy prayed for strength and guidance, but he wondered why she didn't ask for healing as well. Surely God could bring this suffering to an end.

It was a long half-hour before the wail of a siren grew closer. He had expected his brothers to call Dr. Jacobs, not an ambulance, but he supposed it was for the best. Dr. Jacobs couldn't do anything over the phone, anyway.

The EMTs were kind and efficient, and Dad was hooked to oxygen, given an aspirin, and loaded into the ambulance before Adam could even think straight. "Wait, I'm coming with him!"

He clambered in and held his father's hand as the doors shut. He heard Caleb call out, "We'll meet you there!" before the ambulance whisked them down to Grand Junction.

"It was a TIA—a mini-stroke," the ER doctor said. "He's recovering quickly, and you can go in." He looked at the group of them. "Two at a time."

Adam squeezed Maddy's hand, glad she had left Mia with Uncle Dirt, and looked at the others. "Who's first?"

Caleb glanced around, then turned back to Adam. "Why don't you and Lacey go. We'll wait here with Maddy."

Adam took a deep breath and pushed through the door to the treatment area. Lacey followed the nurse to a draped-off cubicle and held the curtain open for Adam.

Dad lay propped up in a narrow bed, his face covered by an oxygen mask and wires running from monitoring machines to his chest. "Hey, kids," he said, lifting the mask to speak.

Lacey rushed to his side. "You had us scared, Dad. Don't ever do that again!"

Adam just stood there, relief washing over him. After the morning's cold, sterile rooms and complicated tests, of course his father would be worn out and stressed. He was just grateful to still have him around and doing well—a stroke could be serious business.

He finally convinced his feet to move and joined his sister by the side of the bed. "We're going to get some answers now, Dad. It will be okay."

His father looked at Adam like he was a clueless child. "Right. I just want to go home."

A doctor came in, a young, swarthy man with a day's scruff for a beard. "Samuel? Good, your family got here. I'm Dr. Abernathy from Neurology. I wouldn't normally have made it over so soon, but I had a—well, I'm here. I've requested some tests for you, Samuel. An MRI, CT scan and ultrasound, among others. And I'd like to admit you for observation for a day or two."

Adam nodded slowly. Dad grumbled. "I have to stay here? But I'm fine."

"Dad, don't argue," Lacey said.

"You might be feeling fine," Dr. Abernathy said, "but we want to get the full picture of what's happening. And prevent a more serious stroke."

"Uh, Doctor?" Adam spoke up. "He just had an MRI today."

Dr. Abernathy flipped through his tablet. "So he did. Good, I'll put a note for the radiologists to do a full read tonight." He looked at his watch. "It's nine-thirty now. I'll be back for rounds early tomorrow. Is there any chance the family can be here about seven? We'll need to talk."

"Of course," Adam said. The doctor left, and Adam met Lacey's glance. He could see the worry in his sister's eyes. "It's all good, Lace. It's only a mini-stroke, and Dr. Abernathy sounds like he's good. He's decisive and knows what he's doing. Dad's going to be fine."

"Not unless you quit talking about me like I'm not here!" Dad grumbled. "And I don't see why I have to—"

A nurse pulled the curtain back. Stern and strongly built, she took command. "Let's get you quieted down, Samuel. You two, out. We want his blood pressure dropping, not rising. Tell the others they can come visit in fifteen minutes." She shooed them into the hallway and pulled the curtain closed again.

"Huh," Adam said, looking at the cubicle in amazement. "I'd like to see her and Dad in a battle of wills."

Lacey shook her head. "Not today. Dad needs to stay calm, not get all riled up again."

They walked through the exit door to where everyone else was waiting. Adam explained what the doctor had said and grinned as he described the nurse.

"So tonight's a waiting game," Micah mused. "Dad can't be happy about having to stay here."

"We've all spent enough time in Emergency Rooms," Caleb said. "It'll take until the middle of the night to get all the tests done. He'll be glad for a bed when they're finished with him."

Adam felt Maddy slip her hand in his. It felt warm and comforting, and he drew her knuckles to his lips for a kiss. "I hope we get answers tomorrow. There has to be a reason for all this."

They sat silently for twenty minutes, except for Caleb pacing. He finally went to the nurses' station, pointed out how long it had been, and got permission to go back.

Thirty seconds later, he returned. "They were just taking him over to Radiology," he growled. "I barely got to wave to him."

Adam sighed. "We may as well go home. There's not much we can do here except get exhausted ourselves."

Caleb crossed his arms over his chest and stood with legs splayed and locked. "I'm staying. He shouldn't be alone."

Adam opened his mouth, then closed it. "If you want."

"I'm staying, too," Lacey announced.

"No," Adam and Caleb said at the same time.

"You can't do anything here, and you need to be bright and cheery for him in the morning, Lace," Adam said. "Caleb, I'll have Wes take care of the horses in the morning."

Caleb relaxed. "Thanks. And bring me some decent coffee when you come back!"

In the early morning, Micah agreed to stay behind long enough to give out the ranch assignments. He'd miss the meeting with the doctor, but would stay longer with Dad afterwards. Uncle Dirt would keep Mia again so Maddy could accompany Adam, but he sent a Thermos of extra-strong coffee in for Caleb. "You tell old Sam if he's tough enough to deal with hospital food, I'll send him some coffee, too."

Adam snorted when he poked his head in the hospital room at six-thirty. Dad was dozing in his hospital bed, but Caleb was sprawled uncomfortably across two chairs, somehow still sound asleep. Adam backed out and motioned to the others. The nurse promised to call them when Dr. Abernathy arrived, and they returned to the waiting room.

The minute hand on the waiting room's old-fashioned clock moved with irritating slowness. Lacey kept popping up and down from her chair until Adam put a hand on her arm to keep her still.

Maddy, on the other hand, rested her hand on Adam's back, rubbing his shirt lightly. The contact helped keep the worry at bay, soothing and comforting, as only Maddy's touch seemed to do.

They sat in silence amongst the comings and goings of other families. Lacey drifted off to sleep, and Maddy's hand moved slower and slower. Adam was left with his thoughts wandering down disturbing paths. His father wouldn't be totally crippled from this mini-stroke, but what did it mean for the future?

A hospital aide finally approached them. "The doctor is here."

Adam nudged Lacey awake and pulled Maddy to her feet. Inside Dad's room, Dr. Abernathy put the scans of his head and neck against a light board and spoke briskly. "Samuel, you've got some major blockage of your carotid arteries going on." He pointed to white areas. "There's hardly any room for blood flow, and frankly, I'm surprised you haven't had a full stroke yet."

Maddy gasped and Adam stared. He looked at the scans and wondered how his father wasn't plain dead yet.

"You're not overweight; you haven't smoked in twenty years. Your cholesterol is quite high, though, and these blockages are what's causing all your problems."

Dr. Abernathy looked at the expectant faces surrounding him. "The good news is that we can fix this surgically. We'll make an incision into the artery, clean out the plaque, and stitch it up again. On both sides."

Dad paled.

"How dangerous is it?" Caleb asked.

"Will this get him back to normal?" was Adam's question.

Dr. Abernathy turned to Caleb. "Every surgery has risks, but this is a quite common solution and most people do just fine. The important point is that it's far less risky than spending even a short time more with them blocked.

"Your question is more complicated," he said, looking first at Adam and then at Dad. He changed the image on the screen. "The MRI shows the damage that's been done. See these areas here and here?" He looked back at Dad. "That's where the brain cells have died from lack of oxygen—the blood wasn't getting to them because of the plaque in your arteries. And the temporal lobe, where these are located, is what controls things like speech and language."

Dad's eyes were hooded, and Adam couldn't tell what he was thinking. Adam looked at the images and thought he understood. "That explains his speech problem with the mini-stroke, but what about his memory and confusion?"

"Problems filtering conversations, forgetfulness, not being able to focus—those are all controlled by the temporal lobe," Dr. Abernathy said.

It wasn't Alzheimer's. *It wasn't Alzheimers.* Adam repeated that to himself a few times, then asked, "So what do we do about it?" Whatever it took, he'd do it. They had the money. His father would get the best care available—therapies, surgeries, medication, whatever.

Dr. Abernathy shook his head. "'I'm sorry, once brain tissue has died, it's irreversible. All we can do is try to prevent more damage."

Adam felt like the air had been sucked out of the room. He couldn't breathe, couldn't move, couldn't open his mouth to protest. He was only dimly aware that Maddy was hugging him.

He looked at his father, who lay with eyes closed, hands gripping the sheet.

Someone was saying something—one of his brothers— but Adam couldn't comprehend the words. He shook his head, but nothing cleared. Pushing Maddy away, he found the door through tear-filled eyes and left the room.

In the hallway, Adam took great gulps of air. He wasn't

used to losing control like this. Then again, he'd never had to face not having his father back before.

Dear God, why this? He's so strong and vibrant. How can you let this happen, especially after Mom?

His heart heard nothing. His ears heard only a cart's squeaky wheel and the orderly's soft shoes following it.

No whisper from God. No reassuring feeling that things would be all right. No guidance on what to do.

He was alone.

Tears welled in Maddy's eyes as she watched Adam leave. He had pushed her away, withdrawn into himself, and left his siblings and father to cope with the news as best they could.

She couldn't really blame him—he needed to be in control of situations, especially the outcomes, and hadn't really faced a time when he wasn't. Not as an adult, anyway. But she was still frustrated that he didn't lean on all of them. They were family, and families depended on each other.

She hugged Lacey, reached to squeeze Caleb's arm, then walked over to Samuel. The doctor's words took up space in her consciousness, but her focus was on her older friend. She took his hand in hers.

"I'm here, Samuel," Maddy whispered. "We're all here for you."

Tears leaked from beneath his closed eyelids. She noticed how thin they seemed, especially compared to the callouses and rough skin of his hands.

She thought of how his life would change. Probably no

more paperwork, no more decisions on his own. Maybe even no more *being* on his own. But he could still be a cowboy. He could still ride and rope and fix fences. He could still pass on his hard-earned wisdom and experiences. At least if…

"Dr. Abernathy?" Maddy said, interrupting Lacey's words to Caleb. "You said the damage is permanent. If he has the surgery—"

"He'll have it," Caleb said.

"—and that fixes the main problem, does that mean his other symptoms won't get worse? The memory and concentration issues won't progress?"

Lacey's mouth formed an O, and Dr. Abernathy looked thoughtful.

"Chances are, no," the doctor said. "There could be some lesions that get worse, but if this is all occlusion-related, then he should stabilize."

Maddy could feel the relief in the room. Samuel opened his eyes again, and she met his gaze with a smile.

"So when's the operation?" Lacey asked.

"As soon as possible. Depends on when there's an opening in the O.R. schedule. Which means," Dr. Abernathy said, turning to Samuel, "no breakfast for you. And probably no lunch."

Samuel grimaced, then brightened. "If what I hear about hospital food is true, then I guess it's no great loss."

Dr. Abernathy chuckled as he left, and Maddy backed away from Samuel's bed to let Caleb in closer. She wanted to check on Adam, anyway.

The hallway was empty of guests; Maddy finally found him slumped in a corner of the waiting room. She knelt in front of him. "You okay?"

Adam twisted his cowboy hat in his hands and shook his head. "Dad's never going to be the same, and I can't do anything about it. I already lost one parent—I don't want to lose two!"

Maddy took the hat from him, brushed it off, and set it down carefully before taking his hands in hers. "You listen to me, Adam Black. There's a lot you can't change in this world —you know that. But your dad is still your dad. He's still the man who raised you, who taught you how to ride and how to rope. And how to be the man you are. You're not giving up now, are you?"

His eyes were bleak when they finally met hers. "There's nothing to give up on. It's final. And God's taking a back seat to it all, just like He did before."

"It's *not* final," she shot back.

Adam stared at the wall. "God stayed away when Mom was killed by that drunk driver. He could have saved her, but He didn't. He saved the driver instead."

Maddy leaned forward, pulled his head to her shoulder and just held him as her heart cried. He didn't make a sound, but she could feel him shudder a time or two.

Help me, Lord. What do I say? She stroked Adam's hair lightly, wondering how any seventeen-year-old could cope with his mother's sudden death without becoming bitter. She knew God was there, waiting to give you solace whenever you asked. Maybe Adam didn't.

Maddy scooted around and sat next to him, keeping his hand in hers. She stroked his thumb with hers, marveling at the difference between them. "Adam, God is here, waiting for us to come to him. He doesn't make bad things happen, but He's always here to help us when they do."

"Yeah, right." His voice was low and defeated. "So what's the point of God being all-powerful if He never uses it."

Maddy leaned her head against the wall. That was a question that would need some long discussions and time for

Adam to ponder. And now wasn't the time, at least not for the whole thing.

"He uses that power all the time," she said quietly. "One of those ways is speaking peace to our hearts. I know He does that anytime I ask, and I know He'll do that for you, too, but you'll need to find that out for yourself. I don't know the other answers, and how I feel about it will take more than a short conversation. What I do know is that right now your father is lying in a bed back there, scared for surgery, scared for the future. And there *is* something you can do about that."

She watched expressions cross his face, watched him go from discouragement to possibilities to determination. He finally inhaled deeply, leaned to kiss her forehead, and stood.

Maddy stood, too, and took his hand just as Micah rushed in from outside. "How is he? I left the ranch as soon as I could."

"Fine. He'll be fine," Adam said. He tilted his head toward the door to the unit, and they walked back down the corridor together.

Dad would be in the hospital for two or three days, so the brothers took turns going down to visit. When he wasn't at the hospital, Adam buried himself in ranch work.

He made sure someone was always on the lookout for strangers, staying somewhat close to Maddy, but it seemed hard to talk to her. Hard to deal with her complete faith. *Trust God and everything will be all right* did little for him right now. Neither did the patient look in her eyes when all he wanted to do was grumble.

Samuel's surgery was a success, and Adam thanked God for that, at least.

"I'm fine," Dad groused on one of Adam's visits. "Don't feel any different, other than having cuts on both sides of my neck. What's been going on while I've been stuck at the hospital?"

"Nothing you need to worry about; everything's good," Adam said.

Dad turned to him sharply. "I ain't dead yet, son."

Adam sighed. "I know, Dad. I just don't want you to have too much stress."

"What's happening on the ranch that would stress me out?"

"Nothing. Really. The spring grass is taking hold, the bulls are still in with the yearling heifers—nothing's changed in the last two days."

Dad gave him a long look. "Don't know whether to trust you or not. You keepin' the cows off the grass? It needs time to get established, you know."

"I know, Dad. I'm doing the best I can."

Dad nodded. "Just don't keep things from me. It's still my ranch."

It was, and Adam didn't want to take it away from him any sooner than he had to. But it added one more thing to be concerned about.

Once his father got home, the best Adam could do was keep a close eye on him. He made sure Dad stayed away from the bookkeeping. He assigned one of the hands to go with him if he wanted to go out with the livestock. And after his father's admission that he'd gotten lost on the range one time, Adam made sure his dad never rode out alone.

And Seth. They'd never gotten a straight answer from Captain Carter, so they'd gathered on Tuesday as normal—an hour of terse conversation while they waited for Seth's chime. It never came.

He must be out on patrol, possibly in grave danger, and there was nothing they could do except wait.

All the while, there was a never-ending list of things to do, things to monitor. He shared an occasional kiss or hug with Maddy, but his mind was usually elsewhere. The only thing to do was keep busy.

He puzzled over Mrs. Evans' situation. Her total

embezzlement was well under the two thousand dollar requirement for a felony, and he'd finally tracked her down in a nursing home. Family Facebook posts had told him she'd broken a hip. Was it even worth pressing charges?

When he wasn't trying to decide that, Adam doubled checked Micah's record-keeping, making sure every newly tagged calf was entered with the proper mama cow. He finalized the placement of the solar wells, arranging for well drillers to come when the muddy season was over.

Everything combined to create a far bigger load than Adam had carried before, but he somehow managed. Except maybe for the time he saw Ty kicking one of the ranch dogs out of the way.

In an instant, Adam had him by the front of his shirt, pushed up against a barn wall. Adam's hand had balled into a fist, and he'd been ready to haul back and let loose until he'd realized Maddy and Dad were talking somewhere nearby.

That had brought him to his senses. He'd shoved Ty away and stomped over to the equipment shed. Maybe Micah had something he could pound on.

Micah hadn't, but he'd been watching with worried eyes all week. Caleb, too, who actually confronted Adam when he stopped to check the grain stores at the stables.

"First," Caleb said, fire flashing in his eyes. "I'm perfectly capable of keeping track of the horse grain myself. You're butting in again. Second, you're stressed and letting your temper get the better of you. You're trying to be Superman, and you're not."

"I am not," Adam snapped. "Butting in or trying to be Superman." He kept counting sacks of sweet feed.

"You are," Caleb countered. "Someday you're going to have to admit you can't do everything on the ranch single-handed. And you don't need to." He pulled Adam around to face him. "Do you hear me, big brother? You. Don't. Need. To."

Adam ignored him and the truth of his statement and headed out to the pastures.

The sunshine and the motion of the four-wheeler calmed him somewhat as he went from group to group among the remaining cows and calves. They looked good: healthy, well-fed, and well-bonded. He paused long enough to watch several calves frolic, running and bucking with all the energy they had.

Something tight within him let go, eased off just a bit, and he suddenly felt like he could talk to God again. *It feels good out here, Lord. I guess I am a little stressed out, but I'm doing what I can to keep things under control. Won't you please do the rest? Heal Dad, and help me hang on until he's back to normal?*

But no matter what he said, God never answered back these days. Not in thoughts, not in feelings. Adam was alone. As usual.

His brothers weren't the only ones to pin Adam down on his workload these days. Maddy pulled him aside Thursday morning, a week after his father had come home from the hospital.

"Do you have a minute?"

He saw the concern in her eyes and tried to evade. "Accounting stuff or something else?"

Maddy pursed her lips. Those pretty lips he hadn't had much time to kiss lately. "Something else."

Adam shook his head. "I'm headed out to check the cows again, then on out to see how the fencing is going. And then I need to go into Beaver Falls and get more vet supplies."

Maddy was determined, though. "It will just take a minute," she said, tugging him into her office. She shut the door. "Adam, you're wearing yourself out. And if you don't keel over from exhaustion, you're going to give yourself an early heart attack if you keep stressing over everything."

Adam leaned against the wall, crossed his arms, and stared her down. "I'm not stressing, and I'm not going to have a heart attack. And calving season is over, so I'm not exhausted."

Maddy's eyes flared. "Do you even know how much you're re-doing or re-checking what someone else has done? I would also guess that half of the things you do could be assigned to someone else. You can't do everything yourself!"

He pushed himself off the wall. "And less than two months on the ranch make you an expert, Miss I-don't-know-what-Ivermectin-is?"

She blew out a deep breath. "I don't need to be a ranch expert to know when you're being a control-freak. You have brothers who have as much experience as you do. You have ranch hands who can do their jobs perfectly well. You can—"

"You can decide that when you're wearing my boots. Until then, your biggest job is to make sure Dad doesn't get hold of the checkbook."

Her jaw dropped, her eyes filled, and she turned away, probably to keep him from seeing her tears.

Tears. How had he come to the point where he had reduced a woman—this woman—to tears? "Maddy, I'm sorry." He took her shoulders and turned her around. No tears, but close.

"Things are rough right now, and I guess I'm a bit overwhelmed, but I didn't need to take it out on you. Forgive me?" He pulled her into a gentle hug.

And she hugged him back.

"Forgiven," Maddy murmured into his shirt.

Now what? He couldn't just walk away after this. "How are you doing these days?"

She shrugged. "Hanging in there. I guess I'm sort of numb right now. Your dad seems much more important than Brock. I mean, we take precautions about Brock, but that's all it needs. And your father—that's life and death."

"No, just figuring out his life now. No death involved, thank goodness." Adam smiled and pushed a lock of hair behind her ear, letting his fingers trail down the length of it. "I'll tell you what. How about I let someone else check the cows—"

Maddy grinned and shook her head in disbelief.

"—and you come with me to Beaver Falls. We can get the vet supplies and then go to lunch."

"Umm…" She leaned into him, resting her head just below his collarbone. "That's sounds wonderrful. I've missed you."

He brushed her wayward curl back again and kissed her gently. "I'm here."

MADDY'S THOUGHTS were filled with Adam as she tidied her desk and waited for him. He was such a complex man—generous, but still hovering over everyone. Steady and responsible, but also over-protective. Kind and loving, but with a temper he kept mostly under control.

She knew where it came from—his need to make everything right—but she'd seen it surface again, and not just in his voice. While she'd been talking to Samuel the other day, she'd seen him shove Ty against the barn. Samuel hadn't noticed, though, and she'd forced herself to continue the conversation. The next time she'd looked, neither Adam nor Ty were in sight.

Could she write his reactions off to stress? Between his father's condition and the worry over Brock, plus all the usual ranch stuff, it was a wonder that Adam hadn't come unglued. But confrontations like that still made her anxious, and she wasn't sure how to handle that.

Actually, Maddy was amazed that she wasn't a walking basket case herself. She had calmed down since the phone call from her sister, partly because of Samuel's crisis, but mostly from the peace that came from trying to trust the Lord. Her faith wasn't so strong to take the apprehension completely away, but it seemed rather distant compared to Samuel's issues.

"I brought you these," Adam said, a welcome interruption to her thoughts. He held out a fistful of spring wildflowers.

Aww. He had never brought her flowers before. And he had picked them himself!

He continued, "I haven't been as attentive as I should have lately, so I thought you might like something special."

Maddy took the flowers, leaning into him and absorbing the strength of being in his arms. The flitting images of his fighting were pushed out by the gentle sound of his voice, the beat of his heart, the touch of his arms.

This time they ordered a Meat-Lover's pizza for lunch.

33

Maddy was still buzzing with happiness the next day. Mia was happy at school and waved cheerfully from the school bus every morning. Maddy had satisfying work to do, and maybe Adam would stop by her office this morning.

Adam poked his head around the door.

Ask and ye shall receive. "Do you have ESP?" she said, grinning.

"Only hoping that a gorgeous lady might be thinking about me." By the time she stood to greet him, he had her in his arms.

"That's quite a hello, cowboy," she murmured when they came up for air.

"I could leave and come in again for a repeat."

Maddy's eyes sparkled. "I don't think leaving is strictly necessary for an encore." She stood on tiptoe, but still had to pull his head down to meet hers.

A very long moment later, Adam gave her one last, gentle kiss. He lifted her hair with his fingers, and she savored the feeling.

"We're not accomplishing much this way," she murmured.

"Oh, I think we've used our time quite well." He buried his face in her hair. "But I suppose you're right. There are other things to deal with."

Maddy sighed and turned to her desk. "I have a final tally for Mrs. Evans' escapades." She pointed to her findings.

Adam took the paper and perused the numbers. "About what we figured. I still wish I knew what I should do about it."

Maddy paused, holding her comment back.

"What?" he asked.

She began to shake her head, then said, "No. I should say what I think."

"Of course you should. And that is?" His eyes gleamed.

"Let it go. Forgive her and move on."

Adam looked like a cartoon character whose jaw dropped completely to the ground. "Let it go?"

Maddy took his hands in hers, rubbing her fingers lightly over his callouses. "Adam, look at it from further away, okay? What Mrs. Evans did was wrong, but the ranch isn't terribly hurt. It's you that's being eaten alive by it. Do you really want to keep feeling this way? If you press charges, you're going to be wrapped up in it even longer."

His stormy eyes turned thoughtful. "You might be right," he finally said. "The only one that's hurt by this is me. Right now, anyway."

"Forgive us our sins, as we forgive others," Maddy murmured.

Adam gave a rueful chuckle. "It will be hard enough to let go of this. Actual forgiveness might take quite a while." He pulled her to him and held her close.

She soaked in his warmth, then said, "You probably ought

to talk to your dad about this. He and your brothers have a stake in it too."

"Dad's not there all the time, remember?"

She leaned back and looked up at him. "Yes, but a lot of the time he is. And he probably has some wise counsel to give, as well as the right to be part of the decision."

Adam stroked her hair away from her face. "You're right, of course."

Maddy grinned. "Aren't I always?"

He sighed, gave her a tender kiss, and headed out.

🐎🐎

ADAM FINALLY FOUND his father out at the stables, grooming Cobbler. That was okay—talking about serious things would be easier with a horse to work on than it would be in the office.

"You've got him looking good, Dad. His white spots are as bright as if you used baby powder."

Dad glared at him. "I did not! That's good old elbow grease you see. No shortcuts for Ranger, here."

Adam sighed. "It's Cobbler, Dad. Ranger was twenty years ago."

Dad looked at Cobbler, then back at Adam. "Of course, Cobbler. But you can't judge a man for getting two Paints mixed up."

Adam smiled along with his father. How would they cope when they couldn't make a joke of it?

"Dad, you remember our problem with Mrs. Evans?"

"Mrs. Evans, sure. Gray hair, glasses, short, and ruled the accounts payable with an iron fist."

Adam grimaced. "That's her, but don't you remember talking about it last week"

"Not really." Dad turned back to brushing Cobbler's tail out. "Remind me again."

Dad didn't remember. Dr. Abernathy's words kept coming back. The damage was irreversible.

Adam set aside the grief that again threatened to knock him down and replayed the situation for his father. "It's not horrible," Adam reassured him. "Maddy's gone through everything now, and it totals about fifteen hundred dollars. Not enough to screw us up too badly. And there are some weird amounts that had Maddy wondering what was up."

Dad shook his head. "Mrs. Evans seemed a good, Christian woman."

"Everyone gets tempted. The thing is, I'm not sure what to do now," Adam admitted. "I was ready to throw the book at her, but it's not enough to make it a felony. And she's in a nursing home with a broken hip now, so it's not like she's carrying on with someone else. So do we prosecute? Maddy thinks we should just let it go."

"It's not like she murdered someone," his father said, "and some things we're just supposed to forgive. Turn the other cheek, and all that."

Just what Maddy had said. "Thanks, Dad." He turned to go, pondering what to do.

Before he got far, Micah appeared in the stable doorway. "Hey, Adam, you in here?"

"Back here with Dad," he called.

"Ty hasn't shown up at all today," Micah said. "I went out to the cabins, and he's still half-drunk."

"What did you tell him?"

Micah gave a harsh laugh. "Nothing. Dealing with personnel problems is your pay grade, not mine, bro."

One more problem. This one was easily solved, though. "Dad, you got any problems with me firing Ty?"

Dad shrugged, but kept grooming his horse. Micah hung back as well. "Have fun," he said, slapping Adam on the back and chuckling.

Adam made his way out to the cabins, admiring the sparsely tidy area. The only cabin with flowers was Maddy's, but that was to be expected with a bunch of rough-and-tumble working men. He frowned as he came up Ty's steps, though. Empty beer cans dotted the porch and doorway, along with a discarded pizza box.

He pounded on the front door. "Ty, you in there?"

He waited, then pounded again. Eventually he heard movement.

Ty opened the door, smelly and bleary-eyed, wearing a filthy t-shirt and jeans that would probably stand up by themselves. "Wha?"

"You're a sorry sight, Ty Hawkins. And you're fired."

Ty gave his head a shake. "What's that?"

"I said you're fired. You have until nightfall to be out of here."

Ty straightened and took a step forward. "You can't do that. I ain't been drinkin' on the job."

Adam narrowed his eyes. "You're drunk as a skunk right now, and you didn't show up for work. Again."

Ty stepped out onto the porch, his breath sour in Adam's face. "I'm a good hand. Do ever'thing you tell me. And you're not the big boss."

Adam braced against the stench. No way was he going to back off the porch and leave Ty the high ground. "Dad agrees you're more trouble than you're worth, I just get to be the one to tell you. So clear out by the end of the day—Maddy will cut your check with two weeks severance."

He smiled inwardly at the coming pleasure of not only

seeing Maddy again, but seeing the last of Ty Hawkins. Unfortunately, that meant he didn't see Ty move.

Ty's fist whipped out faster than Adam could have expected. His jaw took the hit, blowing anything else out of his mind. He stepped back quickly, caught himself, and shook his head to clear it. "Now you're adding assault to the list, stupid."

The other man lurched forward, shoving Adam off the side of the porch and throwing his fist again.

Adam deflected it and gave Ty a gut-punch back. He didn't want to fight, but if he had to, he had to. And Ty wasn't giving up.

34

Drat—Maddy wouldn't have minded another kiss or
two, but an hour after Adam left to talk to his father,
he still wasn't back. There was always later, though. She smiled
at the thought.

She closed up the computer and went down to meet Mia's
bus, enjoying the warm May sun. Mia chattered on their way
back, excited about their family history project at school.
"Was Nonna really born in Italy, Mama? Did she sail on a
boat to get to America? Is she an only child like me?"

Maddy answered happily: no, she was born in America,
but her parents were born in Italy. Yes, they came on a boat.
And Nonna had three brothers and four sisters. All passed
away now, leaving Nonna the only one alive, but Maddy
didn't see a reason to bring that up.

They rounded the curve to the cabins, and Maddy pulled
Mia to a stop.

At the bottom of Ty's cabin steps, he and Adam were
fighting. Full-out. Adam hauled back and hit Ty on the jaw.
Ty staggered and came back with a fake jab and then a blow

to Adam's belly. Adam stepped back to breathe, then took a stance just as Ty reached him. Ty swung and missed, and Adam punched his jaw and slammed him to the ground.

This was no friendly wrestle; they were out for blood. They'd found it already, too—Adam's nose was pouring and Ty had a bloody mouth.

Mia hid behind her leg, whimpering. Maddy's frozen body began to shake. The look on Adam's face was too familiar, too full of fury. Her breath quickened, her pulse raced, and she fought to keep the memories down.

She lifted Mia into her arms, but had nowhere to take her —their cabin was just past Ty's.

Adam had Ty pinned to the ground. He lowered his face and growled something that made Ty struggle to rise. They tumbled over and around, got to their feet, and the fight started again.

Mia's whimpers continued. "Shh, baby, shh," Maddy whispered as she looked frantically for escape. She certainly couldn't stop the fight, but she could take Mia back to the admin building and get help. She stroked her daughter's hair and walked quickly away.

"They're really mad at each other, aren't they?" Mia asked once they reached the main driveway. "Like Daddy got mad at you? Are they going to hit you, too?"

"No, sweetheart, they're not." She wouldn't give anyone the chance, either.

The equipment shed was empty, but she found Samuel in the admin building. She kept her composure long enough to say, "A-Adam and Ty are fighting at his cabin. C-can someone go break it up?"

She didn't wait for Samuel to answer, just raced for her office before she broke down in front of him. Mia calmed down with the unexpected treat of playing a Lego game on her mother's computer; Maddy, not so easily.

She turned to the wall, wrapped her arms around her body, and squeezed for some sense of security. She'd thought she was past the fear, that someone else's fight shouldn't bother her. Maybe it was just that it was Adam fighting. Why did men always try to get their way with their fists? And in front of a six-year-old, no less!

Anger coursed through her, a welcome relief from the fear. Men, power, temper, fists...she'd had enough of it with Brock. More than she ever should have put up with, and she wondered once again why it took women like her so long to leave.

But when she had escaped, Brock had never stopped. He'd confronted her, stalked her, hit her again. They'd been alone every time, but that blow to her face had given her enough evidence for an arrest, not just a restraining order. Unfortunately, he'd gotten a good lawyer and a light sentence, and he was out in a few months.

Which was why she was out here in the first place, where she'd finally begun to feel safe. Like she was surrounded by family she could trust. Like the men around her were decent and honorable, to the point where she was falling in love with one of them.

But now? Now she'd just witnessed Adam pummeling one of his employees, his face full of contempt. She was an expert on that expression even at a distance.

She'd known from the first time she met Adam that he had a temper. He certainly hadn't held back when he'd come roaring up on his horse and yelled at them for letting Mia get into the bull pasture.

She'd told herself that Adam had only been scared at the possibility of serious injury. That although he liked to be in charge, he kept good control of himself. That she could feel safe around him.

That might still be true, but the last twenty minutes had left her shaking. Nerves? Anger? Regret?

All of them.

It was obvious that she couldn't be around Adam. That she'd never feel safe enough.

She sat in a side chair, trying to calm her quivers. Long, slow, deep breaths. She tried to imagine her Nonna's arms around her.

Finally, her heart rate slowed and she could focus on something else. "How are you doing over there, kiddo?"

"Okay. Look, Mama, my car beat the Lego guy's!"

"I see." But Maddy's heart wasn't in the conversation. Instead, it was tearing in half with grief. Adam wasn't the man she thought he was. And as much as she'd come to love the ranch, could she handle being in close contact with a man like him? A man she was in love with but couldn't trust to be around?

ADAM TROMPED up the steps to the admin building, his bandana still clamped to his nose. He was going to have a black eye, too, but the ice for that could wait a minute. "Maddy, are you still here? Can you cut a final paycheck for Ty Hawkins?" he began while he was still down the hall. "I just fired him."

But it was Mia sitting at the computer. Maddy was standing in the center of the room, arms crossed and glaring at him.

"What? He about broke my nose." Adam shifted the bandana to a clean area.

"I'm not surprised. You were really going after him."

Adam clenched his sore jaw. "You saw that?" If she saw it, she should know he didn't start it.

"Of course I saw it." She ground the words out. "I was bringing Mia home from the bus. She saw it too—not what a six-year-old with an abusive father needs to witness. I thought you were better than that, Adam. You're his *boss*."

"He was drunk. *And* he started it." Adam's eyes narrowed. "He didn't show up for work, and when I went to see what was going on, *he* came after *me*. And I've got the black eye to prove it."

"I know what a black eye looks like," she said, eyeing his. "I know what it feels like, too. And I know there's always another way."

"Not always, not when—" Frustration surged, and he broke off. After all the time they'd spent together, for Maddy to know who he really was, she was judging him on this? After all he did to keep the ranch going, to put his own comfort aside for the sake of everyone else, this was the thanks he got?

He was tired, he was sore, he had way too many worries about way too many people. "Look, I can't deal with this now. I've got too much else on my plate. Just cut his check and whatever HR paperwork there is, and we'll talk later."

Maddy stiffened. "You've always got too much else on your plate. You're proud to be the one in charge, and this is what you get."

"Maddy, I told you, I just went out to fire him, not get in a fight."

But she shook her head. "I can't be with a man who solves problems with his fists. My head might understand, but inside myself, I can't."

Had Adam heard her right—she couldn't be with him?

She was throwing away what they had because someone else picked a fight with him? He took a deep breath. "Remember what you said yesterday? 'Sometimes you have to do what you don't like.'" Every part of him hurt, and all he asked for was a little understanding.

But Maddy just looked at him with those big eyes. "I can't change the way I react inside. You don't know what it's like."

"So tell me."

She shook her head. "I can't put it into words any more than I already have."

Adam's head throbbed, making it hard to think. "I can't do this now. I can't deal with more complications, not with everything else."

"You're hiding behind the ranch again." Maddy's worried eyes turned to a glare.

That was enough. "The ranch, yes," Adam snapped. "My dad even more. And we haven't heard from Seth in three weeks. So if you can't understand that sometimes a guy has to fight back, it's no skin off my nose. Maybe I can concentrate on the bigger problems."

Maddy's lips thinned and her glare got more pointed. "Nice to know I'm only a *little* problem. I guess that settles it. Consider this my two-week's notice. I'll post an opening online for a new accountant."

Adam kept his stiff stance. "You do that. I'll stay out of your way tomorrow."

35

This shouldn't be so hard. Maddy stared at the online job site and tried to make the words flow, but they didn't want to come together. And why should they, when she couldn't concentrate on them for more than a quarter of a second?

Instead, her memory filled with Adam's last words and the look on his face, and her heart broke once again. She loved him so much, had had such hopes for them. She'd let herself dream of living on the ranch with him, snuggling with him on the big sofa in the family room, riding up and seeing the eagles with him.

And now it was gone.

Maddy forced back a sob and shoved Adam out of her mind, but still couldn't concentrate on describing her job duties. She set her thoughts on leaving—where she could go and what kind of job she could land on short notice.

Where had to be decided first, and she'd be safer if she moved away from Colorado completely. Utah? New Mexico? California?

California sounded good—it was her fictitious home, after all. She could lose herself in its huge population, and it would be different enough that maybe Adam wouldn't intrude on her thoughts so much. She didn't know how long it would take to get over him, but get over him she must.

California. She and Mia could be packed and on their way in a day or two and leave the whole problem of Brock behind. They could actually visit the beach for themselves. Maybe she could find someone as nice as Samuel to work for.

A job search was only a click away, but Maddy set it as a reward for getting the accounting position posted. Listlessly, she turned back to the description she'd started.

Half an hour of wrestling with words and clicking boxes, her job was posted as open. They'd find someone else to keep the books, and Adam could teach him or her to do things exactly the way he wanted, to put up with him just the way he was.

Something Maddy hadn't been able to do.

If only he hadn't tried to justify his fighting yesterday. If only he didn't have to control everything. If only she'd had a happy-go-lucky last five years. If only she could stop taking things personally.

If only, if only.

But Maddy couldn't change who she was, or who Adam was. There would come a time when he'd use his fists again. A time when she would feel fear course through her once more.

She couldn't depend on him to make her feel safe, no matter how much she loved him.

Which left her trying to figure out how to move on. From both the job and her handsome boss.

That handsome boss was staying outside on the ranch as much as he could and sticking to his own office when he came in. Maddy spent the next few days focused on writing explanatory notes and labeling file boxes to prepare for her replacement. She spent several weary hours each day looking for jobs in California, but nothing was popping out at her. Sure, she could stock shelves or be a cashier, but neither would pay their living expenses. She'd do it temporarily if she had to, but Brock couldn't be *that* close.

Maybe California wasn't such a good idea after all.

At the cabin, she played kickball outside with Mia and decorated cookies with her inside. Her time with her daughter should have been precious, but it, too, was tinged with sadness.

A knock on the door a few days later was accompanied by Lacey's voice. "Maddy? Are you home?"

Maddy let her in. "Where else would I be? Want a cookie?"

Lacey shook her head, but didn't take her eyes off Maddy. "Did you and Adam have a fight? Nobody's talking, but he's sure stomping around the house."

Maddy's throat thickened and no words came out. She shrugged and turned back to the kitchen.

"Look, Lacey, it's a calf!" Mia said, holding up a vaguely shaped cookie with squiggles of icing.

"I see. You look like you're having fun."

"Yup! You should do some."

Maddy watched sideways as the teenager pulled her hair into a quick ponytail and pushed her sleeves up. The two girls decorated a few more cookies, laughing at their efforts, while her own soul felt frozen.

She'd thought she might become a part of this wonderful family. She'd thought she'd found a home in this valley against the rugged mountains. She'd thought she'd found a place to be safe, to let her soul breathe free again.

Evidently not.

How long would it take before the trauma of being beaten would subside completely? Would she spend the rest of her years alone?

She stared out the window at the alfalfa growing, at the mares and foals in the pasture beyond. She'd grown used to country life. She wondered where she would land, what type of place Mia grow up in.

A warm hand rested on her shoulder. "Maddy?" Lacey pulled her away, drew her over to the couch, thrust a mug of tea into her hand.

Maggie took a sip of the mint infusion. "You're mothering again."

"You need it," Lacey answered, sitting next to her. "Is it that bad between you two?"

"Worse." Maddy kept her heartache from coming out in a moan, but she knew it showed in her voice.

"But he loves you!"

"And I love him. But just because two people love each other doesn't mean they'll be good together."

Lacey looked confused. "But if you both say you're sorry…"

But Maggie knew it was naïve to think that love conquered all. Love could soften a person, but it couldn't change who you were down deep inside. She and Brock had loved each other too, at the beginning. It hadn't changed him.

"There's nothing to apologize for," was all she said.

Adam worked outdoors as much as possible through the week. They processed the last six hundred calves, without Maddy this time. Adam spent a couple days doing tractor work and fencing, and then they'd take this herd up to the summer range to join the others. There was plenty to do to keep his distance from her.

The distance didn't help, though.

He was aware of every step she took outside, arriving for work, getting Mia from the bus, walking back to the cabin. Her nervous smile when she'd helped with the first round of calves filled his mind with each vaccination he gave. Her worried face intruded into his thoughts as he stretched and tightened wire. The memory of her laughter and kisses drowned out the tractor's engine.

When thoughts of Maddy did manage to subside, worries about Seth and Dad broke in. They had spent an hour Tuesday waiting for Seth to call, but still nothing. All Captain Carter would say was that he was out on patrol. Which could mean anything from escorting a convoy and braving IEDs and mined roads to taking down a nest of insurgents.

Adam supposed there were other things Seth could be doing, but those two were what stayed in his mind. Both of which put Seth in imminent danger, and there was nothing Adam could do about it.

And then there was Dad.

Samuel Black refused to take any down-time to heal, but the brothers managed to keep him to light tasks. He accompanied Adam to check the livestock, and he helped Caleb with the morning and evening feeds. Dinners were another matter.

Sunday night was one of those times. Dad came sweeping in with a platter of grilled burgers and all three brothers stampeded to the table.

"Good stuff, Dad," Adam said, taking a juicy mouthful.

Micah did the same, but Caleb fixed his burger and left it on his plate while he fiddled with his phone.

"Fixing to call a girl?" Dad asked.

"Maybe." Caleb didn't look up, just swiped at the screen a couple of times.

"Oh, ho!" Adam called out. "Caleb's got himself a dating app!"

"Dating app?" Dad's brow wrinkled.

"Lemme see," Micah said, stealing the phone from Caleb. "Ooh, she's a pretty filly. You going to swipe up on that one?"

"None of your bees' wax." Caleb reached for the phone, but Micah held it out of reach.

Dad looked puzzled. "A filly?"

"Getting tired of dancing with the girls in town?" Adam asked.

Caleb gave him a quick glance. "It's always the same crowd." He stood and reached over Micah's head, finally wresting the phone away.

"So which way are you going to swipe on that one?" Micah repeated.

"That's my business. You find your own girl to date." Caleb stuck the phone in his pocket and reached for his burger.

Micah glared at him.

Adam wondered dully if he'd end up using the same app, now that Maddy didn't want him. Maybe he'd just stay single forever.

Three bites later, Caleb suggested Micah try with Stephanie from Trail's End Stables. "You know, the one who came over when you were covered in tractor grease?"

Micah leaned back and grinned. "I might, if you try taking Janice on rides at the fair again."

Caleb blanched. "Never! I will never go on a whirly spinning thing again, no matter how much a girl begs."

No laughter rose within Adam, although it had been

funny at the time. Caleb's stomach hadn't liked that ride, and he'd ended up puking all over his date.

Samuel, though, looked them with furrowed brows. "I thought you were going to call someone."

Micah and Caleb kept joking, but Adam's thoughts turned toward his father. There had been no more episodes with weird substitutions for words, thank goodness, but the confusion on Dad's face was more common anytime the conversation became lively.

Adam had tried to do some online research—working on his laptop in the house to avoid seeing Maddy—but found nothing the doctor hadn't already told them. He couldn't concentrate, anyway, and gave up completely when a discussion on speech therapy had him remembering Maddy stroking his hair.

He didn't want her to leave.

He wanted to wrap his arms around her, kiss her thoroughly, hug her for a very long time. To hear her laugh, to watch her with Mia, to ride a trail and see the wonder of nature in her eyes. To see the look of scorn from his fight be replaced by the look of love he'd come to know so well.

Enough of that! Wallowing was useless, and Adam had work to do. If he couldn't concentrate on medical research, maybe Caleb had a horse that needed roping practice. And maybe those thoughts of Maddy would stay away.

36

It didn't work. Caleb's young mare knew Adam was jittery, so she became unsettled as well. He kept letting the rope go too soon and missing his target.

He wasn't surprised. Maddy had left a hole in his heart so big he was surprised that blood was still pumping through him. Surely there was *some* way they could make things work. But not if he couldn't talk to her.

He needed an excuse for coming to her office. To talk about Mrs. Evans again? Not really. He'd ask her for an analysis of the projected profit and loss for the year, but they'd already done that. *Be a man,* he told himself. *Just suck it up and sort things out with her.*

His stomach tightened in anticipation. Would she still be angry with him? Would she laugh and not care? He didn't want her mad, but not caring seemed even worse.

He rehearsed again what he would say, but balked as he approached her office. He wasn't ready for this.

He couldn't help peeking through her open door as he snuck past. Her mass of curls cascaded down her back as she focused on the computer screen. She didn't notice him, but his steps suddenly felt like he was trapped in quicksand.

Safe in his office, Adam let out a long breath. He'd have thought two adults could recover from a disagreement without such problems.

Mentally, logically, they could.

Emotionally? Evidently not.

He let his fears take over for too long, staring out the window instead, long enough to notice the shadows lengthen. And then Maddy's voice penetrated his thoughts.

"Do you really think so?"

"I know so, Missy," came his father's voice. "Hasn't changed much since he was a little guy."

Great. Not only was Dad in Maddy's office, they were talking about him! Adam leaned against the adjoining wall, crossed his arms, and listened.

"He's awfully good at what he does," she said.

"Of course, but it's not enough for him," Dad answered. "He'll up and leave someday if he doesn't have someone to anchor him."

Adam fumed. So Dad not only thought he'd abandon his ranch responsibilities, he was trying to influence Maddy? As if Maddy would keep him here when nothing else would?

"We'll just have to find him someone," she said.

Adam froze. His heart cracked in two as he stumbled to a chair.

She had thrown him over that fast? Impossible, unless she had never loved him in the first place.

The thought ricocheted inside him. Could it all have been an act? Why? The ranch had been her hiding place from the beginning—she didn't need to lead him on to be safe.

Had it just been a game to her? She had lied about her

California upbringing, so maybe she had lied about her feelings, too.

He thought of her smile, the way her face lit up when she saw him, the look of love—or what he'd thought was love—in those beautiful eyes.

Adam sank his head into his hands. It didn't matter how he felt about her—if every signal she had given him had been lies, then there was no hope for him, ever. She'd been so true, so real. If it had been fake, he'd never be able to believe another woman's words or actions again.

He strode to the door and yanked it open.

Maddy and Dad were in the hallway. Her eyes met his as she broke off what she was saying. A shutter came down over her face, erasing her expression to nothing.

She turned back to Dad. "Tell Caleb to beware—I'll be on the lookout for the perfect girl." She stepped into her office, closing the door firmly behind her.

Adam stared at his father. They'd been talking about Caleb, not him? He couldn't get any words out, couldn't even move.

Dad just looked at him. "Got a problem, son? Besides the obvious one?" He nodded toward Maddy's door.

"Huh?" Adam's senses began to return. "No. Not at all. In fact…" He was still reeling with his false assumption. She'd been talking about his brother, not him. Their relationship hadn't been a lie. She *had* loved him, as much as he'd loved her. Loved her still.

He brushed past his father, pushing Maddy's door open.

She hadn't sat down yet, was standing by the window. She turned, and their eyes met. And her lip quivered.

Adam shut the door behind him. "Maddy, I—"

"Adam, what are you—" She gave her head a shake as they spoke at the same time. "You first."

He was across the room in two seconds, holding her hands in his. "Maddy, we can't just end like this. I love you."

She ducked her head. "I love you too, more than you know."

Adam tipped his forehead down to rest on the top of her head. "Then why are we doing this?"

He felt her body go still. "I'm sorry I blew my stack that day," he said. "I should never have taken my frustrations out on you. I should never have snapped at you."

Maddy looked up at him. "I think I did as much snapping as you. But Adam—" She looked down again. "It doesn't change anything. I still can't be with you."

His heart broke all over again. "But...why? Why not?"

She leaned her head on his chest. He stood in silence, his heartbeat hammering, waiting for her to speak.

"Because I can't change what I feel inside. I can't change what Brock did to me. What I let him do to me."

"It's not your fault, Maddy!" He nudged her back so he could see her face. "He's the one who hit *you*."

"But I could have left sooner. Before I was damaged inside as well as out." She searched his eyes. "Don't you see, Adam? Even if he never shows up here, I have to get rid of that fear before I can have a real relationship with anybody."

"But can't we—"

"No, Adam." The look on her face was breaking his heart. "We can't. I can't. Not on a ranch where you have to be tough, anyway."

His heart sank to the bottom of his boots, feeling heavier and emptier than he'd ever thought possible. He held her close, breathed in her scent, felt her soft body mold to his, even if he had to let her go. "I love you, Maddy. Just remember that. I don't think there will ever be anyone else for me, so if you get to the point where you want a roughshod cowboy after all, I'll be here waiting."

Adam felt her nod wordlessly. She squeezed her arms around him one more time, then stepped back and turned to the window. He watched her shoulders shake as she kept her head down.

He lifted one hand toward her, then let it drop and walked away.

MADDY HEARD Adam close the door, heard his footsteps as he clattered down the stairs outside before she let herself sink into her chair and cry. It was her own fault, pushing away the man she'd come to love more than any other.

Even after her tears stopped, she stared at her desk without really seeing it. Images of Adam riding Mister, driving a tractor, in the office with the phone to his ear all drifted through her mind. The soft look on his face when he brought her flowers. His eagerness as he sat down to a dinner she'd cooked. Not to mention the intensity of his eyes just before he kissed her.

Maddy sighed and looked at her desk again. She had lined all her pencils up, erasers perfectly even, sharpened points creating a mountain slope from longest to shortest. If only her life were so neat.

She couldn't help Adam being in her heart, and the thought of starting all over again—alone, just her and Mia—made her shrink. San Francisco, San Diego, Sacramento. Maybe even back East. She blanched at the thought. Strange towns, faceless hotels, always wondering when someone would get her real name. It was no way to live, but she had no other choice. She had to do it; Mia would have to adjust again, and this time Maddy wouldn't even tell her mother where she was.

It was doubly hard to think that God had brought her here, given her a place of refuge, only to take it away again.

Maybe it wasn't God's plan for her to be here. Maybe this was just a rest stop on the road to where He wanted her.

If that was the case, she'd better get going. She wiped away her tears, opened up the computer, and started some new job searches. She checked housing prices and tried not to think of what she'd be leaving.

37

"Dad? Caleb?" Adam called out as he approached the stables the next Friday afternoon. He wasn't thrilled with what he had to do, but anything was better than the torture of watching Maddy and Mia walk back from the school bus.

The two came in from the paddock, Caleb leading a slightly lame horse.

"Sanderson called," Adam said.

"From the Lazy S?" Dad growled. "What'd he want?"

"Said he lost a couple calves to a mountain lion, wanted to put us on the lookout."

Mountain lions were regular predators, but this time of year there was usually easier prey around than facing off with an angry mama cow. If there was a mountain lion actively attacking, though, they needed to get a handle on it now. Especially with a lot of very young calves.

"Huh," his father said. "Didn't think Sanderson would bother. Probably just wants us to help hunt it."

"Don't like killing them if we don't have to," Caleb put in.

"Yeah, but we haven't been up on the high range for a while," Adam said. "I figured we ought to head up tomorrow and check things out. Either of you want to come?"

"You bet," said Dad.

Caleb shook his head. "I've got a potential buyer for a yearling coming in the morning. Micah could probably go, though. And a few of the hands."

Adam nodded, an extra thought running through his mind. Maddy hadn't said anything about Brock lately, and while Adam didn't think the guy could actually find them among the hundreds of ranches around, there was a reason "better safe than sorry" was a common phrase.

"Will you keep an eye on Maddy for me?" he asked. "Her ex is still out there somewhere."

Caleb looked down at him. "You're kidding, right? You two really need to make up, and you can look after her yourself."

Adam bit back a retort and simply shrugged. "Even if we could, I wouldn't be here tomorrow. Just stick around, okay?"

"Sure, whatever. I'd better bring a few horses in so they're ready for you in the morning. Dad, can you take Starlight here down to the last stall?"

Adam walked with his father and the black mare.

"In my day, we used to shoot cougars," Dad grumbled. "I suppose you all will want to relocate it or something."

"Maybe. Depends on how wide its territory is, and how much it's got a taste for danger and young beef. Maybe we'll scout out places for some of those flashing lights I've been reading about."

His father snorted as he put Starlight into the stall. "Maybe we ought to build a cabin and put some hands up there for the season."

"We're down to four people, Dad, remember? The others were just for the calving season."

"Right. Is Jesse still here? And Luis?"

"Jesse and Luis are here. And Dax and Wes. But Randy, Lou and the others are gone until next year. And Ty got fired, remember?"

"Is Uncle Dirt still here?" Dad's eyes were worried.

"Yes, Dad. Uncle Dirt's not going anywhere." Adam clapped a hand on his father's shoulder, checked that the stall door was latched properly, and walked with his father back to the house.

So many things to juggle.

"I FEEL like this will never end." Maddy held the phone close to her ear early Saturday morning and kept her voice quiet. She didn't need Little Miss Big Ears to start asking more questions. "Sophie, how did I get into this mess?"

"Aw, Maddy," her sister said. "You didn't do anything but fall for the wrong guy years ago and the right guy when things are still complicated."

Maddy sniffed.

"It's not like you set out to cause problems—they found you. You can blame that rotten ex-husband for everything."

"I want to yell at someone," Maddy whispered. "And then I want to just crumple and cry. Which sometimes I actually do." Actually, she'd done that a lot this past week.

"Maddy," Sophie said firmly. "Who is always there when we need someone?"

"Nonna." Maddy wiped the tears off one cheek.

"No, even Nonna's not always around. Think Maddy— who gives you comfort when you need it?"

Maddy sighed. "God," she said reluctantly.

"Of course. So turn to Him and He'll give you peace. You know He will."

"God and I haven't been very close lately." If Maddy were honest with herself, she'd have to admit that she'd pretty much ignored God while she was so wrapped up with Adam.

She could almost see Sophie shake her head more than two hundred miles away. Maddy chuckled. "You're twirling your hair around your finger, aren't you?"

Sophie laughed. "Of course—I'm thinking! But seriously, Sis, you need to let God handle things."

"Yeah right. He's been hands-off so far."

"Maddy, stop. You *know* He cares. If there's one thing we all know, it's that."

Maddy sighed. "I do know. It's just…I let myself fall in love and now it's all a jumbled mess, Sophie." She was almost wailing. "I feel like there's no hope out there, that I'll be alone and on the run forever."

"I'd give you a giant hug if I could," Sophie said. "So you hang up and get that hug from Mia instead, and then go have a long conversation with the Lord. You'll feel better, I promise."

Simply having someone give her directions calmed Maddy down. She said goodbye to her sister and rested her head in her hands. After a moment, she called out, "What are you busy with, Mia-Mine? Can you come give your old Mama a hug?"

Mia came running from her room and jumped into Maddy's arms. The child squeezed tight around Maddy's neck, and Maddy hugged her tightly back. She held her daughter for a long moment, until Mia leaned away and tilted her head.

"Are you sad, Mama?"

"A little. But your hugs always make me feel better, sweetheart."

"Then here's another one!" Mia drew her into a second long clench.

Maddy's heart filled. Her problems with men might seem overwhelming, but the love from this precious daughter would sustain her through anything.

As would the love from God.

Maddy squeezed Mia one more time, then stood. "Are you fine with your toys for a while? I need some time by myself."

"I'm reading, not playing," Mia corrected her.

"That's good, sweetheart. You can have a couple cookies if you get hungry." Maddy kissed the top of her daughter's head and sent her off to read and play.

In her own bedroom, Maddy dropped to her knees and poured her heart out. She apologized to God for leaving Him out of her life. She asked for strength, for understanding, and that He would bless her with peace and a way out of her dilemma with Brock.

She wanted to pray to have Adam back in her life, but there were such mixed feelings there, such apprehension and regret and hope, that she didn't really know what she wanted.

"Thy will be done, in *all* things," she finally prayed.

Maddy remained on her knees, trying to keep her mind blank and be open to whatever thoughts came. No answers appeared, but she was gradually filled with a sense of love and security, as if the Lord had His arms around her.

She was loved. And if the Lord loved her, He was watching over her. Even if she didn't know how to handle things, that much she did know.

She basked in the feelings for a few minutes, and the glow

stayed with her as she puttered around the cabin. She picked up the phone and called Lacey. "Hey, girl, want to come bake?"

Adam rode along behind the others, his thoughts straying from mountain lion problems to Maddy to his odd phone call last night. Mrs. Evans' daughter had called to tell him her mother was in a confessing mood.

"I'm so sorry," she had said. "It looks like we owe the ranch a bunch of money. Mom got it in her head that the ranch was rich and other businesses needed help and she was overpaying them to 'help out.' I promise I'll pay it back as soon as I can, but it will need to be little by little."

Adam had been shocked—all this time he'd thought Mrs. Evans had stolen it for herself. His heart softened a bit as he thought about what her mental state must be, plus the broken hip. Her daughter didn't sound like they had any extra money, either. And it wasn't like the ranch wouldn't recover—it had been mostly the principle of the thing.

"We couldn't understand why," he'd said, letting retribution slide away. "Thank you for calling. I need to check with my family, but it sounds like you've got enough to worry about. We probably won't prosecute, and you won't need to pay it back. The ranch will be fine."

The daughter had argued about needing to repay for their own peace of mind, and Adam had finally accepted that. But he'd been surprised at how nice it felt to let the bitterness ease away.

He wished there was a way to let Maddy's problems ease away, too. To make Brock disappear, to erase the damage the man had done to her psyche.

Wasn't there any way Adam could help her? To let her know deep in her soul that he would protect her, not threaten her?

Just love her, came the thought.

Huh. Now that things were as bad as they could get, was he finally getting a whisper from God? But if so, it was one without much direction.

"You're awful quiet," Dad said, nudging his horse closer to Adam's.

"Just thinking." There were private parts of his life he didn't feel like sharing, even with his father.

"About Maddy?"

Confound it, did his father know everything that went through Adam's mind?

Adam remained silent, scanning ground and trees for signs of the mountain lion, checking the cattle for clues that a cow or calf wasn't doing well.

"She's good for you, son. You need to make up with her."

Adam snorted. "I wish. Too many other problems involved."

Dad waved his hand in the air, making Cobbler jerk his head in surprise. "Maybe she could help with the problems. I like her, and you put too much of a load on your shoulders."

Before Dad could say anything else, Adam heard a cow

lowing in distress. He kicked Mister into a lope and went searching for her.

It was easy to follow the sound. The cow stood by a huge spruce, her calf out of sight but bawling weakly near the tree.

He prayed it wasn't lion-wounded.

Adam dismounted, dropping his reins and letting Mister stand ground-tied, and followed the sound under the tree branches.

One of the calf's hooves was sticking out of a dark hole. Adam reached in and found the other hind hoof. He grabbed both of them and heaved, hauling a scared calf out into the daylight.

"What happened?" Micah said, riding up with Dad.

"I think he found a tree well left from winter. You know, one of those snow sinkhole things." Adam grabbed a chamois from his saddle and rubbed the calf vigorously. "At least it wasn't too deep."

"I know what a tree well is, Adam," Micah said, dismounting. "I just didn't expect one now"

Adam shoved the calf over to its mother, who comforted it with an all-over body lick. "We ought to send a crew up to fill these things in. See why I'm always double-checking?" He didn't need to look at Micah to know he was rolling his eyes.

"Someday you're going to give up control over everything," Micah said. "And speaking of control, when are you going to forgive Maddy for whatever she did?"

Adam jerked upright. "Who said I need to forgive her?"

Dad looked between them, busied himself with something on his saddle, then left to talk to Wes and Luis.

Micah shrugged. "You guys fought about something, and it must have been big or you wouldn't have broken up. And things like that are never one-sided. So what was so bad that you couldn't forgive each other?"

Adam collected Mister's reins and rubbed the gelding's face, stalling.

"Adam? What exactly happened?"

Adam rested his forehead in Mister's mane. All the private things he'd been holding in wouldn't be held anymore. "She slammed me down for fighting with Ty. She can't deal with any of that. Says she's too messed up inside."

"That's rough." Micah's voice was sympathetic. "She's not ready to move on?"

Adam stroked his horse absently. Mister was mostly shed out now, but soft hairs still came off in Adam's hand.

"No. And I don't know how to fix things for her," he finally said.

"I don't think you can. I think she has to work through that herself."

Adam's heart churned with more. "But I always fix things. I keep an eye on everything I can, and fix anything I can't foresee. But not this, and it's breaking me."

He felt Micah's hand on his shoulder. "I don't think you can 'fix' Maddy—you have to let her work through that. And the rest of it—you don't have to. You've *never* had to. You just have to know that the rest of us will do our jobs."

Adam buried his face in Mister's warmth. He couldn't *not* take care of things. That was how he kept control of things around him. But it was tearing him apart. *How, Lord? How do I do this?*

He twirled a bit of Mister's thick mane around his gloved finger. Peace finally came when he forced an unwanted admission into words. "I don't know how." He froze, wanting to take it back as soon as he said it.

Micah gave him a reassuring squeeze. "Just let go a little. Practice with us first, and then let go a little more with the ranch hands. And just be there for Maddy."

Adam nodded, not lifting his head yet. Letting go right now did not include letting his younger brother see his red eyes. "Maddy's leaving. Maybe not today, but soon. Her ex is still on the prowl."

"What? And we're all up here?"

Adam shook his head. "Caleb's keeping an eye on her, and Jesse's fertilizing the home pastures today. And Maddy doesn't want me around, anyway."

Micah snorted. "She might *say* she doesn't, but …"

Adam pushed himself away from the horse, flipped the off rein back over Mister's neck, and swung into the saddle with one smooth motion. "Maybe that's my first *letting go*: having Caleb watch out for her instead of me. Come on, we've got more ground to cover."

39

By the time Lacey arrived, Maddy's gloom had settled back in. Not about Brock—he seemed far away right now—but the hopelessness over Adam weighed her down even while they watched a video about making profiteroles.

Lacey talked while they mixed the *choux* pastry, her chatter mostly about a boy on another ranch whom she liked. By the time they were smushing the pastry into a bag, Maddy's heart had lightened, and she even chuckled as they tried to pipe the soft stuff. If it were absolutely necessary for the dough to look like small cones, they'd have to start over. If blobs of various sizes and shapes were acceptable, they'd be fine.

"I wonder what the guys will think of these," Maddy wondered aloud. "They're going to be weird-looking profiteroles."

"Most of the guys are out on the range today, so it doesn't matter," Lacey said breezily.

And Maddy hadn't even known. It seemed like only a few days since she was aware of Adam's every move, and yet it also felt like eternity. *Will my heart ever heal, Lord? Will I ever not be broken?* What she wouldn't give to be as carefree as this teenager in front of her.

Lacey was prattling on. "I would have gone with them—they're looking for mountain lion signs—but Brad wants to go riding later."

There was a knock at the door, and Caleb poked his head in. "Did I hear you say Brad Bowen? What happened to Julio? What are you doing with the Bowen kid?"

Lacey tossed her head. "Julio's a jerk, and Brad and I are just hanging out. And since when do you sneak in instead of clumping around in your boots? And did you sell the yearling?"

"Maybe I started sneaking to keep an eye on my baby sister, and no, they're thinking about it."

Maddy just leaned against the counter and watched.

"You're baby sister's all grown up now," Lacey growled.

"Oh, really?" Caleb got a gleam in his eye and advanced.

"No!" Lacey squealed, dodging his outstretched hand. "You can't tickle me, I'm working!"

Caleb stopped at that. "Working? Doing what?"

"Baking!"

He looked around and saw the uncooked profiteroles. "These things? What are they? Besides…interesting?"

Madd grinned, the sibling banter feeling homey and happy, but Lacey glared. "They *will* be scrumptious. *If* we decide you can have any," the teenager declared.

"But they won't be scrumptious if I don't have any?" Caleb teased. Then he grew serious. "Adam asked me to keep an eye on things while they're gone, but I have to take a mare down to the vet—can't wait. Jesse's close by if you need him —I've got him working in the equipment shed until I get back. Uncle Dirt is in the house, too, but you guys be careful, okay?"

He tipped his hat to Maddy, gave a rueful glance at the profiteroles-to-be, and left.

Maddy exchanged looks with Lacey.

"Why does Adam need Caleb to watch out for us?" Lacey asked.

Maddy shrugged and didn't answer, but it was obviously because of Brock. Two weeks since they'd broken up, and he was still looking out for her.

And yet he was gone for the whole day, maybe more, and had said nothing. Then again, it was Saturday and she wasn't in the office, so why should he tell her? Why should he tell her anything these days?

No, Maddy, she scolded herself. *The Lord is looking out for you, whether Adam is or not. Don't worry about the rest.*

She let Lacey's talk brighten her mood again and tried to keep her mind off Adam.

"Brad's going to ride at the Palisade rodeo. I'm going to tag along as his groupie," Lacey confided, once they slid the profiteroles into the oven.

Maddy grinned. "A groupie, huh? Screaming and throwing panties at him? I thought that were just for rock stars."

Lacey scoffed. "Screaming, maybe. Panties, definitely not! Mostly just making sure he knows I'm there and cheering him on. And rodeo has its own rock stars, you know. The bull riders and bronc riders, the barrel racing champs."

"You ever want to be one of those?"

"Nah. Too much stress. I just want to ride horses and watch calves being born. And cook!"

"Speaking of which," Maddy said, turning to check the

oven timer. "These are going to have to cool, but we'll want the bowl and beaters to be chilled for the filling."

"I'll do it!" Lacey washed the beaters and put them in the fridge with the metal mixing bowl.

Maddy smiled at the girl's excitement. "You know, somewhere around here…" If she could find it, she had an heirloom to show Lacey. She dug into cupboards, shifting some things around and pulling others completely out.

She finally cried, "Aha!" and successfully retrieved an appliance from a cupboard corner. By that time, the counters and floor held a cast-iron skillet, a pasta maker, and four sizes of muffin tins. "I can't believe I brought all this with me," she said, looking at the mess.

"I think it's cool," Lacey said. "But what's that?"

Maddy turned the appliance over in her hands. "It's a pizzelle maker. We make special Christmas pastries with it. I didn't think of it before because we're nowhere near Christmas, but I thought you'd like to see it."

She showed Lacey the patterns on the inside and started to explain the thin, not-too-sweet cookie it created, but the phone rang instead.

"Maddy?" came Uncle Dirt's voice. "I just got a weird phone call from Tasha down at the pizza place. She said a guy came in with your picture and she told him you were up here, but then she had second thoughts and wanted to tell you about it. Does that make sense to you? Who would be going around with your picture?"

Maddy couldn't get a sound out. Her eyes flitted from the front door to the windows to Mia's room.

"Maddy? What's wrong?" Uncle Dirt asked.

She opened and closed her mouth a few times, then shook her head. "Trouble. Can you come?" She hung the phone up. "Mia, where are you?"

"In here, coloring," Mia called back.

Maddy spun around. What to do? Keys, she needed her car keys. "Mia, come on!" she yelled.

Why were her hands so heavy? Oh, they still held the pizzelle maker. She needed to put it somewhere. Why couldn't she think where to put it?

"Maddy, talk!" Lacey insisted.

A footstep sounded on the porch, and they both turned their heads.

Maddy shook. "Go get Uncle—"

The door burst open. Brock stood in the doorway, hands held rigidly away from his body and anger contorting his face.

Maddy dropped the pizzelle maker.

40

Adam scanned the high country as he rode. The cows and calves had settled into the summer range fine, dividing into smaller groups and browsing happily on grass. Nobody injured, nobody dead, and no cat marks on the tree trunks.

They rode on, searching for tracks or other sign and checking small clusters of cattle along the way. "If there were a cougar threatening, the cows would be huddled together," Dad said.

Adam nodded and nudged Mister to follow his father, grateful that the older man seemed his usual self today. As long as he didn't get lost again, could Dad be better out with the animals instead of doing the behind-the-scenes work? It wouldn't be hard to arrange assignments so his father was out with the hands most of the time. He could check water and fences, monitor the stock, maybe even help Caleb with the horses.

"Hey, Micah," Adam called, reining Mister in.

"Yeah? Find a problem?"

"No, just wondering about something. Did the doctor say anything about limiting the hours Dad works? Does he need to rest in the afternoon or something?"

"Hmm," Micah said after a moment. "I can't remember anything like that. What are you thinking?"

Adam pointed out how well Dad was doing this whole day and shared his plans.

"Still trying to organize everyone, huh?" Micah said. "I think you need to review the definition of *letting go*."

"Gimme a break. This is me trying to involve you in the decisions. What do you think about keeping Dad outside most of the time? And would we need to schedule things so he can take a midday break?"

Micah stared at him. "Wow, you really are asking for input!"

"If I were closer, I'd slug you right now," Adam quipped.

"If you were closer, you'd still miss," Micah shot back, grinning. "But Dad?" He looked ahead to where the older man was riding toward a grouping of cows. "I think you're right—he's happier out here. More relaxed. And it would help keep him away from the checkbook, right?"

"And the land leases. And the taxes. And—" Adam cut his words off. An uneasiness filled him suddenly, a jittering in his stomach that wouldn't go away.

Micah looked at him with concern. "What's up?"

Adam shook his head. "Just a weird feeling. It's nothing." He peered through the surrounding trees just the same.

"You sure? Sometimes you gotta follow those feelings."

"No, I'm not sure. Maybe it's the mountain lion. But what am I supposed to do about it that I'm not already doing?"

They rode on.

Adam looked at cattle, pleased with their contentment

and good condition. He enjoyed the calves frolicking, the red-tailed hawks floating above, the smell of fresh mountain air. But he was still unsettled.

Was he missing signs of the big cat? Was there something he should be noticing about the cattle? The grass was good, everyone was healthy. He didn't see signs of any large predators—no bear scat, no claw marks on trees.

Anything you're trying to tell me, God? He grimaced at the thought—the Lord hadn't been exactly generous with advice lately.

Then the uneasiness turned to dread. A sense of doom washed over him, made him almost cringe. What? What was it?

Maddy's in trouble.

It came in words in his mind, not a general thought, not a feeling. Actual words. Out of the blue. Maddy was in trouble.

He had to get to her. Now.

"Something's wrong with Maddy," he shouted to Micah, not caring that his brother wouldn't understand. "I have to go!" He spun Mister around and kicked him into a run.

It would take well over an hour at a hard gallop to get back to the ranch. Mister was in pretty good shape, but could he go that far, that fast?

Adam didn't know, and it didn't really matter. All he knew was that he had to reach Maddy.

"You think you can hide from me, Maddy Johnston? A wife can't just run away from her man." Brock took a step inside.

Maddy had become a frozen statue. Her legs wouldn't work. Her mouth wouldn't work. All she could do was stare at the menacing man filling her vision.

"Mama?" came a small voice.

Maddy's mind broke free. "Mia! Back in your bedroom!" She never took her eyes off Brock, but she heard the bedroom door close. Mia was safe. Sort of. Not really.

"Lacey, get Uncle Dirt. Take Mia." At least her mouth was working again.

Lacey took a step forward, but Brock shoved her against the wall. He took another stride toward Maddy.

How could Maddy have ever compared Adam with Brock? The two men couldn't be more different—Brock hit for the sake of hurting someone. Adam had only fought in self-defense and would do anything to protect her. If she got out of this alive, she'd get down on her knees to apologize.

She stepped back, mind whirling, heart pounding. "How'd you find me?" she asked slowly. "It's a long way from Denver." What could she do besides stall him? Where could she go?

The small cabin had no place to escape to. Maddy grabbed the heavy pizzelle maker from the floor and held it in both hands. It would be awkward to swing, but at least it was something.

Brock, on the other hand, needed nothing but his hands. Two more strides and he had a fist wrapped in her hair. "It was easy, thanks to your mother," he growled. "And I didn't even need to drive to all these blasted ranches. Just showed your picture in a few towns. A very nice lady in a pizza place remembered your hair."

Maddy stifled a scream as he jerked her hair painfully— any noise from her would only set him off more. She had to follow Brock's pull, but she swung the pizzelle maker at his shoulder. He let go, and she managed to take a step back.

Just far enough to trip over the cookware covering the floor.

Brock loomed, his fist hauled back and ready. Maddy had never succeeded when she'd tried to fight back before. She knew from experience that all she could do was curl into a ball to minimize the damage. Why, oh why, did this have to be the day that the guys were all out on the range?

There was a scurry of movement behind Brock, beside him. Maddy heard a gasp and a thud.

And then something heavy was pinning her to the floor.

41

Adam reluctantly slowed Mister to a walk. It wouldn't do any good to kill his horse and still not reach the homestead.

He counted the time passing, his thoughts repeating, stammering, pounding. Maddy was in trouble. Maddy was in trouble. He had to save her. Maddy was in trouble. He had to save her.

After three long minutes of walking, he nudged Mister into the slow jog that would let the horse recover a bit, but they'd be covering ground just a little faster. After another three fidgety minutes of jogging, Adam couldn't take it anymore. He pushed Mister into a lope that wasn't as easy as it should have been. He reached down and patted the gelding's lathered neck, murmuring encouragement.

When he reached the first big gate, he came through and left it open. His urgency had grown, and he wasn't going to stop to close it even if there had been livestock in that pasture

.

His thoughts raced ahead of him. If Maddy was in

trouble, it had to be Brock. There wasn't any other trouble to get into, unless she'd gone messing around with the tractors or Mia had gotten into the bull pasture again. But Maddy had a lot more ranch sense now, and those possibilities just didn't stick.

It had to be Brock. It made Adam sick to think of the abusive man on his ranch, threatening his Maddy. *His* Maddy. Whatever problems they had, however complicated Adam's life was, she belonged in it. He had to have her in it. If she could get over her fears.

The good thoughts carried him for a while, keeping time with Mister's three-beat lope. *Kiss*-ing-her. *Hold*-ing-her. *Lov*-ing-her.

But the precious pictures in his mind couldn't hold him forever. Images of Brock filled his head, too, although Adam had never seen the man. He was a lurking, shadowy form storming into the admin building, threatening Maddy.

No, it was Saturday. She'd be at her cabin, with even fewer ways to avoid him. And farther from Caleb's help.

Caleb, Adam prayed frantically. *Send Caleb to help her. He can be there faster.*

That should have calmed him, but the thought rushed in again: Maddy's in trouble.

He pushed Mister faster, fumbling at the last gate. He raced across the pasture to the back of her cabin, pulling Mister to a sliding stop just in time to miss the fence.

"Maddy!" he called, climbing over the fence, almost falling on the other side. "Maddy! Are you there?"

"Adam?" came a shaky answer from Uncle Dirt. "They're okay."

Okay? They?

Was that really possible?

He raced through the back door, came into the main living area, and stopped cold.

Maddy lay curled on the kitchen floor, Uncle Dirt kneeling beside her.

Lacey leaned against a wall, shaking. Sobbing.

And an unmoving man lay face down between them.

"HE'S DEAD, ISN'T HE?" Lacey asked through her tears. "I dragged him off her. I killed him, didn't I?"

Adam looked between them, saw the blood on the back of the man's head, saw the cast-iron skillet on the floor beside him.

"If you did, I'd say good riddance," Adam murmured, kneeling to check the man's pulse. "He's alive," he said, reaching for Maddy and pulling her into his arms. He nodded his thanks to Uncle Dirt and held Maddy close, breathed in her scent, reveled in the fact that she wasn't hurt.

She wasn't, was she?

"Are you okay?" he asked, leaning back to look into her face.

Maddy nodded, then curled up against him again.

Adam reached for Lacey, holding her close with his other arm.

A door opened. "Adam?" a timid, six-year-old voice came.

"Mia!" Maddy called.

Mia joined them, and Uncle Dirt wrapped his arms as far around them as he could. A sustaining family hug for the five of them.

Adam maneuvered them into the living room area, away from the distressing scene. *Thank you, Lord. Just...thank you,* he sent heavenward. He basked in the warmth that filled his soul. Relief. Love. Gratitude.

"How did you get here?" Maddy finally whispered.

"I just had this feeling." Adam chuckled. "I think I started hearing God again. And Mister gave his all."

"He's not—"

"No, he'll be fine. Sore and exhausted, but fine. I need to go walk him out soon, though." Reluctantly, Adam broke the circle. "Actually, I need to take care of this first. I assume this is Brock?"

Maddy nodded, her eyes filling with tears again. "I'm sorry. I didn't mean to bring prob—"

"Hush," Adam said, putting a finger over her lips. "You don't need to be sorry about a thing." He kissed her gently. "Now let me find something to tie him up with."

By the time Adam had him trussed with a belt and 9-1-1 was sending someone out, the others were talking over each other to tell him what happened.

"He just burst in."

"He had Maddy down."

"I couldn't get here fast enough."

"I was so scared."

"Lacey hit him with the frying pan."

They paused for a breath, and Uncle Dirt said, "I'll go down and wait for the cops."

Adam nodded at the old man, hoping his face showed his gratitude. Then he sat on the couch, Lacey under his left arm, Maddy snuggled close under his right, and Mia on his lap, wearing his cowboy hat. "You are two incredible women. No one in their right mind would mess with you."

"I guess roping strengthens your arm for frying pans," Lacey joked.

"You said it," Adam said. If his sister was joking already, even nervously, she'd be okay.

But Maddy shuddered, and he tightened his arm around her. "You're safe now, sweetheart."

"I didn't think this day would ever come," she said. "They'll put him away now, right?"

"And throw away the key, if I have anything to say about it," Adam assured her.

Mia tipped his hat back so she could see him. "Does that mean we can go home now?"

Adam felt Maddy stiffen. The girl's innocent words froze him as well. "I, uh, I guess you could," he said. "You'll be safe from him now."

"Yay! We get to see Nonna!" Mia cried.

Maddy sat up, but kept her eyes on her hands. "Adam, I..." Her voice trailed off.

Adam lifted a hand to her face. "Maddy, sweetheart—"

Lacey shot to her feet. "Come on, Mia, let's go outside for a little."

"Actually," Adam said, glancing to the kitchen where Brock was still unconscious, "why don't you two go look at the horses, and Maddy and I will sit on the porch."

The two girls walked hand-in-hand down the driveway. Adam settled in a porch chair and pulled Maddy into his lap. "Do you think you could ever—"

"I'm not as scared," she interrupted, not really settling against him. " I mean, I am, but..."

Adam felt hope rise inside, tried to tamp it down in case she didn't mean what he thought she might.

Maddy took a deep breath. "I was petrified. I couldn't move even after Lacey knocked him out. And seeing him down, I don't know, changed me somehow."

Adam closed his eyes and breathed out slowly. "So that means..." He couldn't help the hope in his voice. He opened his eyes to find Maddy's full of longing.

"I love you, Adam." She gave her head a shake. "I don't know if I ever really told you that before we broke up. Isn't that crazy?"

"I think we were both afraid to say it—it happened so fast."

"Sometimes time doesn't matter," she said softly. "And I know my fears aren't gone. They're too deeply rooted to just disappear. But you're a protector, not a threat, Adam, and maybe I can get some help to get past what's still inside me."

He kissed her lightly, rested his forehead against hers. "Help is good. Help is always good."

Maddy snuggled against him. She felt so precious there, so right, and Adam cherished the feeling. But he had an admission to make, too.

"Uh, Maddy? My brothers had been doing their darnedest to help me fix what's inside of me, too. I've been a fool, but I'm trying to learn to let go of controlling everything. I'll probably stumble a lot."

"That's good. I mean, the letting go, not the stumbling. But can...can I be around to help pick you up?" Maddy's voice quavered.

"Can you?" Adam laughed. "You'd be hard pressed to make me let you leave!" He sobered as he stroked her hair. He could feel his own eyes shine. With love, with tears—he didn't know, just that he loved the warmth in his soul and hoped she felt it too.

"Maddy, I love you. I love your fire, I love your peace. I'm only half-living if I don't have you in my life. I never want you to leave—I want to watch us get better and better."

Actually, what Adam really wanted was to marry her, but it was way too soon to ask that.

She reached up to caress his cheek. "I *am* fiery, and I

imagine that could cause us a few problems. But we can soften each other, right? Bring out the best in each other?"

"Together. We can do anything together." He bent his head, kissed her lips softly.

"You got that right, cowboy."

EPILOGUE

Caleb turned into the driveway, taking the corner slowly so the mare could keep her feet in the trailer. It wouldn't do to have her scramble and hurt herself again. In the stable yard, he unhooked her tie and led her carefully down the ramp. Once the horse was settled in the largest stall, he left the trailer hitched and headed over to check on Maddy.

His breath caught halfway there, as flashing red lights reflected off the trees and the closest cabins.

Caleb ran, wishing for tennis shoes instead of cowboy boots. An ambulance and two police cars sat in front of Maddy's cabin, and paramedics were carrying a man out on a stretcher.

A stranger. Maddy's ex? Caleb's heart kept pounding despite his relief. Were the girls all right?

"Maddy?" he called, brushing past a cop and through the open front door.

Maddy sat at the kitchen table, across from a police officer asking her questions. Her eyes were red and puffy, and she gripped a coffee cup like it was a life preserver.

Adam stood close, watching her protectively. Every so often, she'd glance up at him and take a shuddering breath before giving her attention back to the cop.

"Lacey? Where's Lacey?" Caleb asked. Was she hurt and already in the ambulance?

Adam looked up and narrowed his eyes. "She's out back with Mia and Uncle Dirt until it's her turn." He turned back to Maddy and rested a hand on her shoulder. "Will you be okay if I go talk to Caleb?"

She leaned into him as if using his strength to bear herself up and nodded.

Adam bent to kiss the top of her hair, then jerked his head at Caleb and strode outside.

Caleb followed, not liking what was coming, but needing answers. "They're okay?" he asked before Adam could speak.

"No thanks to you," his brother snapped, crossing his arms and setting his jaw. "I trusted you to keep an eye on them, keep Maddy safe."

Caleb crossed his own arms. He had to get in his side before Adam got rolling. "I did. I didn't have a choice about the vet, but the girls were fine in the cabin, having a great time cooking. I pulled Jesse in from the field and Uncle Dirt was in the house."

Adam stared at him, working his jaw. He finally sighed. "You're right. I guess it happened too fast for you to have gotten here, anyway."

Caleb jerked his head. That was as close to an apology as Adam ever came. Maybe his brother really was trying to change. "So you burst in and cold-cocked Maddy's ex? How did you get here, anyway?"

Adam gave a wry grin. "The good Lord decided to give

me a nudge. In actual words. As fast as we came down, it's going to take Mister a week to recover."

Caleb looked at the paramedics closing up the ambulance doors, then back to Adam. "And you took him out."

Adam chuckled. "Uh, no. Our sweet little sister swung a cast-iron skillet at the back of his head. I guess he went down so suddenly, she thought she'd killed him."

"Lacey? Our Lacey?" Caleb tried to wrap his head around the thought.

"Don't mess with our ladies, is all I can say," Adam answered. "I need to go back in for Maddy, but Mister's still behind the cabin. I gave him a little water and walked him in a few circles when the police first got here, but do you think you could take care of him for me?"

Adam went back inside to his Maddy, and Caleb shoved his hands in his pockets and walked around the cabin.

"Caleb!" Lacey cried as he came around the corner. She rushed to him, and he enveloped her in his arms. "It was so awful!"

"Shh, baby sis. It's over now. And I hear you weren't just brave, you were awesomely strong! Knocked the guy right out, huh?"

Lacey chattered her stress away, and Mia tugged on his jeans. "My daddy won't bother us anymore," the little girl said.

Caleb let go of Lacey to lift Mia in one arm. "No, he won't." He looked over them at Mister, standing listlessly, his head down, all four feet square on the ground. "Hey, you want to walk to the stable with me? I need to get Mister moving."

Lacey shook her head. "I can't. The police want to talk to me when they're done with Maddy."

"Gotcha. But I've still got to walk Mister." He gave Lacey

another hug, ruffled Mia's hair, and climbed the fence to reach the horse.

Mister's muscles didn't start to move easily until they were halfway to the house. Caleb got him back to the stables and alternated walking with half-buckets of a water/electrolyte mix. "Sorry, bud, too much water at once could make you worse. But you sure did a great job for Adam." He patted the gelding, kept walking, and let his thoughts wander.

The way Adam and Maddy leaned on each other...if Caleb were honest, he'd have to admit he was jealous. Despite the trauma of today, or maybe because of it, they were closer than he'd ever seen them. The looks between them, the touches, the connection...

He wanted it.

He wanted more than just kissing Caitlyn or Susie. More than the fun times dancing and hanging out on Friday nights.

He thought of his new dating app and the girls he'd swiped left or right. He'd messaged a few, talked to one or two on the phone, but nobody clicked enough to want to meet.

So was he destined to spend his life with just the horses? Sure, they were accepting and friendly, and they satisfied a little of his need for giving love, but he sure wasn't going to marry one.

Mister gave him a sideways push with his nose.

"Yeah, I'm not paying much attention, am I?" Caleb responded, rubbing the gelding's face. "You feeling better?" He pinched the skin on Mister's neck and checked his gums —the dehydration was better.

He spent another twenty minutes walking Adam's horse, then turned him out in the arena with a full water trough. "No food for a while, old boy. Don't want a bout of colic on top of this."

Caleb leaned on the fence while Mister rolled in the dirt.

Satisfied the horse would recover, he turned back to the waiting barn chores. He paused as he fixed the grain buckets, though, and pulled out his phone. He stared at it for a minute, then opened the dating app.

There had to be someone out there for him.

The End

Thank you so much for reading
Cherished by the Rancher.
If you enjoyed reading the story as much as I enjoyed writing it, tap here for a bonus scene!

Short Stories

Angel Song (women's fiction)

The Best Christmas Date Ever

ABOUT THE AUTHOR

Jen Peters loves being in love—the look in his eyes that makes her feel pretty, the whispers on the phone at night, the gentleness of his kiss, the security in his arms. She was lucky enough to marry her sweetheart all those years ago, and he continues to sweep her off her feet.

Whether reading or writing, Jen loves escaping into a romantic story to experience it all over again, especially when remodeling their homes gets a little overwhelming. Originally from Oregon, she and her family now live in central Indiana, where an opinionated Cavalier named Bailey reminds her not to take life too seriously.

Learn more about Jen Peters by visiting
www.jenpetersauthor.com

Follow Jen on:
Facebook
BookBub
Amazon

Made in the USA
Middletown, DE
11 November 2021